Kenneth L. Decroo believes you must live a life worth writing about. Before he became an educator and consultant for universities and school districts, he worked for many years in the world of research and wild animal training in the motion picture industry. He holds advance degrees in anthropology, instructional technology, and education. He lives and writes in the San Bernardino Mountains of Southern California with his wife, Tammy. When not writing and lecturing, he loves to ride his BMW adventure motorcycle down the Baja Peninsula to beaches and bays without names. More about his adventures can be found on his blog, http://bajamotoquest.com.

BECOMING HUMAN

Kenneth L. Decroo

Publishing

Dedication

I dedicate this book to my loving wife, Tamara Lynn Decroo. She keeps asking me to tell just one more story, so I keep writing. I love you.

Chapter One

The creatures crouched, intent on the village below. Their clever new leader, Oliver, had picked a jagged outlook where they watched undetected, so focused on the hunt that they hardly noticed the sweltering heat steaming up from the jungle canopy. They could just smell the cooking fires and hear the hollow echoes of chopping. The last rays of sunlight reflected off the river that bordered the village, giving the thatched huts a golden hue. It would not be long now.

Oliver's hair bristled at the sudden sound of drums softly drifting up to them, carried by a light breeze off the river. A flock of birds settled nearby. He sensed they'd have to be careful not to stir them when they moved down to attack. He motioned to the troops to hunker down as they made final preparations and nodded to Danny to help settle the group.

The creatures obediently watched their leader, being careful their movements didn't give them away. Surprise was everything on a hunt, and fortunately, they'd learned that humans were careless.

Oliver waited impatiently for it to grow darker. He liked to time his raids to coincide with the fading light of twilight when they could see better than the humans and be less likely to be seen. Humans had poor vision in the dark and were weak, especially when surprised without their weapons.

He made out the women washing on the riverbank beyond the huts. Their large, full breasts bounced to the rhythm of their work as they slapped their colorful laundry on the slick rocks where they knelt. Their smooth ebony skin glowed in the last glimmers of daylight. Their graceful movements stirred him. Blood filled his loins.

The creatures waited, excited and erect at the prospect of capturing new breeding mates. Their raids had become more frequent because the humans didn't hold up very well after capture, especially the females. They were lucky to get one infant out of them before they died. But at least they produced, and that was critical, besides giving good sport. He'd need to keep control of his band, though. They must be careful not to harm the females in the heat of the hunt like last time. They were, after all, the goal. He didn't care about the rest, although they would make a good feast, as always.

***

"Will you look at that? Those poor bastards don't even know what's about to hit them. They don't have a chance. This is better than goddamn TV!" Bauer whispered excitedly as he looked through his field glasses, watching the hybrids closing in on the village. He wondered why the villagers had no guards or fences.

Deter Vandusen grinned. "Yeah, tell me about it. But why are they taking so long? What the hell do they want, a written invitation? When we finally capture some of these freaks of

2

nature and get them back to the States, we're gonna have to train them better at the art of warfare."

But finally, as though on cue, the creatures stealthy worked their way down the ridge and right to the edge of the village.

"Give me those glasses!" Vandusen commanded.

Reluctantly, Bauer handed Vandusen the field glasses. "It's interesting that they've moved to this side of the river. They're really far from their old digs in the caves." His spirits were high at the prospect of the upcoming entertainment. "But then it makes sense. They've practically cleaned out all the other villages upriver on the other side. My guess is they've got to go farther afield now, where their appetites and sport are—how should we say—less known. I think that's why it's taken us so damn long to find them."

Vandusen pressed against a crevasse in the rock to steady himself for a clearer view. "I'm glad you're so damned entertained, Mr. Bauer." He frowned with impatience and fatigue.

Bauer opened his mouth to respond but shut it, thinking better of it.

Vandusen continued, "I just want to find where their settlement is so we can capture some and get the hell out of this shithole." He stomped his feet, trying to get his circulation going.

They'd been on the run, playing catch up, ever since the counterattack drove them out, and Dr. Ken Turner and the rest had regained control of the compound and some of the creatures. But many of them had escaped, which had brought them here into this sweltering armpit of the world. They'd been squatting for what seemed like an eternity.

"Christ! It's going to get too dark to see the fun," Vandusen grumbled. If that asshole Turner and the rest of his crew had just played ball, he wouldn't be stuck here. Those academics just didn't get it. These creatures were a real find, and if captured and trained for warfare, could change how the CIA did business in shithole places like this.

"Perhaps this will help," Bauer said. Smiling, he handed him a small Starlight infrared scope. "Little souvenir from Nam."

"Thanks, that's better." Vandusen's mood improved at what he saw. "They're finally on the move!" He stood for a better angle. The General had thought of everything when it came to supplies. The Starlight scope gave excellent low-light vision.

Bauer pulled on his shoulder. "Careful! They'll see you."

Vandusen shrugged him off. "We're downwind, and those things are way too focused on hunting." He continued to stand, scanning the events unfolding below, and stiffened when the hybrids moved in. "Finally! They have them backed up to the river. They've cut off every possible escape." His excited voice rose just above a whisper. "They're moving in to cut off the women and hem them in. Brilliant, very sneaky, I take back what I said about them before—beautiful."

***

The village women laughed and gossiped as they worked, unaware of what surrounded them in the shadows of the jungle. They felt tired after their long day, but washing in the coolness of the river was their favorite time together, a quiet time for women only.

The weak rays of evening sunlight faded, and a full moon rose over the horizon. The rest of the village prepared for the evening, back from their daily hunting, fishing, and gathering. The old women busied themselves with the cooking fires and tidying up. The men laughed and told jokes as some worked at stretching the fishing nets out to dry, and others readied their canoes for the next morning. A few wondered why the two young men they'd left upriver where the fishing had been good hadn't returned. They hoped they wouldn't get lost in the growing dark. Other than that, all was well. The old people had food in their bellies, and the children were already bedding down.

They didn't suspect the horror about to visit them.

Chapter Two

Dr. Chris Raven leaned back in his chair on the porch and sipped his coffee. The air felt damp and chill, but he always loved the mornings, about the only time he had to himself—a time when he could enjoy the fruits of his labor: his animal compound, the Wild Animal Training Center, or WATC as almost everyone in the movie business called it.

Fall had arrived. The days were growing shorter. The first snowfall had already whitened the surrounding mountains, and a breeze coming out of the northeast carried a chill. The Santa Ana winds would be coming soon. He'd have to make sure his trainers added extra bedding for the animals. From his years as a wild-animal trainer, he'd learned that cold weather was the great leveler for facilities like his. He lost animals if he didn't prepare properly for the winter.

He loved these early mornings because it gave him a chance to watch his animals waking and greeting the sunrise. In their first awakenings, they revealed more of their wildness and less of their adaptation to captivity. He could learn much about the behavior of his animals by just quietly listening and watching, as he did now, alone with his thoughts.

Their first greetings broke the morning stillness. A lone male lion roared in successions that sounded like someone sawing wood. A peacock sent out cries that reminded him of a woman crying for help. And the monkeys chattered like birds. He stretched out his long, lanky frame until his legs hung over the railing and rocked his chair up on two legs in rhythm to his breathing, eyes closed. Another morning was visiting them, and despite what was happening, all was well at this moment.

He felt especially satisfied this morning, for he'd solved a mystery. For the last several months, his trainers had been noticing the disappearance of several peacocks and other fowl. The only evidence of their disappearance was clusters of feathers blowing across the lawns and walkways. Everyone on the ranch had theories ranging from coyotes to thieves. But today, Chris knew what had happened to the missing birds. He hoped his house guest, Dr. Ken Turner, would be up soon. Ken had come down from his chimp facility at the University of Nevada, Reno, to compare notes on their next steps in keeping their research out of the hands of government. He wasn't sure which alphabet soup was trying to force them to turn their chimps and the creatures they'd found into killing machines—CIA, NSA, DOD or a combination of all of them.

The sound of Ken stepping through the French doors onto the porch jarred Chris out of his thoughts. His boots echoed off the wooden planks.

Chris placed his finger to his lips and whispered, "Shush, watch this." Pointing across the front lawn, in the direction of the chimp cages, he continued, "The mystery of the missing peacocks is finally uncovered."

Ken scooted a chair next to him to observe the unfolding scene. Several peacocks fed near one of the large chimp enclosures. Chimps had sloppy eating habits and usually left an abundance of scraps for the birds to scavenge, so this wasn't surprising, but they foraged differently this morning; something drew the peacocks well within reach of the cage.

"Look at how close they're getting," Chris said. "You'd think they'd have learned by now. Usually, they're way more cautious than this. The scraps must really be tempting."

Ken leaned forward, placing his elbows on the railing, almost spilling his coffee. "Interesting, chimps mainly eat fruits and vegetables, though they're not above enjoying a little fresh meat. It's a good thing the chimps are still bedded down. Those bars are wide enough for one of them to reach out and grab anything or anyone within range."

Chris winced at the image, deepening the wrinkles across his face. "Some of my crew have learned that the hard way. That's why we put up that rail around the cage."

"Obviously, these birds didn't get the memo," Ken replied.

They watched as the peacocks pecked and scratched to the very edge of the bars.

"Now I think we're going to see what's been going on," Chris whispered, pointing to a large heap of blankets the chimps usually used as bedding. "At first, I couldn't understand why the peacocks were becoming so careless—but watch."

"Why's the chimps' bedding outside getting damp?" Ken asked. Standard procedure in chimp facilities around the world was for handlers to provide dry blankets every evening. The chimps went to great lengths to make warm, dry sleeping nests in their den boxes. But not this morning; the pile lay in a damp heap right next to the bars.

But the scientists didn't have long to wonder. From within the folds of the pile of blankets, a biscuit of monkey chow arced in the air and landed on the ribbon of cement that surrounded the cages. It appeared to have been flipped into the air. One of the birds raced to it and within reach of the chimps, intent on pecking the biscuit.

"It won't be long now." Chris had no sooner whispered the words when a hairy black arm shot out between the bars in a blur and grabbed the peacock. Mayhem broke out as a large chimp leaped up, scattering the pile of blankets as the other peacocks took flight in all directions.

The chimp hooted in piercing wails and ran, bipedalling, back and forth, raking the struggling bird against the bars. The rest of the chimps ran out of their den boxes, adding to the chaos, hooting and screaming in excitement. Ken realized they'd not been sleeping but rather hiding in wait. Finally, the chimps settled down to feast, plucking the bird as it still struggled. They grunted as they tore the peacock apart, fighting over it more than sharing.

Chris stood, knocking over his chair and exclaimed, "I've always known chimps are capable of planning, but this takes the cake!"

Ken nodded. "Absolutely. This reminds me of observations in the wild, of them stripping the leaves off sticks before licking the stem and putting it down into a termite mound to termite fish, but in this case, I guess we just witnessed peacock fishing or, more accurately, hunting."

"Yes, exactly, I'd say the score is chimps one, peacocks nothing." They laughed and headed out to check on the aftermath in the primate area. As they passed the big cat arena,

9

Chris said, "It's interesting how much there's still to learn from working with these guys." He stooped to pick up a clump of feathers blowing across the walkway. "We feed them as much as they could ever want. Yet the desire to fish, or hunt, is still so pre-wired in them, they'll go to great lengths to work at it. It's amazing."

Ken watched the chimps from across the walk. "I'm thinking of something Lester once told me about chimps; though I think he was referring to his chimp, Girlie, I think it applies to all chimps we work with, no matter what the circumstances."

"What's that?" Chris asked.

"Our chimps have a foot in two worlds, ours and theirs. It has to be hard for them to balance the behavior they've learned to cope with us with what's instinctual and part of their world," Ken replied.

"That insight is exactly why, in my opinion, Mr. Lester McCall is the greatest chimp trainer who has ever lived and Girlie the smartest chimp," Chris said.

"Exactly, and it goes both ways. I think, more than any of us, Lester has his foot firmly planted in both worlds—he's in sync."

Chris grinned. "You've been to his trailer, right? He doesn't even have a cage for her. They're truly roommates."

"I know. He talks to her all day. And in Africa, Girlie began learning sign language by simply observing my chimp, Mike. She's an intelligent animal, one of a kind."

A chill passed over both scientists at the mention of Africa. But they said nothing, not wanting to ruin the mood. Instead, they watched the chimps at their feast. The younger chimps busied themselves eating the bloody leftovers, grunting and touching the older hunter for reassurance. They were so intent on their feast that they ignored everything else.

It unnerved Ken to think this savageness wasn't unique to these chimps. He'd seen it on a more frightening scale in Africa, but he pushed those thoughts away, for now.

***

Dr. Fred Savage heard the ruckus and intercepted Ken and Chris at the big-cat arena. The chimps had awakened the whole compound, and so the daily routine of cleaning and feeding began.

Chris smiled at Fred. "Let's head up to the elephant barn and check in with Dusty. He's back from Montreal, but I heard he stopped at the Circus Luncheon Club. He may have news of the wider world, if you know what I mean. Besides, he has a new elephant I'd like to see."

The threesome made their way to the back of the compound. They could just make out a large, blue, semi-trailer with the inscription, *Have Trunk, Will Travel. Dusty Smith, Elephant Trainer.* Several elephants were feeding and exercising in a large stockade.

"God, how many elephants does the man own?" Ken asked.

"I'm not sure. They come and go—how many chimps do you have?" Chris asked.

They both laughed, and Ken replied, "Your point's well taken."

"Dusty's been worried about Lester ever since he left for Africa," Chris said as he stopped to pet one of the ranch dogs who'd come to investigate all the activity. "Even though we're friends, I feel a strain developing between us—I'd like to try to clear it up."

"That's interesting; I would've never guessed," Fred said. "When we were here before we left for Africa, all Dusty and Lester did was argue."

"I know, but as much as they argued, I think you'll remember, they were never more than ten feet apart."

"From what Bobby says, they've had a long and troubled history that goes back to Lester's circus days, when his wife was still alive, but they're still friends," Ken said.

Chris shook his head. "Believe me, you don't know the half of it."

Ken and Fred followed behind Chris as they crossed the compound, headed for the elephants. Chris stopped to talk to various trainers, handlers and groomers, slowing their progress, which was to Ken and Fred's liking, as they could spend more time observing the different animals Chris kept ready for the Hollywood entertainment industry.

Ken remembered when Dr. Chris Raven had left academia; he'd watched with interest as he managed to build the WATC into the biggest provider of wild animals in the movie business. Just recently he'd read an article that boasted that, not counting insects and mice, he had over five hundred animals here. Ken paused and looked around in admiration. But Chris hadn't done it without making enemies.

Ken knew Chris relied on friends like Dusty to keep him current with all the gossip about the doings of the animal people around the world. Dusty was part of the circus world, which was small and intimate, and many regarded him as the greatest living elephant trainer in the world. He'd made it clear that nothing much happened inside or outside the big tops around the world that Dusty didn't hear about.

Ken grimaced. *Even in places as far away as Africa.* Ken figured that Dusty's reach must be farther than just circuses. He'd heard tales of many prominent zoos bringing him in to help their handlers deal with difficult elephants. Apparently, Dusty was the only person able to load and transport an elephant who'd killed a trainer.

Chris interrupted Ken's thoughts: "This new elephant, Debbie, did a headstand on a clown in a circus up in Montreal, and they gave her to Dusty as a gift if he'd come get her. He knew if he didn't accept, the circus would put her down, so he and his daughter, Sheri, went up and got her. They just arrived back late last night."

"I thought I heard someone rolling in late last night or early this morning," Ken said. He stopped for a moment to take in Dusty's elephant stockade. "Clearly Dusty is elephant-poor." He pointed at each elephant and counted. "He must have over twenty."

Chris smiled as he watched Ken counting. "I let him winter over one season and that's stretched into more than six years now. But I don't mind. Dusty lets us use his elephants for movie work, and anyway, it's good being associated with Dusty in this cutthroat business. Having him as a friend is more than enough compensation."

Ken had known Chris long enough to know he liked Dusty, and that was enough. Chris didn't have many friends.

"Dusty should be up by now," Chris continued. "I see his daughter filling the water drums over there in the elephant stockade." He quickened his pace and strode up to the young woman. "Good morning, Sheri! Where's your dad?"

She turned off the faucet and smiled. "He's over at the semi. We're going to unload the new elephant this morning. He probably could use some help or at least an audience."

Ken smiled, thinking Sheri out of place amongst the wheelbarrows of manure and smells of animal sweat. Her petite, athletic frame was evidence of a life of heavy lifting and working outdoors with animals. But he noticed she had a grace in her movements that came from the necessity of moving in sync with some of the most graceful animals on the planet, elephants. He realized she was as much a center-ring performer as a trainer, and the trainer she was learning from was the world's best.

"Well, let's take a look at our new guest!" Chris said.

As they strode in the direction of a large, blue and white semi-trailer, they heard the squeak of the trailer doors opening followed by Dusty's deep voice bellowing a series of greetings. "Hello, Debbie. Are we nervous? Easy, girl!"

Dusty didn't acknowledge any of them as they stood behind, watching. "Trunk up!" he commanded. Debbie's six thousand pounds dwarfed his large, stocky frame. The elephant hook he held in his right hand seemed somehow ineffective.

As little as Ken knew about elephants and their behavior, he could extrapolate from his knowledge of chimps that what was unfolding with Debbie was a tipping point. Unloading any

14

wild animal was always an uncertain prospect, but one who'd recently killed someone was especially dangerous. He realized the next few minutes would determine if Dusty would be able to work his new elephant or have to put her down. He had a sudden insight. They were watching a real drama, Debbie's future. Her life, as much as Dusty's, would be determined in the next few minutes.

Dusty concentrated on every movement Debbie made, almost in a trance, and after what seemed like several minutes, he continued, "Come on, girl, trunk up!"

The elephant filled most of the trailer. Her left eye seemed tiny, engulfed in the mountains of wrinkled skin, but it focused only on Dusty. She swayed side to side, rocking the whole trailer. Between high-pitched squeaks followed by low, flagellating rumbles, her trunk slapped against the walls in loud booms.

Dusty repeated his command louder. "Trunk up!"

Finally, Debbie obeyed, and a transition from wild, frightened, and aggressive to obedience occurred before their eyes.

Dusty walked her into the stockade and exercised her in slow but deliberate circles. "Debbie, move up, girl, move up— good girl, Debbie." His voice and gait oozed calmness. Clearly, Dusty was in that special place all who've worked animals have experienced.

"I don't know how he does it, but there you are," Sheri said, watching her dad with admiration.

Ken turned to her voice and realized that she'd been standing behind them holding the largest elephant gun any of them had ever seen.

She smiled as she engaged the safety with a loud click. "Coffee, anyone?"

***

"I stopped at the Luncheon Club before I left for Montreal," Dusty said as he brushed off a stool and took a seat. The group gathered in the elephant barn so they could keep a close eye on Debbie after Dusty had introduced her to three of the calmest elephants. The barn, a large block building with high ceilings, stood next to the elephant stockade and had three tall rollup doors that—open now—gave them a clear view of the elephants carefully greeting each other.

Several other elephants swayed inside the barn in stalls while Sheri fed them flakes of oat hay. She weaved around the elephants, rubbing each as she greeted them and approaching the large bull elephants in a cautious but confident manner. They trumpeted greetings and touched her with their trunks.

Ken watched her at work. *When I die, I hope I come back as one of these elephants.*

"Any news of Lester and Girlie?" Chris asked Dusty, interrupting Ken's thoughts.

Dusty paused, surveying them as though measuring what he'd share. "I found out a lot at the Luncheon Club. Several circuses are passing through right now, headed to their first jump of the season. The club was packed with lots of them. I got a chance to talk to an elephant groomer I know from Carson and Barnes. He told me some 'suits' were asking about Lester. From what I gather, that was a couple of days ago, in Norman." Dusty shifted his weight and leaned his back against the block

16

wall, falling silent. He placed his hands on his pot-belly with his fingers interweaved and began twirling his thumbs.

Looking to one another, they all started to speak at once. Dusty kept his eyes closed as though meditating until Chris won out and asked, "Who do you think those 'suits' are, and what did they want?"

"You know, 'suits.' He thought they might be from the government. They were asking if anyone knew his whereabouts and were flashing lots of cash." Dusty paused, glaring at Chris before continuing, "You gotta know that somebody's going to talk—guaranteed. I told you nothing good would come of getting mixed up with Oliver and those other freaks of nature."

"Dusty, you know as well as I do. Lester insisted on coming with us to Africa," Chris said.

"Yah, but if you and these other people hadn't started messing around with Oliver again, none of this shit would have happened. Trouble follows him everywhere he goes—and that other unnatural freak, Danny, is worse. They're a goddamn menace," Dusty said. He got up and walked past Ken and Fred, ignoring them, to move a water hose overflowing in one of the troughs. "There's more. From what everyone told me, most of the circuses have been visited by these assholes, and worse, there's a lot of people guessing where Lester went and think he's still in Africa."

"When I talked to my wife, Mary, she said questions are being asked up in Reno, too," Ken said. "There's been a lot of people showing up at the ranch. But don't worry, she's used to getting rid of pests. I'm not sure if I mentioned that she's a Hollywood director; which makes her an expert in the brush off."

Chris looked up the drive. "I'm surprised we haven't had a visit here, yet."

"You can be sure you're being watched," Fred said. "Believe me, they'd be swarming all over this place if they thought Oliver, or Danny, or even Mike was here. I don't think they care much about the other chimps we have, not yet, anyway. To them, they're just run of the mill chimps, nothing special. I don't think they get that they're also part of the research."

Ken looked at Fred. "It's good they don't care, even if it's just for now. It buys us some time. I think we need to head back up to Reno. We'll bring the chimps we have here with us. That'll keep everyone confused. Hell, they all look alike to those people, and that might shut up the university for a little while."

"I agree," Fred said. "I think we need to regroup, and I'm sure Mary could use a hand. We need to contact Hunt and Bobby and find out what they've turned up."

"We'll keep our eyes open down here and let you know if any strangers show up," Dusty said. He turned to Ken. "So, your wife is *the* Mary Gibson-Turner?"

Ken nodded. "Yes, she is. The main thing, Dusty, is that we need to get Lester and Girlie out of Africa. We need to get them home."

Before Dusty could respond, Chris interrupted. "I agree. It's unraveling over there. I doubt anyone will be able to hide much longer. I still have the cover of the movie. I've got one last trip no one will be able to question. I still have to haul out the last of our equipment. Hell, the movie wrapped a month ago. I can't stall much longer." Chris paused for emphasis. "We need to make a plan—a good plan, so we can get them out once and for all. The movie is the best cover we'll ever have to bring them back. Customs wouldn't know one chimp from another."

"What's going to happen to Oliver, Danny and the rest of the creatures?" Ken asked. "Are we just going to leave them over there for Vandusen to capture? There's so much to learn from them, so much …" His voice trailed into silence.

They stood deep in their thoughts until Dusty broke the quiet. "Fuck those freaks of nature."

"Don't forget Mike. He's still there," Ken said.

"Who knows, it might be possible to bring them all back," Chris said. "We won't know until we get a hold of Lester and François."

Dusty glared at the three scientists as they said their goodbyes to Sheri, and of course, Debbie. While they were still in earshot, Dusty yelled, "They're still F.O.N.s, freaks of nature."

Chapter Three

"My God!" Mary paused, at a loss for words, before continuing, "Am I talking to myself? We've been over all of this shit. The chimps are not here, and it's none of your damn business where they are, anyway," she sighed. "The courts made it quite clear we're the custodians of all property purchased by the fucking NSF grant." Mary's voice rose, exasperated with the two little bureaucrats who stood at the gate. "Besides, grant money wasn't even used to buy the chimps—I bought them with my own money, goddamn it!"

Mary watched the USDA inspector fidget. She guessed that this skinny, bearded little man didn't like being caught between them. One well-placed phone call from Dr. Mellon or Ken could complicate his career. Mary smiled to herself; obviously he just wanted to get back, as soon as possible, to his usual inspecting work at the US Department of Agriculture. He probably inspected feedlots and dairies. She figured that he, like her, hadn't signed up for this level of politics. She watched as he shifted his weight from one foot to the other, speechless, snapping the paper holder on his clipboard.

Melon jerked it out of his hand and shouted, "Well, are you going to do something about this?"

Mary sighed, glaring from the inspector to Melon, waiting for the inspector to say something. But she quickly realized he wasn't very fast on his feet. "I should think you'd have given up by now. You may recall that the university found in Dr. Turner's favor. We're tired of you dragging every official you can harangue on these trumped-up charges." She resigned herself to the fact that, simply put, this little shit wasn't going to rest until he'd discredited Ken and found where he'd hidden Mike and the other chimps.

From the little drama happening now, Mary felt sure he still didn't know their whereabouts, which was the reason for these frequent visits. She was exasperated at what seemed to be Melon's new tactic: filing charges that Ken was using the research chimps for entertainment, which required a US Department of Agriculture Exhibitor's Permit, hence, the arrival of this new inspector nervously standing in her driveway.

Finally, to Mary's relief, the inspector firmly took the clipboard back from Melon and said while retreating to his car, "I don't think this is an issue in the jurisdiction of the USDA."

Now it was Melon's turn to raise his voice. "So you're not going to do anything about this obvious fraud?"

The inspector paused, picking his words carefully. "I'm not going to get in the middle of what is clearly a legal custody dispute. This is a matter that should be settled between your organizations and the courts." He made a hasty retreat, jumped into his car, and drove off, leaving Mary and Melon glaring at each other.

Melon trembled in rage, losing all the reserve he usually cultivated.

Mary chuckled at the sight, but before she could shut the front gate, he tried to push his way through the gap. "I think it's time to have a closer look around here," he shouted.

Mary grabbed the little man by his tie as he tried to press past her, and two large research assistants ran toward him.

Thinking better of it, he wilted and stepped back through the gate. "Alright, but I'll be back. You'll be hearing from the ethics committee very soon if I have anything to say about this, this …"

Mary shut the gate with a clang and left him to his rumblings. The assistants watched closely until Melon sped off in his car, throwing gravel at their feet, then they laughed and headed back to their work.

***

Two agents stood in the thick grass of the pasture, hidden in a grove of cottonwoods, across the road from the ranch.

"Now that was interesting," one agent said as he pulled out a photo of Melon from a file in his backpack.

"You think?" the other agent said.

The first agent put the photo back. "It seems this Dr. Melon is stirring things up a little bit."

The other agent slipped on his own backpack and said, "Let's go. The General may need to have a little chat with that professor before he screws everything up."

While they gathered their gear, getting ready to head out, one agent asked the other, "Where in the hell is that can of insect spray?"

***

Mary muttered to herself, ignoring a group of research assistants who'd been drawn by the ruckus. The phone rang just as she reached the back door of the main house.

"God, what now?" she shouted into the empty house. Actually, she hoped it was Ken or Fred; she expected them back in Reno any time now.

She'd encouraged them both to remain incognito ever since the university hearing. But she wanted them back now. She'd thought it would be easier to explain the absence of Mike and the other signing chimps if they appeared to be on the road. Besides, with her movie contacts and the WATC making a movie, it would be the perfect cover if they needed to go back to Africa to help bring back Lester and the chimps and, maybe, even one of the creatures.

However, Mary realized from this visit that Melon wasn't buying any of it. She suspected he had surveillance on both the WATC and their ranch, but she was pretty sure he didn't know the whereabouts of the chimps or what had taken place since their absence. So she felt hopeful that the plan was working in some ways, though barely.

I'll kill them both if they're drinking at Franks.

She answered the phone.

Chapter Four

Lester and François watched in horror as the soldiers tidied up the dead. Their gruesome effort was like putting the pieces of a macabre jigsaw puzzle together—picking up and sorting the scattered, stiff limbs, and searching for the bodies to which they belonged.

Lester covered his face with a red, paisley bandana in a feeble attempt to avoid the sweet smell of rotting corruption. Clouds of hungry flies spewed from the bloated corpses, making them hesitant to disturb the dead further. Sweat from the relentless tropical heat soaked the soldiers' tunics as they hastily dug shallow graves in the red clay.

"I want this whole operation wrapped up as soon as possible. We've got a long way back, and I don't like being exposed out here with such a small force," François said as he looked nervously around, surveying what little was left of the village. Though almost completely destroyed, the savageness of the attack concerned him more than the destruction of the dwellings. In all his years as a soldier and mercenary, he'd never seen such a brutal scene. It was as though whoever or whatever was responsible wanted to completely obliterate the village and everything in it. Nothing, including the livestock, was left alive, and, more horrifying, some of the dead had provided a savage feast.

"Do you notice what's missing?" Lester asked as he examined the rows of bodies. He turned them all face up, then absent-mindedly rearranged the dismembered limbs so they'd be anatomically correct.

François kneeled down for a closer look at the line of corpses. "There're no females." He motioned a soldier to take photographs. "We're going to need some evidence of this— some photos. I don't have the words to describe this mess."

"I don't want to think why they're absent," Lester said in a trembling voice.

François unlatched his holster nervously. "It's obvious. God help them."

"I don't think God's at work here. They—"

"We can talk about this when we're safely back," François interrupted. "Let's clean this up, bury the dead, and leave this behind."

"I'll never be able to put this behind," Lester said.

Ignoring Lester, François continued, "We'll have to remove all traces of this—this massacre. This side of the river is more populated. I'm afraid the details of this will get out if we don't act quickly and thoroughly."

Lester nodded and hastily helped with the gruesome cleanup. "I don't think it will matter. This'll be discovered soon enough and bring outsiders into the area."

"Then let's get humping. At least out of respect for these poor souls." François barked orders to the soldiers to muster. "Finish burying the dead. There's evil here."

***

On the riverbank, two fishermen from the village hid under the cover of the brush near several shattered fishing boats. They clung together, barely moving for fear of being seen by the soldiers of the white men.

The evening before, the fishing had been good, and, intent on harvesting their last fish traps and resetting them, they'd remained out later than usual. The other fishermen had teased them and left early, hurrying back to their wives before dark.

The fishermen had been returning home, but were still out on the river, when the creatures attacked. The beasts had been so intent on their gruesome work that they'd not noticed the fishermen silently floating downstream in their dugouts. From the middle of the river, they'd watched helplessly, frozen in horror. They'd managed to paddle quietly to shore and hide in the reeds, where they remained in fear of their lives, with no idea of what, if anything, they could do to thwart such brutal savagery.

They'd watched some of the creatures drag the young women off into the jungle, while the rest turned the village into a killing field, followed by a morbid feeding. The fishermen stayed in hiding as the creatures finished their grim work. They covered their ears to shut out the screams, then after the creatures had left, ashamed and overwhelmed with guilt, they'd wandered aimlessly among the dead until they heard the coming of the soldiers.

Now, they watched the grim cleanup. They would wait until the soldiers left, then drift downstream to warn all who would listen.

Chapter Five

"I can't believe Mike had any part in this," Lester said as they marched back to the compound in the fading light. He was having trouble keeping pace. Night was coming, and the soldiers were in a hurry to get back home.

François glanced nervously from side to side along the trail. "Just try to keep up, my friend. We'll have plenty of time later to try to make sense of this. Just concentrate on getting the hell out of here and back to the compound." The loud screeches of a troop of howlers startled them, and the men quickened the pace. François continued, "We don't want to be caught out here after dark. We've still a long way to the ford."

Lester nodded without saying anything. He knew François was worried about the river crossing. As the only passable section across for miles, it was a perfect place for an ambush. He noticed the soldiers were unusually somber and figured that, like him, the atrocities they'd witnessed at the village had shaken them. The growing darkness put him on edge as they trudged on.

Finally, Lester heard the babble of the river gushing over the shallows of the ford. He watched as François sent several men ahead to scout the crossing. As they waited, the insects fed relentlessly. Lester was startled but relieved when one of the men appeared out of the moon shadows and signaled the all-clear.

Lester could see more easily in the river ford. His eyes had grown weaker since they'd embarked on this journey. He wasn't sure if it was the strain of the adventure or that he was just growing old. But, fortunately, a full moon had risen early, illuminating the way. He felt vulnerable out in the open and realized that François felt the same, as he'd ordered several men to peel off the line to guard their flanks. François watched at the edge of the stream as they waded against the swift current, carefully picking their way among the slippery rocks. Though his heart thumped at the occasional muffled swear word when someone slipped, he felt relieved that they were about to reach the other side—their side of the river.

Lester wasn't sure if his fatigue came from the long trek they'd made over the last two days or the strain of being on edge, but once they were safely on the other side and had started down the trail to home, he relaxed a little, smiling as the familiar jungle sounds returned. He could tell that the whole party felt relieved to be on *their* side of the river. His energy returned, and he quickened his pace to keep up with the patrol. He, like the rest, knew this part of the trail well and was happy to hear subdued chatter rise from the ranks again with an occasional muffled laugh.

This was the very spot they'd been reunited with Girlie and Mike after the attack on the beach by the creatures. It seemed like years since that day, but he realized it had only been a few months. He wondered how Mike, Oliver and Danny were doing somewhere out in this forsaken jungle. He missed his friends, especially Bobby. He quietly laughed to himself as he thought about the antics of that little midget and wondered what Fred and Ken would think of the photos they'd taken. And

Hunt, he actually missed him and his old friends at the Circus Luncheon Club. Had they all forgotten him and Girlie? He wanted to go home.

He looked down at Girlie and squeezed her hand. She quietly hooted and touched him behind his leg. *I wonder if things will ever get back to normal?* He had the feeling they'd left death on the other side of the river. But a chill passed over him, and he wondered if they might not be running right into its embrace. He knew the creatures could be very patient, and it would not take them long to learn this side of the river.

***

Oliver watched in the shadows as the humans crossed the river carrying their firesticks. He felt the heat rising in his body and he began panting. His lips opened to make a trumpet hoot signaling his troop to attack, but he quickly covered his mouth, knowing he couldn't stop the noise once he began to make it. He could just make out Lester and Girlie in the failing light. He looked over at Danny and realized that he stood ready to charge, his hair bristling.

He still felt awkward making the signs the little chimp had taught him, but he'd try as he knew their power. He first looked at his troop clustered behind Danny, gripping their weapons and baring their teeth, then he moved near Danny and tapped him several times before signing, "Stay."

Danny looked at him and back at the troop before widening his mouth, panting. He shook his club toward the humans but dropped it, then extended the back of his empty hand toward Oliver.

Oliver kissed the back of his hand.

Danny stayed.

Oliver felt the troop gathering around as he embraced Danny.

Chapter Six

It grew dark as they reached the last ridge overlooking the flickering lights of the compound. Lester felt a light breeze and smelled the faint aroma of cooking, reminding him of how hungry he was. It had been a long trek up the river, and returning on an empty stomach made it even worse. He figured he wasn't alone in this, as François had been reluctant to stop to eat in the haste to reach their side of the river. Images of the creatures' handywork had haunted him the whole way back.

"Home at last," François said to Lester as he squinted in the growing darkness. "We need to be especially careful on this last leg, my friend."

Girlie, clearly agitated, looked back behind them and tried to pull away. Lester gripped her hand tighter. Her coarse, black hair stood on end, puffing her up. *A classic chimpanzee piloerection,* Lester thought.

"Easy, Girlie, what's wrong?" he whispered. Feeling uneasy, he scanned their surroundings, trying to pierce the darkness. "I'll feel a lot safer when we get out of this damn jungle and can rest inside," he said to François.

The Belgian nodded. "I think she senses something. We might be being followed. That's why we're not using the main trail. I learned the hard way, from my time in Indo-China with

31

the French Foreign Legion, to be especially alert when within sight of camp. That's when your troops are tired and may let their guard down. It still amazes me, but these creatures are capable of sophisticated tactics. They could easily set up an ambush."

Using the cover of tall grass, François quietly led them off the trail and down along a creek, which trickled out from a tunnel that lead under the outer wall of the compound. He whispered in his radio to signal their approach to the guards on the wall above, then wasted no time unlocking the gate and leading his men through the tunnel. The last thing he wanted was for the creatures to discover this secret entrance.

The men relaxed as they took in the familiar surroundings and made their way to the kitchen. They were finally safe and at home, "inside" as Lester had said.

François smiled at the thought of a hot shower and a nice, tall bottle of Black and White. He exhaled and said, "Okay, men, smoke 'em if you got 'em." The men laughed for the first time in a while, and Girlie hooted in relief. But she couldn't help looking back at the secret gate.

***

The creatures watched quizzically as the last of the humans disappeared into the dark hole below the wall. Oliver motioned his group to follow him down for a closer look. He knew they had to be careful, as a watchtower had a clear view of the area. But it was dark, and the searchlight on the wall cast many shadows they could use to blend into and creep through.

Oliver felt curious but cautious. He signaled the group to wait in the tall grass away from the gate. The locked, iron gate that led into the darkness below the wall perplexed him. He gingerly pulled on the padlock and bristled when it rattled and echoed up into the tunnel. He pressed against the iron bars, trying to get a closer look, but it was too dark. Danny tapped him on the back and pointed at a guard shining a beam of light above them on the wall. Oliver signed, "Hide," and seven black figures froze, blending into the darkness, until the human moved further along the wall, away from them. When the human's light beam stopped zigzagging into the darkness, Oliver motioned his group to leave. The brush rustled as they silently retreated, like fading shadows, back into the forest.

For now, Oliver would wait. He had a treasure, something very special, hidden back in the caves, something he'd kept secret and safe ever since the raid on the compound and their escape— something he needed first before they could return.

For now, he'd have to wait. But he could be very patient.

Chapter Seven

"Cut! Okay, people, one hour. The food truck's out front." The assistant director picked his way through a maze of lighting cables and apple crates, almost tripping on a transformer in his haste. He shouted to catch Bobby Waiter's attention, "Bobby! I've got a message for you."

The midget shaded his eyes as he looked back into the brightness of the set. He could just make out the silhouette of the AD approaching, waving a folded paper.

I wonder who's calling at this hour? Bobby had to reach up even as the tall man stooped to hand him the note. He frowned and read the note, but quickly put on his best poker face when he noticed the AD still hovering over him.

"I need to use the phone in the production office," Bobby said.

"Of course. Bad news?"

Bobby tried to keep his voice level and without emotion. "Are you writing a book?"

"Sorry, Mr. Waiter. I'll unlock it for you."

Melon watched, hiding in the shadows, taking little notice of the crew as they rushed to dinner. He smirked at the odd contrast between Bobby's compact-but-well-proportioned frame next to the lanky AD. Melon sighed as they made their way up the steep, wooden stairs to the office above the studio floor. Resigned that he couldn't follow them without being noticed, he made his way out the fire exit into the night. He had much to share with his government friends.

He wondered where Vandusen and his crew had disappeared to. It had been months since he'd heard from any of them directly. Ever since his meeting with Vandusen in Reno, the checks made out to his research project kept coming in, and they were sizable. Childs had been his go-between for a few months after he'd first introduced him to Vandusen, but even that nervous, little grad student had fallen off the radar. He hated that his only method of communicating was posting to some P.O. Box. He didn't like being left in the dark. But a phone call—someone had called that midget, and it was so important they'd interrupted his work. It could be anything from his agent to one of Dr. Turner's people. He was going to have to stay close to this little shit.

***

"Hunt! What's going on?" Bobby asked, puzzled why his friend was calling since they planned to meet that evening at their favorite deli, Canter's, on Fairfax in Los Angeles.

"I don't think we should meet tonight—I think I'm, or maybe we, are being followed," Hunt said. His feminine voice sounded more strained than usual.

"Who do you think it is?" Bobby asked. "Hold on just a minute." He looked out through the blinds of the window, which gave a clear view down to the studio set below. Everything seemed normal, but he had a sense of foreboding and a feeling of impending danger that had been with him on and off ever since they'd returned from Africa. He kept half expecting Vandusen and his agents to suddenly show up. Only recently, during a meeting, he'd nearly jumped out of his skin, scaring a whole production crew, when someone dropped a tray of coffee. And now, this call from Hunt. He, like the rest of his friends, questioned if it'd been worth getting wrapped up with Ken and this mess.

"Bobby, are you there?" Hunt asked.

"Yes, sorry, I was checking to be sure I was alone."

"Can you get away and meet me at City Lights?" Hunt asked.

"I thought we were meeting at Canter's," Bobby said.

"I'm hiding out at the Baths."

Bobby smiled to himself. The "Baths" is what Hunt lovingly referred to as his favorite recreational spot in the Castro District of San Francisco. Hunt was known to disappear for weeks and when asked what he'd been doing, he'd simply reply that he'd "gotten the works."

Bobby thought that maybe making a trip up to the homosexual district in San Francisco would be the perfect place to disappear for a while and go unnoticed, even for a midget. People minded their own business there, as many didn't want to be recognized.

"Bobby, are you still there?"

"Yah, Hunt. We wrap tomorrow, so I can meet you Saturday evening."

"Great, get a cab to City Lights in North Beach—I'll meet you upstairs."

Bobby hung up the phone and tried to make out what all this meant. Who would be following Hunt? He was pretty sure, or at least he hoped, that Vandusen was still stuck in Africa. He'd have to be more careful and maybe take a vacation, a long vacation.

Someone down on the set was playing a CD on the sound equipment as they hustled to break the set down. He couldn't make out all the words from the noise of the crew working.

Take to the highway, won't you lend me your name ... want to pass that way again ... Sail on home to Jesus ... I guess my feet know where they want me to go ... walk on down, walk on down ...

He shook his head. "James Taylor—fucking fitting."

Chapter Eight

"These work great as rifles. They may even be better 'cause they're silent!" the Belgian said, as he opened the bolt and handed the dart gun to Bauer.

Bauer lovingly stroked the finely machined blue steel of the barrel with his large, rough hands, then he shouldered it and took several imaginary aims above the treetops before handing it to Vandusen, stock first.

Vandusen didn't know the gunrunner by any other name than the "Belgian." He sneered at the short, portly man tottering on two skinny legs that seemed disproportionate to his rotund pear shape. He couldn't tell if the flushness of the man's cheeks came from overindulgence or the tropical heat, but when he came close enough to smell his foul breath, the answer was obvious: both.

"It'll do the job you wish, my friends." The Belgian flashed a gapped smile. "With the right tranq—like, say, ketamine—it'll knock your prey helpless without killing it." His brow furrowed. "It was very useful in that recent unpleasantness over in Chad." He paused and caught Vandusen's eye. "Both sides found it useful for gathering intel, as you people like to call it."

Ignoring the shadowy reference, Vandusen aimed at imaginary targets. The dart gun felt like a toy in his arms as he hunched over and aimed down the dusty road, but it was in good shape, almost new, and it'd been oiled, worked over by someone who obviously cared for precision mechanisms. He thought it as much a work of art as a well-crafted tool. But then the Belgian was known for the quality of his products.

"How much?" Vandusen asked, knowing that tranq guns were hard to find in this part of the world and very expensive. African governments, who often wanted to capture rather than kill dissenting subjects, snapped them up, leaving few available for others.

"What's its range?" Bauer looked out into the distance as though measuring and tracking prey.

The Belgian cocked his head and gazed down the road. "I'd say twenty meters, more or less."

Bauer smiled and reached for the gun. He ran his hands over the polished-walnut stock, took several syringe darts and CO_2 cartridges from the case and checked their fit in the receiver. He figured its bore to be .50 caliber, more or less. Except for the shortness of its barrel, it reminded him of the sniper rifles his agency found so useful. "Will the gun do the job?" he asked as he handed the weapon back to the Belgian.

The Belgian paused before answering, careful not to divulge what he suspected the job might be. "I've sold a lot of these systems to the local traders. They swear by them, but you have to get the dosage right. Ketamine can be tricky, but a well-placed dart will do the job on almost anything you want to drop but not kill."

Vandusen gave Bauer a knowing look, but before he could speak, the Belgian continued, "The dosage is everything. If you get it wrong, you'll kill the animal. Apes are especially touchy. Even when you get it right, there can be side effects."

"Like what?" Vandusen asked.

"Respiratory failure or, worse, hallucinations similar to LSD. It's important to get as close as possible to the animal you want to capture."

Vandusen frowned at the prospect of using them up close and personal on the hybrids. But as dangerous as it would be, he thought it worth a try, especially since he wouldn't be the one delivering the darts. That's what he had Bauer for, after all. He smiled at the thought of Dr. Turner and company experiencing side effects. These dart guns would be his best chance at capturing them alive, and he'd need them in order to continue the experiments the Soviets had started.

"How much?" Vandusen asked again. He winced at the price the Belgian demanded, but then nodded, realizing the guns were his best chance of capturing some of the creatures alive. "How many do you have?"

The gunrunner nodded enthusiastically toward his tiny African assistant. He climbed into the back of the dusty Land Cruiser and brought out three more cases.

"We'll take all three and all the darts you have," Vandusen said, then he counted out gold *Krugerrands*.

The Belgian broke into a broad smile and reached out his hand.

Vandusen weighed killing the fat bastard and his sidekick, but thought better of it, knowing they'd need more arms in the future, and this gluttonous pig was the only game in town or jungle.

The Belgian concluded the transaction as quickly as possible, wanting to put some miles between himself and these shady characters. He'd dealt with agents of all kinds lurking in the shadows along the Congo River, but these two and their group of mercenaries were different. He felt a chill every time their shark-like eyes held his. He hastened to load the guns and bid his client goodbye.

Chapter Nine

Bobby thought Hunt had picked the perfect place to meet. When he stepped into City Lights Bookstore, though the pungent scent of jasmine filled the store, making it hard for him to breath, he was relieved to find it packed, even for a weekend. That made it easy to blend into the assorted crowd. He paused to take in the office types in their I'm-important-and-work-for-a-living suits, the bearded and sandaled students, the hippies in tie-dyed t-shirts, and what he thought must be the last remaining hipsters from the Beat Generation.

He realized why it was so crowded when he recognized Lawrence Ferlinghetti, owner of the place and a renowned Beat poet, giving a reading of *Landscape of Living and Dying*. Bobby thought he must be the most famous poet in San Francisco since it seemed as if the entire counterculture of North Beach had turned out.

He crept upstairs as quietly and unobtrusively as he could, but everyone was so intent on the reading that he needn't have worried—that is until some old treads creaked under his weight. Luckily, only a few absently looked in his direction. He expected the upstairs to be crowded with tourists trying to pass for poets. Hunt had mentioned on his last visit that one of the best collections of counterculture books in America lined the shelves, hence the so-called poets. But tonight, he found it empty except for Hunt sitting at a small, oval table in the darkest corner.

Hunt smiled, exhaling in relief, as Bobby slid into a chair beside him. "Hell, I've been worried about you!" he whispered, making his lisp even more noticeable.

"Honestly!" Bobby said, amused. "You fags sure like your drama."

Ignoring his comment, Hunt leaned toward him and continued, "Melon is back, and I'm pretty sure we're on his radar. He's been asking around the district about me, but more importantly, all of us. And worse, Mary called, and said he and some other government lackey had been by the ranch in Reno." He paused as two stringy-haired blondes came up the stairs and waited until they'd found a table on the opposite side of the room. "This whole business has the feeling of more than just Melon."

"What do you mean?" Bobby asked.

"Vandusen and the rest of that bunch."

"Vandusen!" Bobby hissed. He paused, massaging his temples before continuing, "I was hoping they were still trying to haul their butts out of Africa." He looked around nervously, noticing the two girls for the first time. "Do you think this is a safe place to be meeting?"

"Yes, it's fine. My guess is even Melon knows how much he'd stand out here—especially tonight."

"What do you think he's up to now?"

"Melon? The same; looking for leads on Ken"—Hunt leaned closer, lowering his voice even further—"and maybe the creatures."

Bobby frowned. "Hell, you think he actually knows about the creatures? God, is this ever going away?"

"Maybe, and not likely. If Melon is tagging along with Vandusen, then this thing is gonna grow. It's certainly not over. Vandusen wants the creatures—and Melon wants the chimps. They know what they can do with them, or they think they know. It's obvious, Vandusen's willing to do anything to get them—the creatures, that is."

"I don't like what that means," Bobby said.

"It means we're in a shit show." Hunt shifted in his chair and winced in pain.

"Hunt, you all right?" Bobby asked.

"Fine. Just had a long evening at the Baths." Hunt stretched before continuing, "They'll have to go through us first, though." He stood, looked around the room, smiling at the girls, and motioned Bobby to follow.

The reading continued on in earnest, making it a breeze to slip down the stairs and onto the busy sidewalk.

Out on the street, Hunt had to yell over the Saturday night crowd in North Beach, San Francisco. "Come on! I know a more private place where we can get some help in contacting Lester and everyone." Hunt stopped and leaned down to Bobby. "I have an old friend that owns a bar, but more importantly, she's one of those ham radio nuts."

"A what?"

"You know, she has a shitload of radios and talks to people all over the world. They send each other cards—kind of like radio pen pals."

"That could actually work!" Bobby exclaimed, then lowered his voice to continue, "We could find out if Vandusen is still in Africa." He had to almost trot to keep up with Hunt's strides as they weaved through evening crowds toward the Castro District and the Twin Peaks Tavern.

Chapter Ten

Weekday afternoons at Frank's Bar and Cafe were always quiet. A few warehouse workers off from the morning shift were shooting pool for pitchers of beer before heading home to their wives and families. Scotty, the bartender, held court at the U-shaped counter where the unemployed and unemployable counted out the price of a drink in loose change and slid it across in piles on the worn Formica. Hamburgers sizzled and hissed on the grill in the back, filling the bar with an appetizing aroma.

Randi, a full-time college student turned part-time waitress, busied herself getting ready for the three o'clock rush when the next shift at the surrounding warehouses changed. She glanced at a table in the corner. "One of my professors is here."

Scotty smiled. "I'm glad they are. They saved this place."

"What do you mean?" she asked as she filled a pitcher.

"When all the upscale sports bars started popping up all over town, our business almost dropped to nothing."

The waitress looked over at the two professors.

"Those two started coming in with their friends and colleagues," Scotty said, "and business is booming now, thank God."

The waitress laughed and brushed a strand of blonde hair from her face. "Where else can a college student, like me, come into a place and hear teamsters arguing over who will be their next steward, and at the same time, grad students discussing what Kant actually meant by ether in *Critique to Pure Reason*." She'd wondered about the facelift this old sagging bar had received. But looking around at the murals dating back to the forties, the ornate pool tables and photographs of the city when it was still the *Biggest Little City*, she realized it hadn't lost its old-school, Humphrey-Bogart-in-*Casablanca* charm.

"Whatever; what the hell is *ether*, anyway?" Scotty chuckled. "But you know, when those guys are in town, everyone says you're more likely to find them here than in their offices." They both laughed, then Scotty continued, "Finish this tray and take it over to them. I need to go into the walk-in."

***

Doctors Ken Turner and Fred Savage sat in the back, away from the door, poring over a pile of letters and papers they'd dumped out of a wrinkled manila envelope. They had to rearrange everything when the young, blonde waitress brought them a pitcher of Hamm's and two large, steaming bowls of chili. The latter sat on oval plates along with red-plastic baskets of fries and hamburgers, fresh off the grill.

Putting her hands on her hips, she smiled and asked, "Will there be anything else, professors?"

"Not right now, Randi. How's your genealogy project coming along?" Fred asked as he filled two frosty glasses.

She frowned. "Oh God; I'm still struggling with the differences between matrilineal and patrilineal exchanges of wealth." She paused, glancing sideways at Ken before continuing, "I could use some tutoring tonight if you're free."

Fred smiled. "But, of course, I always have time for one of my favorite grad students. How 'bout we meet at the Bull 'N Mouth around nine tonight?"

She nodded with a provocative smile.

They watched as she glided away.

Ken smirked, shaking his head. "Still the dedicated professor, I see."

"Of course, teaching has its own ... how should I say? Intrinsic rewards."

"The limits to your dedication have no bounds. But I have one question."

Fred took a long draw from his mug and set it down noisily on the table. "Ask away."

"How come it's only the good-looking female grad students you seem to be in the habit of tutoring?"

Fred paused, watching the waitress stretching up on her tippy toes to reach more plastic baskets above the grill. Her t-shirt rose. revealing her shapeliness. "Just lucky, I guess." He continued to stare for a few heartbeats as the young woman lingered. She seemed to sense him admiring her and reached higher, apparently enjoying it. "Beautiful women really do have all the power."

"Careful; that road leads to ruin," Ken observed.

Fred laughed. "I know. Think of Chaney. If that young man isn't careful, he'll end up putting more women into houses than HUD."

Both professors laughed as Scotty toasted young Fred from behind the counter.

Ken reached for a letter. "Now, back to business. Read this letter from Lester." He watched as Fred read, ignoring the couple who greeted them in passing.

Fred frowned as he read. He finished, looking concerned, but before Ken could speak, he began reading it again. This time he scribbled notes on the back of the envelope. Finally, he laid the letter back on the pile, carefully avoiding the puddle of condensation that had pooled from the frosty mugs, picked up the envelope, and examined the return address and stamps.

"Lester and Girlie are still in Africa." Fred moved his fingers as though counting, tapping out the months in the air. "At least five and a half months after we left."

Ken frowned, the wrinkles accentuated his thin, chiseled face. "Yes—and from this account, still no sign of Mike, Oliver or Danny."

Fred nodded. "At least we know Lester and Girlie are safe, or at least they were when Lester sent this. I was worried about Girlie. She's an old chimp."

"She may be old for a chimp, but she's tough, for sure," Ken interrupted. "I'm more worried about where the hell Vandusen and his gang are. I'm pretty sure they're still in Africa or they would've shown up around here by now."

A loud crack sounded at the pool table, startling the professors. Someone had just broken a rack, but both scientists looked around as though half expecting Vandusen and his band of agents to come busting in.

"Don't forget what it was like to be 'guests' of the CIA or whatever organization they serve," Ken added.

Fred nodded. "It hasn't been that long ago that we barely escaped being kidnapped by those assholes in this very bar." He paused, checking to see if his last statement had sunk in before continuing, "And don't forget Africa. That whole group is ruthless, and they'll stop at nothing to get their hands on the creatures, or our chimps for that matter, to use for their own warped purposes."

Ken open his mouth to speak but could only manage to nod.

Fred picked up several more photos and began sorting through them. "Most of these seem routine. They just show the repairs and improvements since the raid."

Ken picked up a photo from the pile and held it up to the light that hung over the booth. "It looks like François and his Belgians have been busy putting the compound back in order."

Fred nodded. "It looks pretty much back as it was." He continued organizing the photos into piles. The images drew him back to Africa. It seemed like ages since they'd discovered the *Orion* on that lonely beach on the coast of the Congo. He wondered what secrets must still be on that wreck and when, if ever, they'd get back to search it, and, more importantly, find their star chimp, Mike.

Ken leaned toward the center of the table, almost spilling his beer. "Don't forget the creatures. These hybrids are the anthropological find of the century." He paused. "Maybe of all time."

Fred waited for a group of students to pass. Fortunately, they noticed the professors were deep in conversation and were polite enough not to stop. "It's apparent the Soviets pulled it off and bred humans and chimpanzees successfully. But how, especially with the limited technology they had in the thirties?" Fred's face flushed and he clenched his fists. "Vandusen and these government agents are complicating everything. They don't care for the scientific implications of all this. All they want is to use these creatures for their own purposes. They corrupt everything they touch." Fred stood up to pace but realized he was hemmed in as the bar filled up with the afternoon crowd. He sat down and shrugged.

"Earth to Dr. Savage," Ken said, pulling Fred back to the work at hand.

"Sorry." Fred continued to separate a group of photos that depicted several destroyed villages.

"I thought we'd lost you, amigo."

Fred lowered his voice. "Take a look at these. I think we should've stayed."

Ken took the stack of photos carefully, holding them by the edges as some were stuck together with sticky emulsion. "Christ! Look at this set of pictures. This is really disturbing." Ken handed the stack back to Fred. "While they're very much like the villages you and I saw on our scouting parties with François—they seem fresher."

"Fresher?" Fred raised an eyebrow. "That's an interesting choice of words." He paused, watching several people entering the bar and noisily greeting friends as they found a booth. "But I see your point. All the villages we'd come across were destroyed long before, and little was left of them but ruins—certainly no bodies."

"Exactly, but look at this photo. They've lined up all the bodies into rows as though to order them … maybe … or count them before burying them," Ken said.

"A body count—Lester must have arrived right after this happened. I can't imagine dealing with this gruesome mess," Fred said.

Ken leaned toward Fred and whispered, "It's more than a body count. Look closer. There's something not right about these bodies. They almost seem reassembled—put back together."

"Yes, some of the arms and legs are not quite right. Are they?"

"Nope, but there's more. Look at where the river is in relationship to the mountains—and how far away the village is from the banks," Ken said.

"They're on the wrong fucking side of the river!" Fred yelled.

"Hush!" Ken whispered. "People are looking." Ken smiled and waved at several people who were looking over at them before he continued, "I think you're right. The creatures have crossed the river and are at it again."

Fred shook his head. "God, I hope they know what they're doing over there. This is going to get out of hand."

"I'm sure they do. But, remember, they were powerless after the raid by Vandusen. All the creatures escaped along with Oliver and Danny. It was a cluster fuck. Look at the photos.

They've spent a lot of time just making the compound secure again," Ken said.

"You're right about it being a cluster fuck, for sure. But I think there's more to worry about." Fred took a sip of beer.

"Like what?"

"Mike, Oliver and Danny. Think about it—they've spent their whole lives with humans, and the last time we saw them, they were together," Fred said.

"And your point?" Ken asked.

"Mike knows sign language. He can teach the creatures to communicate on a higher level than they've ever been able to do."

"Crap."

"No, holy crap."

They sat silently, caught up in their own thoughts and not noticing the waitress who automatically brought them another pitcher. They were going to need it, and many more.

Chapter Eleven

"Well, it's time to check-in—I suppose," Ken said with a sigh.

Fred drained his glass. "Better not put it off any longer."

Ken gathered the photographs, slid them back into the envelope and tucked it out of sight in his satchel, then they left the bar and headed to the president's office located in the main administration building of the university. They walked across the quad in silence, pausing to step over a rope where a sign dangled, reminding them to "Keep off the Grass." Ken laughed at the marijuana leaves someone had sketched around the borders.

Some student has way too much time on his hands.

He smiled, trying to remember back to the time in his university life when a sign like that was the most excitement he got in a day. "I can't believe it's been a year since the hearing."

Fred nodded. "In this very building."

"Well, at least we're not going to another one. We're just having a little chat with the president." Ken stopped and leaned back, trying to pick out the window of the president's office.

"Yah, but the stakes always seem the same every time we enter the administration building," Fred said.

"Just our careers. Relax, what could go wrong?" Ken said, smirking. It seemed like a lifetime since he and his colleagues had been jerked from their comfortable routines and thrown into the shadowy world of intrigue and danger that they found themselves in now. Those proceedings had added further strain to his already testy relationship with the school's administration, but he didn't care. He'd been, and was still, outraged at the recommendation of the hearing panel to make their research more "practical." An interesting choice of words, he thought, knowing it was just a code word for playing ball with the shady government types. He sighed, knowing this meeting would probably be another attempt to force them to get "practical."

"I can't believe the university doesn't realize this so-called 'grant' money has strings attached to it." Ken's voice rose, catching the attention of several students reading on the lawn. "It's no more than a bribe. It doesn't bother them that we'd be implementing cruel and unethical practices on our chimps." He quickened his pace.

"Careful, Ken. Keep your voice down," Fred said. He was having trouble talking and keeping up but managed to say, "I have a feeling the president and his lackeys may have found out about our investigation into hybridization, and, worse, the research the Soviets conducted."

Ken slowed down to a walk. "Melon's probably at the bottom of this—at least here at the university. But somehow, I think Vandusen is pulling the strings. I wish I'd never dragged everyone into this mess."

"You didn't. We all came along willingly. I wish I knew an easy way out without raining disaster on us, the chimps, and the creatures, though. We need to keep our mouths shut."

"You're right. I wonder how much the president really knows, especially concerning Childs. I bet he knows plenty, or, worse, is part of a scheme to get us to fall in line."

Ken couldn't even be sure if Vandusen's people actually represented the government. He wasn't sure of anything anymore. He looked over at his friend, but just couldn't admit that his thoughts kept looping back to the fact that since their orderly world of research and teaching had been turned upside down, wouldn't it be better to just give up, come clean, and get this nightmare over?

He was so deep in thought that he hardly noticed the students and faculty who greeted them as they made their way up the steps. He did, however, think it odd that a university policeman waited to escort them. He felt the policeman's uneasiness as he joined them in the elevator, and couldn't help but break the silence by tapping the policemen on the arm and saying, "Now, I call this service."

The officer glared at both of them, and Ken thought better of continuing his taunts.

When they stepped into the reception area, he paused to admire the rich, walnut paneling being installed by an army of workmen. He followed the policeman, being careful not to trip on tarps spread over a new parquet floor. Without saying a word, he pointed at piles of planks lined along the walls ready for the carpenters. The workman paid him little attention, too busy struggling to move a tall ladder and hoist a crystal chandelier up to the newly vaulted ceiling.

I wonder where they got the money for these little upgrades? Ken caught Fred's attention and realized he was thinking the same thing.

He had to weave around even more drop cloths and ladders to enter the reception area of the president's office. The pungent odor of fresh paint assaulted him. A secretary coldly greeted them and ushered them into the office where the president stood smiling behind his desk.

Ken thought the little man acted unusually amiable. *Out of character for this pedantic little bastard.* The last time Ken had seen him was at the formal hearing. The president had been so angry he'd refused to acknowledge or look at him. He'd stormed out of the room in a rage. But, now, he was half expecting to be invited to sit around his desk and sing "Kumbaya."

"Ah, Dr. Turner and Dr. Savage, at last! How good of you to take time out of your busy schedules to meet with us." The two scientists took notice of his use of "us." They looked around the room, but they were alone, at least for the moment.

The secretary returned, rolling in a cart with a carafe of coffee and assorted rolls. The wheels bogged in the thick, newly laid carpet.

Ken, making little effort to hide his disgust for the expensive decorations, observed, "It seems there's been a lot of remodeling and upgrades around here since our last visit. Your office is well appointed."

Ignoring Ken's sarcastic tone, the president smiled and answered, "Yes, it's quite nice, isn't it? A little gift from one of our newfound donors. Aren't these new bookcases beautiful? They're handmade from Germany, I believe."

New donors! I can guess who they might be. Ken could just control his anger, but he couldn't hide his disdain upon noticing an antique, leather-bound volume of *Mein Kampf. How fitting,* he thought.

Undaunted, the president continued, "Some of our new donors have taken a real interest in your work and are eager to gift you anything you or those precious chimps might need. I wanted us to get together this morning over coffee and start out on a new footing—start over, if you will." He walked out from around his desk and motioned them to sit at a small conference table. "Please, let's get comfortable and chat. We really want to help."

First 'us' and now 'we.' Ken was losing his patience.

Without asking, the president began ceremoniously pouring them cups of coffee. "The rolls are delicious, fresh this morning. I think they're from the bagel shop across the street, student owned, I'm told."

Ken and Fred hesitated before accepting the offered plates. The meeting was obviously rehearsed. Ken thought it a classic example of what he called "insincere sincerity"—a behavior he'd unfortunately grown accustomed to since entering the world of university politics and grants. He still didn't like it.

Fred interrupted, growing impatient: "I'd appreciate it if we could get to the point. As you might guess, we're very busy with our work and need to get back to our chimps."

A flicker of anger crossed the president's face, but he quickly got back in character. "Ah, you see, that's just what I admire about you both—so dedicated to your work and the chimps." His manner hardened, becoming less jovial, and he kept glancing to the door as he buttered a roll. "That's partly what we wanted to talk to you about this morning. It seems you have some chimps that are—how should I say?—misplaced."

There's the "we/us" again.

Ken interrupted: "The findings of the hearing made it quite clear that we're the legal guardians of our chimps. Besides, you needn't worry, they're all accounted for."

"Really? Part of the findings made it quite clear that the university was to be kept apprised of the location of all the inventory that is part of your project. It seems we're not all on the same page with that." The president's voice trailed off at the sound of the door opening.

Melon entered, accompanied by a young sheriff.

Ken and Fred stood abruptly. "So this is what this farce is all about!" Ken exclaimed.

The sheriff stood silently, blocking the door.

"Well, well!" Melon said. "After spending the better part of this year trying to arrange a meeting, where should I find you but at a chance meeting with our esteemed president. Do wonders never cease?"

The president quickly retreated behind his desk.

Glaring at Melon and barely controlling his anger, Ken said, "We have nothing to say to you that hasn't already been said at the hearing. Now, if you'll excuse us."

Ken and Fred made for the door, but the young sheriff quickly placed his hand over the handle of his pistol. "Sirs, if you will please sit down."

"Why? Are you arresting us?" Ken asked.

"Not at this time, but my orders are to have you wait. My lieutenant would like to have a word with you concerning a missing person."

They both knew to whom the sheriff referred: Childs.

"And if we choose to leave?" Fred asked.

"You'd be disobeying a police officer's directive. I'd have no choice but to arrest you. But hopefully we won't have to go that far." The young officer's Adam's apple bobbed nervously, and he unsnapped the strap on his holster.

Ken and Fred returned to their seats.

Melon smiled, but the crackle of the sheriff's radio stopped him speaking further. The young man turned it down and opened the door.

A stocky man in his forties with disheveled, thinning blond hair entered. He adjusted his tie and pulled at his off-the-rack, loosely fitting sports jacket in a careless manner. "Let's see. I've met everyone here but Dr. Turner and his esteemed colleague, Dr. Savage, both who, I might add, need no introduction around these parts.

"My name is Lieutenant Detective John Sandy, and as you can guess, I work for the Washoe County Sheriff's Department. Dr. Melon was kind enough to inform me that I might be able to catch you both here this morning." He nodded to Melon. "Many thanks, sir." He looked back at Ken and Fred and added, "You're hard men to catch!"

Ken interrupted: "I'm not sure what you mean by 'catch', but could you please tell us what this is all about?"

"Of course. I'm assigned to investigate the disappearance of a certain university graduate student—a Mr. Gordon Childs." John Sandy paused, observing the two scientists closely. "You both knew this student, correct?"

No one spoke while the detective casually busied himself at the coffee table.

Ken finally broke the silence: "I believe he was auditing my primatology class and had dropped by the compound a few times. But I wouldn't say I knew him. Our project draws a lot of people. We can't be expected to remember them all."

The detective nodded to Fred. "And you, sir?"

"He gave me a ride once from the airport—I think he was looking for work. As Dr. Turner mentioned, we get lots of types wanting to join up with us."

Melon could hardly contain himself. "Really! I—"

The detective continued, cutting Melon off abruptly: "Thank you, Dr. Melon, but I'll do the questioning here, if you please." He smiled at Fred and pulled out a small notepad. "We understand you were in Africa very recently."

Fred hesitated. His mind raced back to the events that took them to Africa, and he wondered how much this inquisitive detective actually knew. But he realized that their passports would reveal their travel itinerary and nothing much more. "Yes, we were on sabbatical, serving as technical advisors on a movie."

"Interesting—Mr. Childs apparently was in Africa at the same time."

Ken jumped in: "It's a big continent. What are you driving at?"

The detective smiled. "That's right; it's a continent, isn't it? I always think of it as a country—but I was never very good at geography in school."

Fuming, Melon could contain himself no longer. "Short of a geography lesson, what in the hell are we doing here?" he shouted. "Arrest them! Clearly, they're responsible for the disappearance of Mr. Childs."

Ken and Fred both caught the special emphasis he put on "disappearance." In unison, they stood to leave.

Ken, ignoring Melon, said to the detective, "We've told you all we know concerning Mr. Childs. If you're not prepared to charge us with anything, we're leaving."

"Really no need to get so formal here, professors. Please understand, you both just may have been the last people to see or speak to Mr. Childs before his disappearance. I was hoping you'd cooperate with my investigation and help me close the case." The detective paused, seeming to read the strain between the two professors, Melon and the president. "I wonder if you'd be kind enough to join me downtown and give me a statement? I think we can be more productive if I speak with just the two of you."

"So we're free to go?" Ken asked.

"Well, yes and no. Let's say you're free to go if you agree to come down to the station and give me statements for my investigation."

"When?" Ken asked.

"How 'bout now?" The detective opened the door. "I can give you a lift if you need a ride."

"Thanks, but we can drive ourselves if it's just the same," Fred answered.

"Then it's all settled. After you, professors." He ushered them to the door with a sweeping motion.

The meeting was over.

Melon's protests could be heard all the way to the elevator. In spite of the circumstances, Ken and Fred couldn't help laughing. Detective Sandy joined in for a moment, but then his manner grew serious, and as the elevator doors closed, he said, "Now let's talk a little more about you two.

Chapter Twelve

The Twin Peaks Tavern was packed, and to Hunt and Bobby, it seemed as if everyone from the Castro and the Tenderloin mixed with the young, straight, and upwardly mobile must be out for happy hour. They had to push their way through a crowd jammed three deep to even get near the long, ornate bar where several bartenders frantically worked to keep everyone in drinks.

Hunt yelled several times before his soft, high-pitched voice finally registered above the din with a young, petite bartender. Nodding, as though they were expected, she motioned them to follow and sashayed up the stairs. Her cropped, black-dyed hair, highlighted with a bright-orange streak, contrasted with her fine features and ivory skin. As she progressed up the stairs ahead of them, they couldn't help but notice her studded, calf-high motorcycle boots and tight-fitting shorts.

"Bobby, just stick close and let me do the talking," Hunt said, as they followed the bartender up the stairs. "We're going to meet Lori, one of the owners of this place." Hunt paused, looking around, and whispered, "She's been a ham radio enthusiast for years and thinks her equipment can reach François and Lester."

"You're kidding. We could really talk to them?" Bobby asked.

"That's what she says."

They stirred to action when they noticed the bartender waiting, tapping her boot, at the top of the stairs.

But Hunt stopped to greet numerous patrons, slowing their progress. It was no surprise to Bobby, since Hunt was a regular in this most irregular place. It seemed that Hunt was a kind of a celebrity everywhere he went, known from the Circus Luncheon Club in LA to the Twin Peaks Tavern in San Francisco. Bobby smiled in admiration.

"This place has a long history that goes back to the beginnings of the bohemians." Hunt stopped to embrace someone, then continued, "There was a time when writers like Kerouac and Ginsberg came here to mix with the hippies of Haight-Ashbury. But now, everyone comes here, even the straights and ultra-straights. It's owned by two lesbians, friends of mine. You might say it's one of the most avant-garde, gay spots in the city. The only place I love better than here are the baths."

"Well, it sure looks like everyone comes here now," Bobby said.

Hunt looked over at some young college students and grinned. "You're right. Young straights come up here on Saturday nights wanting the adventure of mixing with us. I think they want to prove how open and egalitarian they are." He paused on the stairs and chuckled. "After a few too many Cosmoses, some find out just how open and egalitarian they really are—especially around closing time."

Bobby laughed. "So you could say lives are changed here."

The bar was a renovated fire station dating back before the San Francisco Earthquake and Great Fire. Originally, the engines and equipment had been kept at the ground level where the bar was now. The second floor, where they were headed, had been the sleeping quarters for the firemen. It now had additional booths and afforded more privacy than the floor below. So, if someone really wanted to be private, they went to the second floor and held forth in one of the back booths where the lighting was poor and everyone minded their own business. That was the attraction of the Twin Peaks Tavern.

Hunt picked a good place, Bobby thought.

As they made their way further up the stairs, Bobby noticed memorabilia of the station and history of the bar interspersed on the walls; old photographs of fire crews hung beside portraits of transvestites. It seemed to Bobby that everyone had a place in the tavern.

Hunt smiled when he saw Bobby looking at the photos. "In its own way, this place has been able to bridge the gap between the straight and gay cultures of the city. All are welcome as long as they leave their prejudices and politics at the door."

Hunt and Bobby waited at the top of the stairs while the girl with the orange streak cleared a booth, then disappeared through a full-length mirror on the wall—a secret door left over from the Prohibition days.

They were just finishing their second Cosmos when the girl reappeared from the mirrored door and motioned them to come in.

"A woman of few words," Bobby said.

Ignoring him, Hunt led the way through the mirrored door. Obviously, he knew the way and had been there before.

They entered a small room full of radios and other electronics, and an older woman turned from her desk and greeted them. "Hunt, my dear!" she said, her voice with the rasp of a longtime smoker. "Where in the hell have you been?" They embraced, as old friends often do after a long absence.

Bobby was taken and amused by the contrast between them; the woman seemed more masculine than Hunt. The woman wore an oversized, white t-shirt with a pack of Camels rolled up in one sleeve and paint-splattered jeans that spread wide at the seat. A faded radio call sign was stenciled across her chest. He could just make it out between the stains and holes of her ragged shirt. Her disheveled appearance contrasted with her sharp and bold manner.

"Please make yourselves at home," she said, as she busied herself clearing dog-eared magazines and books from a worn couch. "Hope you'll excuse the mess. I don't often get visitors up here in my shack."

Bobby realized they must be standing in a ham shack. While he'd heard of people who practiced the hobby of ham radios, this was the first time he'd actually met anyone who did this sort of thing. A slew of electronic equipment packed and stacked the little room. Two of the biggest pieces looked to be some kind of radios or transmitters, but Bobby couldn't make heads or tails of anything else. Cables and wires ran in every direction; he had to be careful not to trip in the tangle strewn across the floor.

Photographs of people surrounding radios or posing on mountain tops with large antennas covered the walls. Cards with call signs from all over the world were pinned up on the wall behind what looked to Bobby to be a large radio. In front, a tall chrome and black microphone sat on a table scattered with logbooks and various cords.

"God, is this some kind of mission control?" Bobby asked.

Lori laughed. "Actually, it is, sort of." She smiled and reached her hand out to Bobby. "So you must be Bobby Waiter. Hunt has told me a lot about you."

"And you're Lori. As you've probably guessed, Hunt has reciprocated," Bobby said while shaking hands.

"Now that you've established your little mutual-admiration society, shall we get down to business?" Hunt asked. He took one of two chairs at the table and motioned Lori to follow. "So, Lori, as you might've guessed, we have a problem." Hunt paused, looking around the room. "We have some friends who may be in trouble in Africa, and we need to reach them."

Lori nodded. "What part of Africa?"

Hunt hesitated.

Sensing his reluctance to divulge too much, Lori continued, "Sorry if I seem to be prying, but it's important to know exactly where the radio is you're trying to reach."

"The Congo," Bobby said.

"Well, now, that's going to take some doing. We're going to need some real output and a bigger antenna."

"So you can do it?" Bobby and Hunt asked, almost in unison.

"Sure, but it'll take a little time."

"Like how much?" Hunt asked.

Lori frowned as she opened a large world atlas. "How much money do you have?"

"Enough," Bobby answered. Smiling and patting Hunt's shoulder, he continued, "I'm just finishing a movie. Hell, I'm rich, at least for a week or two."

Lori laughed. "Well, that's settled. You'll get along just fine around here. I'll have to do some research, order more equipment." She looked around the room as though mentally rearranging it. "And install it—I won't order it all from the same outlet, though—two or three weeks, at the most."

"Can we help?" Hunt asked.

"Only if you want to slow me down."

They laughed, and Bobby began counting out hundreds.

***

The bar was closed by the time Bobby and Hunt made their way downstairs. The few remaining servers and bartenders were so busy cleaning up, they didn't notice them.

The contrast with just a few hours before was marked. The streets, damp from a recent drizzle, were vacant. Their footsteps echoed down the empty streets as they made their way to the BART station. Bobby found it unsettling to realize they were completely alone.

"Should we find a phone booth and call a cab?" he asked.

"No, BART isn't far." Hunt craned his head around and quickened his pace.

"How far?"

"Depends on if we take a shortcut through that alley over there or stay on these streets," Hunt replied.

"I vote for the streets," Bobby said.

They continued in silence past the alley and tried to pick up their pace, but the few streetlights that still worked cast more shadows than light, and they had to be careful picking their way along the cracked and uneven sidewalks. The Castro was an older part of the city with crumbling infrastructure, and navigating it slowed their progress, making them nervous.

Finally, Bobby broke the silence. "I can't explain it, but I feel like we're being followed."

"I think we're just tired," Hunt said.

"Tired of what?"

"Secrets, Bobby, secrets; I'm sick of it."

Bobby glanced around. "Let's not talk out here."

It began to rain.

"Christ! That's all we need," Bobby muttered, buttoning his jacket.

"There's BART!" Hunt exclaimed. He quickened his pace, making Bobby have to jog to keep up.

The glow of the lights of the BART station blinded them when they stepped out of the shadows onto the empty platform. The contrast between the decaying concrete and brick neighborhood of the Castro and the shiny, chrome and glass station was eerie, and, strangely, they felt even more exposed and in danger in the bright lights of the station than they'd felt, moments before, on the dark streets. Hunt squinted as he tried to read the rolling electronic route schedules on the screen, and Bobby fumbled for change at the token machine, then paced, being careful to stay out of the shadows.

Suddenly, the whole platform rumbled under their feet, startling them, and they felt the swoosh of air from the tunnel before they saw the train approach.

Hunt smiled in relief. "That's us."

When the door hissed open, they jumped into the empty car of the yellow line to the airport. It had been a long evening.

***

The General watched from the far side of the platform just out of the blinding light. Nudging his aide, he whispered, "Hurry up! Follow them."

The aide jumped into action, boarding the train several cars up from Bobby and Hunt.

All the pieces are finally falling into place, the General thought.

When the train left the station, he beckoned a black sedan waiting in the darkness. It drove up beside him, and he paused, looking around, before sliding into the back and tapping the driver. "Let's get to the airport. I need to get back to Reno, so we can gather up a few people. I think it's about time we had a little reunion, so we can tie up some loose ends—I hate loose ends."

The driver nodded and turned onto an empty street. "You want me to call for some back-up?"

The General looked up from a small address book and nodded. "Yes. We're going to need a specialist on this operation."

The driver smiled. "I know just the person. She's an expert in … persuasion. I think you know who I mean."

71

The General nodded. "Yes, I do. Tell her to bring her tools—all of them."

"She usually does, being a woman who takes real pride in her work, a true professional."

They both laughed as they merged onto the Bayshore Freeway and sped into the night.

Chapter Thirteen

Melon raced down the crowded front steps of the university muttering angrily to himself. He ignored the rude remarks from students jostling to avoid him and stopped in their midst to look for the detective, Dr. Turner, and Dr. Savage. Being passing period and the beginning of the fall term, the admin building was packed. It would be difficult to find anyone in this crowd.

After all the money the NSF had given to this podunk excuse for a university, someone was going to pay and pay big—especially that poor excuse for a college president. The idiot just didn't understand how the game was supposed to be played.

Dr. Turner and his crew would be sorry they'd ever crossed him. If it wasn't for him, they'd never have received a grant in the first place—a grant that had given them a pretty comfortable situation. He couldn't believe how ungrateful the lot of them were.

If it hadn't been for me, they'd still be scraping and begging for crumbs to keep their project limping along.

He felt exasperated to think that they didn't even acknowledge the potential of their work and the rewards it could bring to all of them. He'd tried to explain to them that the government had fat purses just waiting to be dipped into—if you knew how to open them. Even the shadowy elements Vandusen represented could be quite cooperative.

Ungrateful shits!

Melon was so engrossed in planning his revenge that he didn't notice two agents swooping in on either side of him until one grabbed his arm with a vise-like grip. He winced, startled.

"This way, if you please, Dr. Melon," the big, muscular man said in an intense and menacing voice.

Another agent dropped in behind them and followed as the pair escorted Melon toward a sedan parked at the curb, its rear door open. He made a feeble attempt to struggle by pulling back from the door, but the men unceremoniously shoved him into the back seat and up against another agent. The man glared, pushed him off, and motioned him to sit quietly. A large, dark man slid inside after Melon, pinning him in the middle. Melon, who was never at a loss for words, found himself speechless.

***

Except for the General and his adjunct standing at the corner of the building, the crowd didn't notice Melon's predicament. The General smirked as he watched the sedan speed off, disappearing down the road that led out of town.

"Vandusen better get back soon," he said to his adjunct. "I mean like yesterday, or we're going to have to make some readjustments. Go make the call."

Deep in thought, the General stared down the road, and then, as though shaken out of a dream, joined the throng of students entering the building.

It's time to have a little chat with someone special.

Chapter Fourteen

A stale smell mixed with whiffs of urine and sweat assaulted Ken and Fred as they entered the stuffy reception area of the cramped Reno police headquarters. Clearly, it hadn't kept up with the growth of the "Biggest Little City in World." From the looks of the crowded station, crime was booming. Loud voices and the scraping of chairs echoed off the black and white checkered linoleum floor. Everything about the place was chaotic.

Ken thought how much this once-sleepy little town had changed in the decade since he'd packed up and settled to assume his post at the University of Nevada, Reno, but the shouts of two prostitutes being roughly escorted to a booking window jarred him out of his thoughts. He and Fred followed the detective through a maze of desks, manned by an army of officers who answered a chorus of ringing telephones. They carefully worked their way around the ruckus, and no one paid them much heed as they crossed the room toward a little glass cubicle that Ken assumed was Detective Sandy's office.

Ken smiled, and gesturing his arm in a sweeping motion across the room, he observed, "It looks like the progress the city fathers worked so hard to achieve has resulted in more than they expected."

John Sandy ignored his remark, holding the door open. "Please, sorry for the mess. Just clear a place and have a seat."

A blinking fluorescent lamp hanging crookedly from the water-stained ceiling drew Ken's attention. The hum of its faulty ballast explained its flickering glare. He squeezed through a clutter of haphazardly stacked files and looked at the clippings and mugshots pinned up on the back wall, behind the desk. The different groups seemed to be for the different cases on which the detective worked. From the extent of them spreading across the wall, it seemed to Ken that the man had a full caseload. He studied several photographs in the largest display. Pictures and diplomas had been unhung and haphazardly set aside to make room for the growing collage.

Ken leaned against the wall on one hand and took a closer look at a press clipping that included a grainy photo of Oliver. "That's not a very good picture of Oliver. I've seen better over the years," Ken said.

Detective Sandy smiled and pointed at the clippings. "You've lived a busy life, Dr. Turner. After reading all these, I feel like I already know you. I have to say, you've covered a few miles while on your vacation—sabbatical, I think you called it. You mentioned, back at the president's office, that you got as far as Africa, but we were interrupted before we got to what exactly you were doing over there."

Ken felt uneasy with this line of questioning. How much did this young detective know about their doings? Beads of perspiration trickled from under his arms, and he wondered if the detective noticed his uneasiness. He had to calm himself. But all these clippings made him feel exposed. It was as though a spotlight had flooded all over their dark secret and all could see every detail of what they'd been up to.

He couldn't explain it, but again for some inexplicable reason, he had the urge to come clean and put an end to all this mess, right now and in this office. He was tired of all the deceit and lies they'd had to perpetuate to hide what had happened. He'd almost forgotten what it felt like to just attend to teaching and research and live a normal life, absent of all the secrecy. But then, he remembered Mike and the rest of the chimps. They were the ones really at risk, and he would do whatever was necessary to protect them. He'd even lie if that's what it took.

"As I said, we were working on a movie as technical advisors," Ken said as he took a seat.

Detective Sandy smiled. "As you said, Professor. But if you'll excuse me, it seems quite a departure from your regular work. I know you were ... how should I say, distracted at the chancellor's office, so I'll ask you again, did you happen to run into Mr. Childs during your *technical advising* over there?"

Ken noticed the subtle but incredulous emphasis the detective put on *technical advising*. "I'll say, again, Africa is a huge continent. The chances of us meeting up with Mr. Childs would be very slim."

"I'm not sure that actually answers my question, Dr. Turner." Detective Sandy's voice and manner grew more interrogative and serious. "So you're saying none of you saw Mr. Gordon Childs during your time in Africa?"

Ken realized that the detective suspected more than he was letting on, and he, and whoever he was working with, were likely closing in on the truth. And further, he suspected the country bumpkin manner of the detective was just a cover to put them off guard. Ken needed to pick his words very carefully.

Fred gave him a sidelong glance of warning as Ken answered, "Detective Sandy, I will say again, we have no knowledge of the whereabouts of Mr. Childs or much less care."

"So you haven't seen him?"

"No."

The detective now addressed Fred. "So, Dr. Savage, do you have anything to add to this … story?"

"Mr. Childs wa— is a real pest. I think he's been trying to secure a position with us, but he's really not qualified. We've given him the brush-off several times, but he just doesn't take the hint and keeps pestering us."

"I see. You don't know his whereabouts?"

Looking at Ken for reassurance, Fred replied, "No, we don't, and as I said, we don't really want to."

Spreading his arms, the detective said, "Well, that puts my investigation at a standstill. You have nothing more to add?"

"We'd really like to help," Ken said, "but I'm afraid we're at a loss as to how. We can't tell you the whereabouts of Childs if we don't know." He stood, dumping a pile of folders off his chair. "If you don't mind, we need to get back to our work."

Detective Sandy took a deep breath before exhaling. "No, no more questions at this time, but certainly stay in touch, and don't leave town without contacting me."

"Then we'll say goodbye, for now." Ken motioned Fred to follow.

Detective Sandy's eyes hardened as he watched the two professors make their way out of the station. He picked up his phone, rang the duty sergeant and said, "I want those two gentlemen followed. I want to know every move they make from now on, day or night."

He ended the call and paced his empty office. "Technical advisers, indeed. Those two know more than they're letting on, and sooner or later, I'm gonna find out what the hell they're up to. Then let's see how long they hold up under some good old-fashioned interrogation."

He turned to the wall of clippings again, wondering what had interested Dr. Turner about the clipping of Oliver. He'd seemed surprised at seeing the photo. Detective Sandy pulled the staple from the clipping and his heart raced as he read. *There must be a clue here somewhere.* He grabbed his magnifying glass and looked more closely at the photo.

"*Steinwasen* Park. That's it," he shouted.

Several of the officers in the outer office looked up from their desks at the young detective pacing and talking to himself, but only for a moment—they were getting used to it.

Detective John Sandy was on the hunt now, but his prey was very clever. The photo that startled the professor had been taken in *Steinwasen* Park, probably the last place Oliver had resided before arriving in the U.S. It could be a stop on the underground smugglers' route he'd read about. He needed to make some calls and find out what about that place made the usually cool professor nervous. The detective felt almost embarrassed when he realized how much he loved the hunt.

***

"Well, that sure as hell went well," Ken said. "We're genuinely fucked." He honked the horn of his suburban as he weaved through snarled, downtown traffic. "This place is getting way too crowded."

Fred nodded. "That detective definitely knows a lot more than he's letting on. But how much? Remember, he's a cop, and that's what they do." Fred kept his voice calm, knowing that would help keep Ken from "red alerting," as Mary called it.

"What do you mean?" Ken tapped his fingers on the steering wheel as he waited for the traffic light.

"You know. He's acting like he knows more than he really does to get us talking," Fred replied.

"Maybe, but I don't think we want to wait around long enough for him to fill in the blanks. Did you see that clipping of Oliver standing next to the old circus wagon?"

"Yes, I've seen a lot of those pictures. Oliver worked in the circus most of his life. What of it?" Fred asked.

"In that clipping you can just make out the sign on the gate in the background," Ken replied, "that little gypsy camp, *Steinwasen*, is where Oliver and probably Danny were smuggled from."

Fred nodded. "If I remember correctly, Dusty said it's near Ramstein Airbase in Germany."

"Yes, which is conveniently located near all military and government transportation coming in and out of Africa." Ken paused as he concentrated on weaving through a knot of traffic slowing behind a tour bus. "In the old days, it was a breeze to transport anyone or anything through that base without even the military knowing, and from there—well, anywhere. I came across several references to that park when tracing the origins of not only Oliver but also some of our own chimps."

"Our own chimps? Hell, that's illegal." Fred frowned.

"Not that long ago, we really didn't care where our chimps came from as long as we got them for our research," Ken said.

"I doubt the detective is going to be too concerned with where our chimps came from."

"Sure, but if he begins asking questions there, the hybrids are sure to come up. From what I'm learning, that little gypsy camp comes up in several accounts concerning the backgrounds of Oliver and Danny and probably other creatures we haven't even heard about." Ken reached to the backseat for his briefcase. A car honked and Ken swerved back into their lane.

"Let me get that before you kill us!" Fred grabbed his case and set it on his lap.

"I've got some information on that place," Ken said. "I was meaning to take a trip there to see if we can find out more about where and when Oliver came to the States. But more importantly, did other hybrids pass through there? Someone over there has to know."

"I'm thinking that if you know about this, and, now, that detective is suspicious, it's only a matter of time before Vandusen will figure it out, if he hasn't already," Fred said.

Ken grimaced. "Yeah. We need to take a vacation to fill in some blanks. Germany should be nice this time of year."

Fred shook his head. "You heard the man, 'don't leave town' or some other silly crap. I don't like it."

"He said not to leave town without contacting him." Ken smiled. "That's why God created answering machines. We'll leave him a message."

The traffic lightened as they made their way south down Virginia Street towards the ranch and Mary, and the next adventure.

Chapter Fifteen

"Well, I guess you see where all your money went." Lori beamed as she wiped off the new equipment. Two large consoles sat where the old equipment had been. "It took some testing, but we have them locked in now. It was hard to get the times right between them and us, but we hit the gray line perfect, last night around eight. They weren't happy since it was five the next morning for them, but we got a good signal."

"I'm almost afraid to ask, but what's the gray line?" Bobby looked closer at the equipment that had cost over a week's pay. He was surprised at the heat that radiated off the units' powder-coated metal housings. He ran his fingers over the embossed names on the radio sets: EF Johnson Viking Ranger and Hallcrafters SX-100. Strange names that meant nothing to him, but he'd paid a lot for them just the same. It felt as if they were in some kind of NASA project headquarters.

"We can get a really good signal bounce off the line between day and night especially with the solar cycle we're in now. We call that the gray line." Lori pulled out a manual and pointed at a row of numbers. "Here, look. Solar Cycle Twenty is pretty good right now for reaching out. So we took advantage of it."

Growing impatient with the technical talk, Hunt interrupted, "So they're expecting us?"

"Yes, I did what you asked. They're expecting a radio communication when you guys arrive in Africa. We said you'd be there in a couple of weeks," Lori answered, frowning at Hunt.

"All right, then. We'll let Dr. Raven and the rest know we have a plan." Bobby got up to leave.

Lori held her hand up. "Hold on just a minute. You've got to come up on the roof. I want you to see the new dipole antennas you bought me and the place where we're setting up the new vertical antenna you're going to buy me."

Bobby shook his head and sighed, but he filed behind Lori and Hunt and climbed up a steep ladder that led to the rooftop.

Lori's voice echoed down from the top of the ladder. "The roof works really well. We're about two and a half stories up here, so we don't have to erect much of a tower to get above everything and avoid interference from the other structures."

Bobby stepped off the ladder and onto the roof, immediately taken by the sweeping and unobstructed view of the city. Streams of lights crisscrossed the city, defining the grid of streets below. The Bay Bridge sparkled across the bay.

"It's beautiful up here, isn't it?" Lori said as she gazed over the city.

"In all the years I've been coming here, I've never been up on the roof," Hunt said.

"This is a special place for special people," Lori put her arm around Hunt and looked over at Bobby. "I'm going to need more money to finish the vertical antenna."

Bobby reached in his front pocket and began counting out hundreds. He sighed. "Say when."

Lori smiled. "Keep counting, dear."

Chapter Sixteen

"I've run into those creatures once before, and believe me, once is enough," Gabriel said.

Gabriel, the tracker, was having difficulty sizing up his new acquaintances. For the last several months, he'd been hearing about the adventures, or more like misadventures, of these two foreigners, Vandusen and Bauer, blundering their way through the jungle, but he'd never met them before today.

The stories about them seemed beyond belief, and he'd dismissed them as just another group of tenderfoots lured into the jungle seeking hidden treasure or some other silly crap. It seemed the bush was full of these types nowadays. But he was beginning to realize that there was a method to their madness that, in some ways, made them far more dangerous than the typical outsiders. Judging from their manner and the gear they were packing, Vandusen and his crew had powerful backing, but that didn't mean anything if he couldn't trust them to pay. He was going to have to be very careful with these two.

Gabriel knew not to act too eager to cooperate with them. He thought as fast as he could talk, and thinking on the fly was what he did best. But as seriously as he took these two, what they were asking was crazy. It made no sense. The last thing he wanted to do was run into those creatures again. The last encounter had almost cost him his life, and he didn't want a repeat performance. But there was money to be made if he led them on with finesse and skill. After all, the jungle was like a vast ocean that could swallow up secrets with a little help. A plan turned in his dark mind.

Vandusen grew impatient with the tracker's indecision. "We're interested in finding these creatures for their, how should I say, scientific value. We're willing to pay double your rate. And there's a fat bonus for you and your men if we capture some alive."

Vandusen realized that this strange Portuguese tracker was probably the only hope for them to leave this hellhole with some of the hybrids, but he didn't trust him. For that matter, he didn't trust anyone in this godforsaken part of the world. He needed someone who knew the jungle and had knowledge of how to find and catch one of these creatures. More importantly, he needed a man who could be bought, for now at least. And the Belgian had assured them that Gabriel was that sort of man.

From all accounts, Gabriel was some kind of great white hunter. Though 'white' might have taken it a little too far; his silky black hair and dark skin betrayed his Portuguese descent. His intelligent, dark eyes seemed to take in everything. But worse, they burned with an intimidating fire. They would have to be very careful with this one. *But then you never know what might happen when we don't need his services anymore,* Vandusen thought with a smile.

"I'll give you a list of what me and my men will need to get started," Gabriel said, "but, for now, I want a week's pay up front and four bottles of Vat 69." Ignoring Vandusen's less-than-favorable reaction to this, he began scribbling a list on a wadded piece of a sack. "And let me take a look at those dart guns of yours."

Vandusen motioned to Bauer. "Mr. Bauer will take care of everything you need."

Bauer handed Gabriel a case containing the dart guns along with a box filled with vials of ketamine. He pulled out a folded map from his back pocket. "Let me show you where we last saw those damn things."

"No need, I know exactly where they are this time of year." Gabriel smiled.

Even in the sweltering heat of the African sun, Vandusen felt a chill pass over him.

Chapter Seventeen

Ken's heart raced when he caught sight of the ranch. The intense emotions he felt surprised him, and the tears welling up made it difficult to navigate the last few yards of the drive. He turned to speak to Fred, but a loud chorus of greeting hoots interrupted him before he got a word out.

He laughed, his mood changing. "Well, Fred, there's no denying it. We're finally home."

Fred nodded. "It's good to know there's at least one place in this world we're welcome."

Mary met them at the side door of the house. Smiling, hands on her hips, she raised her voice, trying to be heard above the riotous noise of the chorus of chimps. "The wayward travelers finally return!" Shaking her head at the hopelessness of the task, she turned and led them inside.

Ken stepped inside, overwhelmed by a sudden and inexplicable wave of relief. He was home. Before Mary could speak, he pulled her close, felt her passion, and drank in her perfumed and yielding lips. He'd been away too long from her delicious spell.

Fred smiled and slipped away, leaving them in each other's embrace.

Outside, he greeted Mark Chaney and Consuelo, who'd walked over when they'd seen him and Ken drive up. "We should head over to my room for a while. I think Dr. and Mrs. Turner are going to need a little time to—catch up, if you take my meaning." Fred smiled as they led the way, walking hand-in-hand.

It seemed Mark had adjusted well to post-doc American life; especially after having to leave his university in Kent so abruptly. He just hoped he wouldn't lead this young lady astray. He and Ken felt she was one of their most promising graduate students. They continued up the gravel drive toward Fred's place, or the Doll House as it was lovingly referred to by those who knew the ranch's checkered history.

"So where do we go from here?" Mark asked. He sat close to Consuelo in the comfortable way that defined them as a couple.

A lot's gone on since we left, Fred thought, smiling to himself.

Embarrassed by his attention, they shifted slightly apart. Chaney continued, "We've had several visits from Melon and the university people since you've been gone, and each one's getting more aggressive. It feels like the noose is slowly tightening." Mark paused, looking at Consuelo as if for reassurance. "I don't think we can go on like this much longer. We either have to come clean or get the hell out of Dodge."

"I know what you mean, Mark; I feel the same way," Fred said. "Actually, we both do, Ken and I, that is. But I don't think 'coming clean' is an option. We've just got back from the sheriff's station and there's a detective there who seems to know a lot about us, and—"

Mark interrupted: "That's just what I mean." He paused, putting his arm around Consuelo. "We feel like everything is closing in on us. I'm worried—really worried."

Nodding, Fred said, "We need to get in touch with Lester before we do anything. These letters are not working well. There's too much delay." He hesitated before continuing, "Also, we've found a clue that may show us how Vandusen and his men are coming and going so easily. We may know how Oliver got here in the first place."

"A clue? What do you mean?" Mark asked.

"We think they're using a military base in Germany."

"Germany? That could be a direct flight from the Congo with the right connections, and Vandusen certainly would have them." Mark stood and walked over to a world map pinned on the wall. "Smugglers would have those connections as well."

"Yes, but first we need to contact Lester and François," Fred said.

"Hunt and Bobby are working on it," Mark said. "A few days ago, I got a strange call from Hunt. But you know Hunt; it's hard to pick through all his drama. He says he and Bobby contacted someone in San Francisco who can help us—using some kind of long-distance radio, but he's afraid they're being followed."

"Hell, we're all being followed—probably a ham radio. I wouldn't worry too much if Bobby's with him. I don't think anything scares that little guy." He looked out the window toward the main house. "A ham radio—that could work."

Ken lay in bed enjoying the view as Mary combed her thick, red hair. Through the partly opened door, he could just make out the rest of her naked shapeliness in the bathroom mirror. She smiled when her hazel eyes caught his gaze in the mirror. She opened the door the rest of the way and turned, exposing her fullness.

"Well, professor, it's obvious you've been away for a while."

Ken covered himself, surprised at his embarrassment.

Still smiling, Mary moved gracefully across the room like a Celtic goddess, slowly pulled the sheets away, and whispered, "Ready for another session?"

***

"What are we waiting for?" Fred said to Consuelo and Mark. "Let's stop talking and gather everyone and go!" He moved to the door, opened it, and found Ken and Mary standing there grinning like two schoolchildren who'd just returned from playing hooky.

"Go where?" Ken asked, his fist still positioned to knock.

"Well, we're sure in a good mood, aren't we?" Fred said. He couldn't help but smile despite all their concerns. It pleased him to see the calming effect Mary had on his friend—though he suspected Ken's apparent change in mood was from more than just her presence.

Sensing the couple's embarrassment, everyone laughed—something they hadn't done for a long time.

Ken and Mary listened while Fred filled them in on what Bobby and Hunt were up to, and they talked into the night. Now that they were together and back at the ranch, all their cares seemed somehow manageable. It felt as if they'd stepped back in time. A time when they only had to worry about teaching, research, and where the next grant was coming from. They missed those times.

Ken realized it had been months since he'd spent any quality time with his chimps. He especially missed Mike and Girlie. He worried about them and his friends, and wondered if they were all right. He decided that tomorrow, no matter what, he would spend the day with the chimps at the ranch. Even if the world ended, he was going to spend it in the company of his chimps. He needed to meet the new ones they'd acquired in his absence. He wanted to take his mind off Africa and all the rest of their troubles, even if just for a while. And he actually did have research to do.

But tonight he would spend with Mary. He squeezed her hand and they left. Consuelo and Mark followed. Fred picked up a bottle of wine from his bookshelf and made a call. A grad student needed tutoring.

***

When Ken woke, Mary was still sleeping. He gently tried to untangle himself from her smooth, fragrant body, but she awoke with passion, and he floated back under her erotic spell, thankful that it wouldn't be the last time.

An hour later, he kissed Mary at the door, zipped up his Carhartt coat against the morning crispness, and made his way in the direction of the chimp cabins. The sun hadn't risen high

93

enough to melt the frost still on the roofs. The icy crystals made them look like sugar-glazed, gingerbread houses. The frozen ground crunched under his steps, interrupting the silence of the morning. He reveled to be in his old routine again, back where he belonged, and inexplicability, he felt safe.

An idea kept turning in his head. He couldn't stop thinking how easy it would be to just come clean with everyone and give up this deception. After all, it wasn't as though they had actually committed a crime. They'd just gotten wrapped up with the wrong people in their search for Oliver, which, while not what they'd received the grant to do, wasn't against the law.

Perhaps the police would even help protect them once they understood how this whole crazy mess got started. *After all, that's their job, isn't it? To serve and protect.*

He took the split in the drive that led to the building where they usually exercised the chimps, the play barn as they called it, and quickened his pace in anticipation. A staccato of greeting hoots and a rustling in the trees above startled him. He looked up, and to his surprise, a young adolescent chimp came swinging down, limb by limb, to greet him.

The chimp unceremoniously plopped in front of him and signed, "Who you?"

Surprised, Ken automatically signed a reply: "Me, Ken. Who you?" Since Ken wore glasses, he made his name-sign by holding his index finger and thumb slightly apart and tapping his glasses. Name signs in American Sign Language usually denoted a unique attribute or characteristic of a person. Signing chimps had mastered this in surprisingly creative ways.

The young chimp watched him intently, head cocked to one side, and responded clumsily by swinging his right arm up and awkwardly brushing his open hand across his big floppy ear, several times.

Ken remembered that they'd recently acquired an adolescent chimp named Dar from Yerkes National Primate Center. He'd been told the chimp had big floppy ears. The name sign fitted him perfectly.

Dar danced and hooted before continuing signing, "You, me, play hide 'n' seek?"

The little chimp used the appropriate "open-face" kinesics that should accompany a question, and Ken had the sudden insight that this, more than vocabulary, confirmed that Dar possessed language. So he did what any researcher would do in this situation and asked, "Who, it?"

Dar bounced and, while hooting in guttural, hoarse sounds, signed, "Me hide, you chase." He disappeared over the roof as quickly as he'd appeared, leaving Ken standing alone, stunned and unsure if their interaction had actually happened.

In a flash of insight, he realized he'd never go to the authorities. He wouldn't "come clean." Rather, he'd do whatever it took to protect his chimps and the project from Vandusen, Melon, and the whole sinister lot. He couldn't imagine these bright and innocent creatures being forced to kill and maim, and, worse, doing so as expendable machines for the government.

Relieved this course was finally clear, he laughed, breaking the silence that surrounded him, and gave chase.

After all, he was "it."

Chapter Eighteen

Lester felt relieved that the radio station was finally working again, and he was eager to communicate with his friends in the States. Since the movie had wrapped, he guessed Chris would be returning to Africa soon to pick up the last of his equipment. And afterwards, he knew Chris wouldn't be coming back, at least not using the movie as a cover.

When Chris had left with the movie crew, he'd assured Lester that upon his return, he'd find a way to get him and Girlie home. If he and Girlie were ever going to get home, it would have to be on this last trip, but coordinating it would be another thing.

Lester had refused to leave with Chris. He'd wanted to try to find out where Mike, Oliver, and Danny had disappeared to. He feared for their safety with Vandusen still on the loose. Nobody knew where or when he and his agents might show up again. The whole compound had been on high alert for months, and the strain was beginning to show on all of them. Life was getting complicated, and Lester felt that time was running out. He'd watched, with interest, the flurry of activity to repair the radios and antennas. François had confided to him that their survival depended on it.

Since the attack on the compound by Vandusen and his company, Lester hadn't been able to stay in touch with the outside world. The radio station had been one of their first targets, and as a result, they'd lost all communication. He had painfully watched the radio technicians beg, borrow, and steal the equipment needed to get back on the air, but it had taken them months.

"I feel like we've been thrown back into the Dark Ages," Lester had said several weeks ago as he'd handed François an envelope addressed to Dr. F. Savage.

Since the raid on the compound by Vandusen and his men, they'd had to send all Lester's messages by runners through the jungle to the boats that ran up and down the river. He smiled to himself thinking *boats* was a pretty ambitious word. Most of the traffic he'd seen on the river consisted of native dugouts powered by rusty outboard motors, except for a decaying cutter that plied its way up and down the river in a hit-and-miss fashion following no schedule.

Getting a message through to anyone in the outside world had been a daunting task, and it'd been even rarer to get a reply. He'd been frustrated with some of the first replies as they'd been hard to make out. They wrote cryptically for fear of a message falling into the wrong hands and had learned to read between the lines. In the jungle, much could, and did, happen to the runners.

"It's not just the ease of sending messages that will improve now we've got the radios working," François said now, looking at the technicians for effect. "All resupplying will be easier and safer. You know there's always a chance of some merchant, trader, boat captain, or some other pain-in-the-ass snoop getting suspicious and following our people back upriver to us. With a radio we can get back to having our supplies dropped off way upriver when we're sure no one is following us." He shook his head. "I'm worried this once lonely region is getting too crowded. It seems like the river is getting busier with every month."

"Everyone is on edge," Lester said.

François shrugged. "You know most of our scientists left after the raid, and, honestly, without them, there really isn't a reason to remain." He got up and opened a shutter. "I mean, we lost the creatures they were here to study."

"Vandusen saw to that." Lester frowned, concerned at François's tone. "What are you getting at?"

"We're running out of time here. We need to close up shop and move on."

"Move on? Move on to where and to what?"

"You were at that village. You saw what happened there. We might find a new mission protecting the villages."

Lester winced at the mention of the village. He'd accompanied the Belgians on that last patrol looking for Mike and evidence of the creatures. It hadn't taken them long to lose the trail and for the mission to turn into a wild goose chase. After bogging down in the swampy regions on the other side of the river, they'd given up and had decided to head back. That was when they'd stumbled onto the massacre. While they hadn't found Mike, they'd confirmed that the creatures had crossed the river and were near.

The horrifying images of the death and destruction still haunted Lester. He'd been reluctant to send the photos, not wanting to alarm his friends, but when the photographer had handed him the developed images, he'd decided that they needed to know just what these hybrids were capable of. So he'd taken a chance and had sent the envelope with one of François' most trusted men.

Finally, Lester had heard from Bobby, and his letter had contained details of how they could make radio contact. "It's like Bobby read our mind," he said, nodding to the letter in François's hand.

"Yes. His friend has a radio and has given us everything we need to make contact." François smiled.

The details Bobby had sent confused Lester, but they seemed to make perfect sense to François and his radio technicians. Lester had never seen the one-armed Belgian so excited. Being military, they were in the habit of using shortwave radios to stay in touch with each other and the outside world. After being blind for so long, they were excited about being able to communicate again.

There'd be no more delay. But they'd have to be careful in what they said over the airwaves for fear of their transmissions being intercepted. Lester figured the Belgians already had that worked out.

He looked around the radio station again, amazed at how busy the Belgians had been over the past several months. While it was not as elegant and well organized as before, or "strack," as François would say, it was functional.

Lester stepped out onto the landing of the radio station to get some relief from the heat and noticed they'd re-erected several of the antennas and stretched wire between the towers in east-west and north-south orientations. He thought the tallest of these antennas must be at least forty feet.

He pointed. "Why are the antennas so high?"

François shrugged in his typical Belgian manner. "We have to clear the jungle canopy to transmit. Most facilities in this part of the world communicate with radios, so it causes little suspicion, my friend. Not to worry; what could go wrong?" He smiled and shrugged again.

Lester shook his head. "I'm not sure." He stepped back in the radio shack. "Vandusen and his agents are still out there, somewhere. And then there are the creatures to worry about."

François spread his arms. "Leave it to you to keep us all grounded, my friend. I think we've learned from the massacre that the creatures that escaped during the raid may well have regrouped with those in the wild."

Lester reread Bobby's letter as the technicians busied themselves testing their equipment. He didn't understand most of the radio lingo, but François had been animated when he'd read the index card Bobby had included in his letter.

Scribbled in Bobby's fine hand were several radio call signs and lists about frequencies, times, Lat/Longs and other information that was Greek to Lester. He smiled, remembering François running across the compound, waving the card in one hand as his armless tunic sleeve flopped. The guards had watched their captain with amusement.

Lester and Girlie watched as the technician busied himself unscrewing the metal covers on the equipment, replaced tubes, and soldered wires.

Girlie tried to climb onto the table to get a closer look as the technician flipped through various military radio manuals, running his finger down columns while adjusting dials with his other hand.

"Girlie, leave it!" Lester ordered. "Leave the man alone, for chrissake."

Girlie whimpered and signed, "Help. Play."

"Not now, Girlie," Lester said. He'd been amused at first, then later, amazed at how quickly Girlie had picked up sign language. She used the signs now whenever she wanted something, instead of using her begging gestures. What seemed like years ago, Ken had explained to him that the gestures chimps used were pre-wired and common to chimps universally whether in the wild or in captivity.

But Lester preferred to speak to her more than sign. He'd held one-way conversations with her since she'd been an infant, and he wasn't about to change now. After his wife, Karen, had died, his conversations with her had given him a kind of peace, and, in fact, they still did.

The technician nodded and said, "We're almost ready, sir—*pret.*"

"Ready for what?" Lester asked.

"To power up a signal and send out this call sign," the radio technician answered, holding up the card Bobby had sent. "We'll try to reach your friend Bobby." He set the index card against the radio where he could read it as he continued to refer to different dog-eared books and manuals. He turned the pages as he scribbled in a notebook. Occasionally, he looked up from his

101

work to adjust various knobs and dials. Sweat trickled down his forehead, causing him to push his glasses back up his nose.

Lester handed him his bandana. It was late afternoon and the breeze had died, making it humid in the tiny radio shack.

"*Merci*, Lester," the radio technician said. Scooting his chair back, he readjusted himself and paused, collecting his thoughts before he began to tap dots and dashes on a Morse code key.

At the sound of the transmission, Girlie did a slow summersault in his direction and placed her head inches away from the key. She smacked her lips in time with the dots and dashes.

The technician paused. "I think maybe our friend Girlie will learn Morse as fast as she learns the sign language." They both laughed, and Girlie hooted and stomped.

"Easy, Girlie, let the man work," Lester said. While he didn't know Morse code, he could tell the technician was repeating the same series of dots and dashes several times and then waiting. On hearing only static, he made several more adjustments to the dials and tapped the series out again.

Another technician came in carrying a Royal typewriter in a case that he opened and placed on the table next to the radio technician.

Girlie ambled over to him as he took a seat. He smiled at Girlie and nodded to the others. Girlie tilted her head at the serrated sounds as he shifted a lever and loaded the paper into the typewriter. He rearranged the machine, reached his fingers out over the keys, and typed in the air. Frowning, he scooted the chair back a few inches. Now satisfied, he placed a set of earphones on his head, nodded to the radio technician, and waited.

The radio technician tapped out code again and paused. They both stared at a speaker hanging on the wall as though they could will it to answer.

After what seemed like hours, Lester stood to leave. But the technicians didn't stir and kept at it, sending out what Lester had learned was the call sign Bobby had mailed. The technicians' patience impressed him.

François opened the door a crack and popped his head in. "Any luck?"

The technicians shook their heads in unison without looking in his direction. The key operator tapped the code again and looked at François. "Let's give it a few more minutes, sir."

François nodded and turned to leave just as the speaker came to life. The radio technician smiled and nodded to the typist, who began typing in a flurry, his fingers a blur.

Lester leaned over the typist's shoulder and watched the words unfold.

"It's in English!" Lester exclaimed. Girlie hooted, joining in on the excitement.

"But of course," the typist said, still typing with a smile on his face.

As the minutes ticked by, Lester watched a kind of routine develop. The radio technician keyed the dashes and dots and then waited as the typist typed incoming code.

Lester could hardly contain himself. He wanted to read the message, but François told him it distracted the typist when he stood too close and tried to read over his shoulder, so he paced, waiting for the communication to end.

François took a seat and listened with his eyes closed. His lips moved as though wording the code to himself.

"Ask him to repeat that. The signal is fading in and out," the typist said.

The radio technician nodded and began tapping again.

"I think we're losing them," the typist said.

"I'll try to get us to shift to a different frequency," the radio technician said. "Make a note of the time."

The typist nodded and looked up at a large military clock on the wall above them. "It's weak but a little better. Try to hold it."

The technician shook his head. "It's no good. We better finish up. We're losing our bounce." He looked at Lester. "It's probably all we're going to get tonight. But we did pretty well. We were lucky and got a phenomenal bounce off the atmosphere, but it's fading fast. That's typical down here below the equator."

François smiled. "Tomorrow's another day. We'll keep trying until we get it right."

The radio technician nodded to François before turning to the typist. "I'm signing off now."

The typist nodded and stopped typing. He stretched his interlaced fingers until they cracked, "*Fini.*"

The radio technician keyed some final information and exhaled.

The typist stood and spread his legs apart, then paused before he leaned back, placing his hands on his lower back and rotating side-to-side. "This was good, *bon*. We've established communication."

"Yes, but it's gonna be sketchy. Our window is tiny and our band narrow, I think," the technician said.

"They didn't have a strong signal. Do you think we should make some adjustments to the antennas?" François asked.

The typist shook his head. "I think we started a little early."

"Possibly, but I think we should start trying different times before making any adjustments to the equipment," the technician replied.

"The person on the other end was fast, very fast, and I think a woman," the typist said.

"How can you tell?" Lester asked.

"I agree," the technician said. "You can tell a lot about the person on the other end from the rhythm and cadence of the keying."

The typist rolled the typing paper out of the machine. "Let's take a look at this message."

Lester was surprised as he took the sheet from the typist. All the back and forth, dots and dashes, covered only two single-spaced sheets of transcription. "I'm going to need some explanation here. There's a lot of abbreviations I don't understand and partial words," he said.

"Not to worry, we'll get you up to speed in no time," François said, snatching the message out of Lester's hand. "Now, this is good, *bon*. We're in touch again!"

Lester let him scan it, then took the sheet back and held the message at an arm's length. He'd lost his reading glasses in the raid and found it frustrating to read in general but small type was the worst. "What the hell does this mean?"

"The first part of this message is just typical protocol, call signs and Q signs pertaining to frequency strength and other things. The second paragraph is the real body of the message," François replied.

"Q signs?" Lester asked.

"They're abbreviations to save time and energy—and when using Morse like we're doing, they save on keying," the technician told him.

Lester wanted to tell them what he thought of all this hocus pocus but thought better of it. He felt frustrated, wanting to be able to find out what was going on in the real world without all these obstacles. But clearly there was much to know about radio communication. It wasn't going to be as easy as he thought to send and receive messages with Bobby. Radio communication was a language of its own, and it would take some time to learn the abbreviations and special signs. Though radio operators used them to save time and make messages clearer, to Lester the Q signs were as clear as mud.

"What the does ##### mean?" he asked.

"Their signal strength was weak with a lot of static so we missed some words," the radio technician replied. "The great distance between us make for poor reception."

Lester rubbed his eyes before looking again. "And the partial words with spaces?"

"You'll have to try to make sense of them by using the rest of the message," the typist said. He blew out a sharp breath. "The signal was very weak. It kept fading out. I couldn't get it all."

Lester handed the message back to François. Clearly, he needed his and the technicians' help to make sense of Bobby's message. "How about you translate this into plain English?"

François grinned. "Sure." He looked down at the sheet. "Bobby says Chris will be returning in the next few weeks." François stopped, frowning, and reread part of the message before continuing, "Once they're in Africa, we'll have less than a month to clear out." He handed the message to the typist. "I can't make this part out. What's he saying here?"

Everyone waited as the typist reread the message. He handed the message over to the radio technician, then said, "Once Chris's back, he'll radio us. We'll have very little time to clear out."

"I think it's best we keep this to ourselves until I've had a chance to share it with everyone," François said, holding their gaze. "They need to be prepared for this kind of news—hell, so do I. We might as well bring our operation here to an end when Lester goes. The last of the movie equipment leaving is a good cover for shifting things around and for anyone wanting to get out of Africa without a fuss. What it means, though, is that we'll have only a few weeks to wrap up a lifetime of work."

None of the Belgians spoke; they sat deep in thought.

"Our ride home is coming, and we're running out of time," Lester said. "We still don't know where Mike or the rest of the creatures are, and then there's Vandusen to worry about." Looking at François, he said, "As you would say, 'what could go

107

wrong?' God only knows." Everyone laughed as Girlie climbed into Lester's arms. He was amazed at how much they took in their stride these days. But it wasn't surprising after all they'd been through. Clearing his throat, he continued, "I'd like to try one last time to at least find Mike before we pull out of here—if you'd do me that favor."

François held his gaze and said softly, "Yes, why not, my friend, one last adventure; one last patrol before we leave."

François walked across the room and opened a window. Evening was coming, and without a breeze the humidity remained high. He leaned against the sill and looked down on the compound. The last rays of sunset reflected off the metal roofs, and bats fluttered at eye level, intent on feeding. A last chorus of jungle sounds greeted the evening.

I'm going to miss all of this, François thought, scratching Girlie's back absentmindedly as she leaned against him. *Where will we go, I wonder?* Still looking out the window, he said, "We'll head for the caves. It's the most logical place for them to go after taking captives, which it looks like they did." When he turned from the window, tears ran down his wind-worn cheeks. Embarrassed, the technicians looked away and busied themselves tidying up.

Lester realized that leaving the compound would be the end of a way of life for François and his people. He hadn't thought about it before, being so intent on finding Mike and getting home. It dawned on him that, while they hadn't intended it, their search for the creatures had led Vandusen and his agents straight to the compound. They'd brought devastation and loss to François and his people. *What will happen to them. Where will they go?*

Lester would be returning home to his friends, but it would be different for them. François had spent most of his life hidden away in this remote part of the world. While they'd had brief and sporadic contact with the outside world, this place that they'd carved out of the jungle was the only home they knew. François and the other Belgians had nowhere to go. That had been the price of their commitment to the creatures and the research.

Lester promised himself that he and his friends would find a safe place for them. They would bring them back to the West. But how?

Girlie hugged François and licked his tears. She whimpered and panted in his ear between smacking her lips in soft kissing sounds.

Pulling out of Girlie's embrace, François laughed and said, "It's good to know that someone cares, Girlie."

Girlie stomped her feet and hooted upon hearing her name.

Laughter filled the little radio shack as evening shadows grew and the jungle settled into the stillness of night. They had each other, and at this moment, in this distant place, that was enough.

Chapter Nineteen

"The caves will be our best bet this time of year," Gabriel said while overseeing the offloading of supplies and equipment from a rusty M34 cargo truck.

Bauer and Vandusen watched Gabriel's men form a relay line and begin unloading boxes and bags. From the dents and bullet holes riddled across the hood and door, the truck had obviously seen action and better days. When one of the men attempted to open the tail gate, it fell to the ground. Vandusen shook his head; none of what he saw instilled him with confidence.

Gabriel strode over to the back of the truck, gathered up a number of M-14s under one arm and grabbed an ammo can in the other.

Vandusen frowned, looking at the weapons. "As much as I'd like to, we're not out to kill them. We want to take them alive."

"Yes, but we also want to come back alive," Gabriel replied as he threw one over to Vandusen.

Vandusen cocked the bolt, pointed it at the treetops, and pulled the trigger with a click.

Bauer stepped out of Vandusen's line of sight. "We were on the trail near the caves about a month ago and found nothing but stones and bones."

"It will be different now—the rains are coming," Gabriel said as he stacked the rifles—butt down in pyramids of three. "They like the rain even less than we do. We'll have a good chance to catch them with their guard down."

"What's our next move, then?" Vandusen asked.

"Creep along the river until we reach the caves. Wait to follow a hunting party as they leave the caves and ambush them far from the help of their brothers; easy—*facil*," Gabriel said, his eyes cold and expressionless.

"That may be easier said than done." Bauer looked over to Vandusen and his men; they hadn't forgotten their last encounter with the creatures.

"Yes, that's why we have the rifles and these." Gabriel pulled a MK-2 hand grenade out of his vest.

"How many of those do you have?" Vandusen asked, his admiration growing at the tracker's preparedness. He wished they'd had a few at their last encounter with the creatures. He thought Gabriel was beginning to live up to his reputation as some sort of "great white hunter."

"We probably have enough," the tracker replied as he motioned one of his men to open a splintered wooden box. It contained dozens of grenades packed in wood shavings. "I'd say more than enough."

Vandusen could just make out the faint stenciling of US Army on the side of the box.

"So what are we waiting for?" Bauer asked.

"First light—at dawn—we'll move out." Gabriel stared into the jungle. "It'll be cooler, and we've a long way to go."

Looking at his men, Vandusen said, "So that's settled. Get your equipment ready. Let's get it right this time. If we're successful, nobody gets hurt, and we go home."

Vandusen watched as Bauer helped one of Gabriel's men shoulder a manpack of one of the radios the General had supplied. He wasn't surprised that he'd supplied them with the latest equipment. The General was quite thorough when outfitting a mission. These AN/PRC-77s were pretty new. They'd replaced the old 55s and worked somewhat better in the tropics, being solid state rather than tubes. He smiled as the man struggled to heft the fifty-some pounds of equipment. *Better him than me.* The General hadn't missed a thing. The radios were paired with TSEC/KY 38 NESTOR devices that scrambled and kept voice traffic secure. But he'd learned in 'Nam that they were heavy and, worse, didn't like dampness. Hopefully the humidity wouldn't be enough to cause a problem.

The first clap of thunder speared them into action. The sky had been darkening all afternoon, threatening rain. It let loose just as Vandusen's men began packing their gear.

"Let's get a move on or you'll be living and sleeping in wet gear," Vandusen ordered his men.

Over the past year, Vandusen had learned that the rain gave no relief from the sweltering heat of the jungle. It only added to the humidity, which was enough to drown a man. Their clothes were already drenched, so they hardly noticed the dampness, but the heat grew unbearable, making it feel like sweat was boiling out of every pore. He slapped his neck at the first sting, reminded that with the humidity came insects large enough to have facial expressions. He wondered if he'd ever get out of this godforsaken place to the air conditioning and iced drinks of home. At that moment, it felt unlikely. The jungle would swallow them all into its darkness, leaving them to wander for eternity.

***

Vandusen and his men slogged through the jungle. The rains had been relentless all day, bogging them down. Small rivers flooded the trail, turning the red clay into a slippery mess that clung to their boots, making every step a struggle. And worse, a humid steam rolled out of the trees, making it difficult to see more than a few feet in any direction. The jungle brooded and no life showed itself.

Gabriel worried about their lack of progress. He often disappeared for hours before reappearing to urge them to step it up. They'd been out since dawn and still had a way to go if they wanted to reach the abandoned village for shelter. His plan was to head upriver to the last village the creatures had overrun and use it for their base.

Vandusen had been against staying anywhere the creatures had been, especially somewhere they'd attacked. It unsettled him, not to mention the effect it had on his men. They were still unnerved by what had happened on their last encounter. But now, he'd go to Hell itself to get out of this deluge. Darkness was coming early, aided by the pouring rain. They'd be lucky if they didn't get stuck out on the trail for the night, exposed and vulnerable.

Worse, all their equipment was dripping wet, including their weapons and ammunition. They'd wrapped the dart guns in plastic, but they couldn't be sure they'd stay dry enough to work when they needed them. And without the darts they wouldn't be able to take any of the creatures alive. Vandusen's mood grew as dark as the weather.

"Where the hell's that Portuguese gone again?" Vandusen asked no one in particular. "The rain's getting worse." They'd been following close to the river for several miles but had had to cut their way into the jungle to higher ground as the banks had begun to overflow at the low spots of the trail, making it impossible to ford. "Christ! This is getting impossible," Vandusen said as one of his men caught him by the arm, saving him from falling into the greasy mud.

Gabriel suddenly reappeared. "It's not far now," he said from under his drab, olive poncho. He looked back at the column of men and shook his head. "Get your men together; they're strung out way too far, and move to higher ground. Stay off the trail; it's washed out just ahead, and try to stay close together. Believe me, you don't wanna get lost out here." Before anyone could tell him what they thought of this last remark, he disappeared into the growing mist as quickly as he'd appeared.

Bauer motioned the men to close ranks, and they trudged on in the slippery mud. Vandusen remained stoic. The vegetation was so thick and matted with interwoven vines, they had to use machetes to cut a path that paralleled the flooded trail.

The jungle was silent of anything or anyone, except for the occasional loud splat off the dripping lank canopy. Bauer had learned that animals were rarely seen in the bush. Instead you heard their faint stirrings in the shadows. But there were no shadows in the failing light, just the flat one dimension of the fog. The only good thing about the rain and fog was that everything seemed to be hunkered down. That is, everything but them. The cloak of humid steam seemed to swallow every living thing.

"What's that I see up ahead?" he asked one of his men.

Before he could answer, the cloaked form of Gabriel loomed up again. He paused, surveying the group. "The village is just ahead, but there's a problem."

Vandusen exhaled loudly. "What now?"

"There are people in it."

"People or creatures?" Vandusen asked as he unholstered his pistol.

"People."

"I thought it was abandoned. Who in the hell would be out in this mess?"

"I've sent a scout up for a closer look, but they look to be military—soldiers," Gabriel replied. "They've set sentries and have cooking fires, not going to any great lengths to be covert, and they're in force." Gabriel jogged down the jagged line of men. "We need to close ranks and pick up stragglers."

Bauer sprang into action and followed him down the line.

"It might be a patrol down from Banana investigating what happened to the village—word has to have gotten out," Bauer said as he gathered his men. "Let's get off the trail and hunker down."

Gabriel didn't answer. He busied himself gathering the stragglers and setting up a perimeter. It looked as though they'd be spending a wet night in the jungle.

Chapter Twenty

Pinned between the two large, muscular men who leaned hard against him in the back of the car, Melon found it difficult to move. The rich leather seat engulfed him, yielding to their combined weight. A streetlight illuminated the front seat and the back of the driver's head as he turned the sedan off the highway and down a two-lane country road.

"What in the hell are you doing? Who are you?" Melon asked as he twisted, trying to make some space around him.

The man who'd shoved him into the sedan glared at him and said, "Relax and keep your trap shut."

Melon struggled to sit up, but one of the men pushed him back between them.

"Look, you're making a big mistake," Melon said. "If you know what's good for you, you'll stop right now and let me out." His voice came out strained. He craned his neck around, trying to get his bearings. He realized that the sedan was speeding out of town into the darkness of the country. "When you find out who I am, you're going to be really sorry. Now, stop and let me out." Melon's hands trembled and he struggled to catch his breath. He didn't know who had abducted him but figured they had to be associated with Vandusen, so he decided to try a different tack. "Look, when Mr. Vandusen finds out what you're doing here, you're going to be in big trouble."

Laughing, one of the men said to the driver, "Did you hear that, Carl? We're going to be in big trouble." They all laughed, even louder.

"Just relax and you might just live through this." The man looked straight ahead, ignoring Melon, and spoke in a hard, mechanical voice that lacked all emotion.

Seeing a pickup truck parked by a mailbox, Melon yelled, "Help!" and began to squirm with renewed energy.

The man squeezed his arm. "I told you to shut your hole and sit still."

Melon jerked his arm loose from the man's grip and reached across to the door handle. The man grabbed him by the wrist. The power of his grip shocked Melon, but before he could pull away, the man twisted it until it snapped.

Melon screamed. "You broke my wrist!"

The two men laughed even harder than before.

"It's a good thing we have the windows up. Christ, he sounds like a little girl," the man said as he released Melon's arm. "Now, shut up before I do the other one."

Melon held up his arm and continued screaming. His wrist hung lopsided.

The man grabbed his wrist again and twisted it. "Does this hurt?"

Melon screamed at a higher pitch.

The other man grabbed Melon's other arm. "Watch this!"

Carl, the driver, looked in the rearview mirror and yelled, "Shut that asshole up. I'm trying to drive here."

"All right, already." The man released his arm, then smiled and slammed his elbow into Melon's temple.

"Are you nuts? The General wants him in one piece," Carl said.

A sharp pain spread across the side of Melon's head. Sparkles floated across his eyes. The inside of his sinuses fizzed spreading to the back of his head. He tried to speak several times, but nothing came out as his words seemed disconnected from his thoughts. He tried to swallow as a wave of nausea rose to his throat. As if from a great distance in the darkness, he heard an echo of someone saying, "Stop the car, dammit; stop the fucking car," and then there was nothing.

***

"Now you've really done it," Carl said as he watched the two men try to wipe blood off Melon's face. They had him seated with his head leaning against the open rear door, his legs splayed out on the gravel of the road side. They'd gone to great lengths to place him out of view of possible passing traffic.

"What do you mean 'you?' You're the one who wanted this sorry ass to shut up," one of the thugs said as he wiped chunks of vomit off the arm of his blazer. Frowning, he asked, "Why don't you get your ass over here and help us?"

"Hell, no—puke makes me puke." Carl swallowed several times.

"Holy Jesus! You can put a bullet behind someone's ear but you can't deal with puke," the man said.

Both men smirked as they hurried to clean their clothes and the seat of the sedan. Lucky for them, it would be dark in a few minutes on this lonely country road. The last thing they needed was some pain-in-the-ass Samaritan stopping.

"Just clean the sorry fuck up and let's get going before someone stops—the General's waiting and not going to be happy," Carl said as he raised the hood of the sedan. "What does the General want with this piece of shit, anyway?" Both men stopped cleaning and stared at him. Realizing his mistake, he added, "I'm just saying. Of course, it's none of my business—just saying."

"If you're so interested, you can ask the General yourself." The thugs shot each other a knowing look before returning to wiping up the last chunks. They all knew it was best not to ask questions. The General didn't like questions, just doings.

Carl walked around the raised hood. "Hey, look, the prince is waking up."

Melon moaned and put his head in his hands. His head was throbbing and the world was spinning. Panic filled him when he realized he'd not had a bad dream. He tried to push up with his hands, but sharp pain jabbed up his arm. He winced and lowered his elbow.

"Just stay put," Carl said. Looking at the two men, he continued, "You've had a bad fall."

They all laughed.

"Listen, if you're going to puke any more, do it now, you sorry shit," one of the thugs said, throwing a soggy towel in Melon's lap. "Yah, poor baby can't stand puke." He laughed and pointed at Carl.

Melon's vision was blurred, and he felt woozy. He tried to sit up again, but one of the men shoved him back down and said, "I said, just keep your sorry ass down for a minute. You've had a bad fall." The men smirked at their joke.

"Okay, the car's clean enough now. God! Do you smell that?" Carl fanned his hand in front of his face. He squinted and gagged.

"Never mind that—we've got company," one of the men said, jerking his head towards the police cruiser slowing down as it drew near.

"Shit!" the other said. He pulled a flask out of his pocket and emptied it all over Melon.

The other man patted him down with his handkerchief.

Carl drew himself up. "Let me do the talking."

The cruiser drew to a stop in front of them. A moment later, a sheriff got out and wandered over to them.

Carl slammed down the hood. "Good evening, officer."

"What's the problem here?" The sheriff shone a flashlight on each of them.

"One wrong word out of you and you're dead," one of the thugs whispered to Melon.

Carl had a clear view of Melon, but the sedan blocked the sheriff's view to the other side. "The usual tourist problems, sir. I'm taking this fare to the airport, and he's obviously had a little too much to drink. We're trying to clean up the mess he made in the back seat and tidy him so he can board his plane." Carl watched the sheriff walk around to the other side of the car.

"Are you all right, sir?" the sheriff asked Melon as he knelt down and shone his flashlight in his face.

Melon felt fingers tighten like a vise on his arm.

"I think he passed out, sir," Carl said. "We've telephoned the casino and let them know he may miss his plane."

"Looks like he bumped his head," the sheriff said as he stood. He looked from Melon to the other men and covered the butt of his pistol with his hand. "May I see some ID?"

Melon interrupted. "I think I need to go to the hospital."

"I can call an ambulance for you, sir." The sheriff walked over to his squad car.

"Follow him." Carl motioned one of the men in the direction of the flashing blue lights. He could just make out the silhouette of the sheriff leaning over the console from the passenger side of his cruiser, then he saw a flash and heard a dull pop. The sheriff staggered upright, turned, looking straight at Melon, and rolled off the side of the road. Two more dull rapports came from the ditch.

"Good job! We need to tidy this up right now—did he get on the radio?" Carl asked.

"I'm not sure," one of the men replied and beckoned the others to help him drag the body up the slope.

Melon watched in disbelief as they opened the trunk of the cruiser and threw the sheriff inside. It bounced from the weight of the body. Melon's nose burned from the pungent odor of gunpowder. He thought of slipping away, but knew they'd kill him if he tried. Instead, he slipped his hand into the vest pocket of his jacket and tossed several of his business cards under the sedan.

"Turn those lights off and let's get the hell out of here," Carl ordered, then looked at Melon. "Load this piece of shit up. I know where we can get rid of his car."

Both men grabbed Melon and dragged him, his feet trailing, into the back seat of the sedan.

The driver narrowed his eyes at him and said, "That little stunt of yours, about going to the fucking hospital, just got him killed." He looked up and down the road. "Let's move out. We've been lucky so far."

One of the thugs climbed into the cruiser; the other sat beside Melon, and a moment later both cars raced into the darkness, leaving only a cloud of dust—or so they thought.

Chapter Twenty-one

The whole station was abuzz when Detective Sandy returned to his office. The morning shift after Saturday night was always busy picking up the overflow from the third watch.

He slid into his chair, leaned back on its two legs and exhaled. Looking up at the peg board ceiling, he noticed several brown water stains for the first time. He reached for the phone to call maintenance but realized it was just a delaying tactic from navigating the routine Sunday morning crap lying in front of him on his desk.

He stretched to reach what looked like an unusual pile of messages, pulled several off a spike, and began reading. Most were the typical day-to-day phone messages with information and leads on various complaints: car thefts, disturbing the peace, pickpockets, break-ins, shoplifting, civil disputes, and neighborhood noise complaints. Their little station had gotten busier since the completion of several new casinos, and, worse, a new element had been attracted to Reno to prey on the increased tourist trade, which kept him busy.

He picked up the phone and began assigning calls to the deputies working the morning shift. After passing each one off, he wadded it and tossed it into a round metal trash can across the room. A cluster of crumpled wads representing petty crimes surrounded the can on the floor.

"Two points!" Sandy yelled as a wad thumped into the can.

The door opened and his captain stepped in. "Busy at work, I see."

"Sorry, sir, just cleaning up the messages from the night shift. All pretty usual stuff so far for a Saturday night."

The captain frowned. "I can see." He kicked a few of the wads aside as he made his way to Sandy's desk. "I think this should perk your interest." He handed Sandy a file and picture of one of their deputies.

Sandy leafed through the file. "Deputy Johnston. I don't think I know him. Looks like he's a rookie. Just started with us a few months ago. Missing since last night after he called in a traffic stop."

"Yes, nice kid—I know his family," the captain said.

"Maybe he just forgot to punch out," Sandy said.

"No, I had the duty sarge call his house. He hasn't come home according to his mom." The captain stooped to pick the missed shots off the floor.

"Where was his last call?" Sandy asked.

"A traffic stop on Holcomb Lane," the captain answered, staring up at a city map behind Sandy's desk.

"What time?"

"About 0200 hours—his shift started at 1800 hours and ended at 0600." The captain looked up at the duty schedule charted on the wall.

"What about his dinner break?" Sandy asked.

"He stopped at Franks and had a burger and left, according to the bartender. He seemed to be in good spirits and acting normal according to the waitresses and patrons. He was a regular for their chili and burgers."

"Did dispatch try to make contact after he made the traffic stop?"

"No, he radioed in first and stated he was wrapping up a disabled sedan. Let me see—Black Buick—Nevada plates, personalized—Mapes 1. Sounds pretty routine."

"Mapes 1? Like in the Mapes casino, do you think?" Sandy asked.

The captain shrugged. "Maybe. I'd like you to follow this up personally."

"Ten-Four, Cap—I'll get on it as soon as I finish getting through these." Sandy held up the few remaining phone messages.

The captain nodded and started to head out but paused at the door. "Keep this on the low down for now. We don't need a lot of press on this, complicating everything—plus it's bad for morale. For now, we're just checking on a new deputy who may have forgotten to punch out."

Sandy nodded and watched his captain work his way through a maze of desks toward the exit. It was getting well into the morning shift so most of them were empty. He'd have to get dispatch to radio additional beat assignments now.

He wondered how it was possible for a deputy and his cruiser to go missing in a small town like Reno. A missing rookie sheriff and his vehicle was going to spread like wildfire once it got out, and get out it would. It would be news. He sighed and began prioritizing the rest of the messages in stacks. That is until he came to a missing person call.

He held the message, reread it, then stared into space, piecing together what he knew. Based on the time recorded on the phone log, Dr. Melon had last been seen at the university getting into a black sedan. This would've been shortly after he'd escorted Doctors Turner and Savage to the station. A student had observed him being escorted into a sedan by two men in suits. He swore to himself at the absence of the student's name or phone number on the report.

The duty sergeant hadn't filed it as a missing person since it was the department's policy to wait for forty-eight hours to lapse before doing so. But when Sandy saw Melon's name on the phone message, he got the ball rolling by creating a report immediately, sending a deputy out to take statements, and filing the report to get it out on the wire service. He didn't believe in coincidences, and the disappearance of both Melon and the deputy on the same evening made him suspicious.

He picked up the phone and called dispatch to get the report of exactly where Deputy Johnston had made the traffic stop the night before. He discovered that the deputy had been way out in the country on one of the back roads leading to the airport—a puzzling fact. Even more curious was the plate he'd called in: "Mapes 1."

Detective Sandy became antsy and decided it was time to get out of his office and do some real police work. But before he headed out, he ran a DMV check on the plate. He had a hunch that the vehicle was connected to the Mapes on Virginia Street, and if that turned out to be correct, he'd pay a visit to the casino.

But, most importantly, he wanted to take a drive down the country road where they'd last heard from Deputy Johnston.

Sandy's suspicions grew. He may have been one of the last people to see Dr. Melon, and his disappearance occurred the evening after his visit with the president of the university. A possible casino connection was even more disturbing.

Five casinos had been built in the last couple of years, and his department was beginning to deal with more cases which looked and felt like organized crime and the activities commonly associated with it. Kidnappings and murders were on the rise. They'd increased their force and now even had a bunco section. Reno was beginning to feel more like a big city than the sleepy little gambling town it had the reputation of being.

There are a lot of balls in the air on this case, he thought.

His suspicions were only hunches, but his hunches had always served him well. They'd gotten him promoted. Hunches were good.

He wondered how the two professors might be connected to the disappearances. He didn't think they were capable of crimes like kidnapping and possibly murder. But just the same, two people were missing who'd been connected with them: first, Gordon Childs, and, now, Dr. Melon. He had a hunch that foul play surrounded these disappearances.

It seemed unhealthy to have a close relationship with the good professors. At least for some. He racked his brain searching for the common string connecting them to these disappearances, but nothing jumped out at him. First things first; he'd take a drive out into the country.

In spite of all the new construction of the past few years, Holcomb Valley still had the feel of the old Reno where Detective Sandy had grown up—horse and cattle country with most spreads on considerable acreage. Horses grazed in the deep, rich grass, creating a scene that hadn't changed for a hundred years. It was hard to believe anything violent could happen in this genteel and peaceful countryside.

As he wound through the landscape of pastures lined with white-rail fences, Sandy tried to put himself in Johnston's patrol cruiser the night before. There would've been little, if any, traffic along this road. Only locals used it. But a local might have noticed a black Buick sedan as out of place—maybe.

He guessed that if anything had gone wrong that evening, this would be the stretch—isolated with most of the homes set back at the end of long driveways well off the country lane. The white-clapboard houses had two stories with green roofs and large, covered porches. Sandy pulled off at a wide spot to think. His hunches always came to him as he mulled over how events might have happened.

Closing his eyes, he visualized the young deputy cruising down the country lane. He must have seen something that caused him to pull over and make a stop—but most likely not anything out of the ordinary for him not to call for back-up. He ran the plate, which was routine, and later called to say he was wrapping up. A rookie working alone was unusual, and it was getting dark. So he must have stumbled onto something. Any clues would be on this stretch of road. Anywhere else would've been too open and visible. But it'd be a long shot. The road went for several miles before it crossed highway 395.

A pickup coming to a stop in a cloud of dust next to a line of tilted mailboxes jarred him out of his thoughts. A rancher got out of the pickup, and Sandy walked over as the man posted some letters and flipped up the red metal flag.

"Good afternoon, sir."

The rancher smiled. "We must be having a regular crime wave out here. You're the second sheriff that's been out here in a day."

"You saw another sheriff?" Sandy asked.

"Last night a car passed me, and someone yelled out," the rancher said. "Couldn't tell who it was. It just startled me. Didn't pay much attention until a sheriff passed by a little later and stopped up the road or at least I think he stopped. It was dark by then, but I could see blue lights flashing up the road a few miles. Didn't pay much attention."

"Where did all this happen?" Sandy looked up the road, squinting into the sun.

"I was sitting on my porch up at the house." The rancher pointed up the drive. It led to a house on a hill.

"May I take a look?"

"Sure."

Sandy pulled his sunglasses out of his shirt pocket, got back into his car, and followed the rancher up the drive.

From the porch, he could just make out a wide spot on the road where he guessed lights had been visible. Pointing in that direction, Sandy asked, "Over there?"

The rancher nodded. "Yes, at that turnout. I couldn't make out anything in the dark but the blue lights flashing. I figured the sheriff had pulled over some hooligans. They mess with our mailboxes out here, especially on Saturday night. I've called it in several times, but you guys haven't done anything about it," the rancher paused, "at least until now. The damn hippies keep moving in. It's those new casinos bringing in a bad element."

Sandy stared up the road, thinking that the rancher may have witnessed more than a mailbox molester. He thanked the rancher, then drove back to the road and down to the turnout.

At first, he found nothing that would give a hint that the young deputy had stopped where he stood. And even if he had stopped there, it could've been nothing more than a routine check of a disabled vehicle. The deputy hadn't requested a tow truck, but the car could've had a car phone. Discouraged, he started back to his patrol car but changed direction when he noticed several black birds clustered around a damp spot in the sand. They flew off squeaking at his approach. Crows or ravens? He couldn't remember what set them apart. He knelt for a closer look, and flies scattered when he touched the dampness. He wrinkled his nose at the smell. His fingers now had the distinct odor of vomit.

On looking back toward his vehicle, he noticed a larger stain and swore at his carelessness—he may have just walked through a crime scene. After a closer look, he suspected it was blood.

On the way back to his cruiser to get on his radio, he noticed some litter on the ground and found several cards scattered in the sand. They looked like business cards, and their pristine condition indicated that they hadn't been there very long. He picked one up by its edges and realized he'd solved part of the mystery: Dr. Melon had been there. The cards appeared to have been tossed in the sand on purpose.

The professor had been there, in this wide spot in the road, and not long before. He would've been able to drop the cards under the cover of darkness. But what would've made him so desperate as to leave them as a sign of his presence?

He took a slow walk around the clearing, being careful not to step on any vehicle tracks or the damp spots. Deep in thought, he pieced the evening together. Melon must've been out of the car at some point. Different foot prints, especially around the damp spot that appeared to be blood, indicated that several people must've been out of the vehicle with him. Next to the blood, he found an impression in the sand and drag marks that ended by car tracks. The signs were starting to make sense, but it was time for the experts, the technical people.

After radioing the station for his captain and the crime lab, Sandy sat in his car deep in thought. The crime lab's meticulous procedures would shed further light on all this, but he already had the big picture pieced together. The vomit was probably Melon's, and the blood the deputy's or both of them. They'd stopped to deal with Melon, and Deputy Johnston—alone and, worse, a rookie—had most likely stumbled on them in the darkness. A wave of guilt passed over him when he remembered that he hadn't assigned him a partner as they were short-handed. Sometimes he hated his job.

He'd still have to find out what happened to Deputy Johnston, and to where he and his patrol car had vanished.

Who did this? He wondered, then whispered to himself, "First things first. Why would anyone do this?" He'd learned from his years in law enforcement that the *why* would lead him to the *who*.

As to who, the student had reported two of them with Melon and another driving. But where did they go from here? He stared down the narrow country lane and could just make out the skyline of the casinos in the distance. A jet took off from Reno Airport in a steep climb as it banked east.

I think it's time to pay a visit to the Mapes.

Chapter Twenty-two

The sentry peered into sheets of rain. "Did you hear that?"

"Yes, it sounds like someone's hacking through the bush, and not that far away," François replied, cupping his hand to his ear. In spite of the possible danger, his men couldn't help but smile, amused at the comical figure he struck while leaning forward with his hand cupped to his ear, his other sleeve, absent an arm, flapping and dripping in the rain. François usually kept the armless sleeve of his tunic neatly pinned in half, but the arduous hike through the jungle had pulled it loose.

Guessing what his men found amusing, he turned on them, scowling. "What's so funny? I can give you something to do that'll wipe those idiotic smiles off your dumb faces."

The smiles disappeared at the thought of what such tasks might be.

"Listen!" François commanded.

The men strained to listen but could hear no sounds apart from the patter of rain.

François and his men had been lucky to make the village before the rain began. While the going had been rough, at least it had been dry. Their trek from the compound had taken two laborious days, but the journey had been uneventful for the most part. They'd seen no sign of Mike, Oliver or Danny, or the creatures.

François looked at a young lieutenant and said, "I'm kicking myself for ever promising Lester to make one more trip looking for Mike."

The lieutenant nodded.

"I care about the little chimp," François said, "but don't forget he ignored Ken and Lester and left with the creatures. The only way we're going to find Mike is if he wants us to find him. I'm much more worried about who, or what, might be accompanying him."

Before Ken left for the States, he and Lester had promised to search for Mike; but it seemed impossible given the vastness of the jungle. François knew better than anyone that nothing was ever found that didn't want to be found in the jungle, and it seemed that Mike didn't want to be found.

But he had bigger worries than finding Mike and bumps in the night. Lester had been struggling to keep up with them for most of the trek. While his aging friend didn't say much, François knew he was suffering, taking longer to get back on the move after each stop, not talking and apparently turning inward. François had noticed some of the soldiers helping him to his feet, and he seemed to have a perpetual grimace on his face. Concerned, he'd ordered his men to head out a little slower after each rest stop to give him a chance to catch up. But towards the end of the day, he and Girlie lagged too far behind to catch up. After an especially long wait, he'd ordered some of his men to drop back to escort them and help take up the rear.

When thinking back on it, François realized that over the last several months, Lester's progress had been getting slower on each patrol. He wondered exactly how old Lester, and for that matter, Girlie, really were. He guessed from Lester's circus stories, he was at least seventy, and Girlie had to be in her late fifties. This was rough country at any age but especially when age caught up. François fiddled with his sleeve, trying to pin it. He wasn't getting any younger himself.

"How long has it been since we arrived here?" he asked one of his aides who came over to help pin his sleeve.

"Three hours or more, sir."

"Well, at least they're coming in from the opposite direction of the chopping noises." François gazed over the shoulder of the sentry. "Something's definitely out there, and it's people—not our people, and not the creatures, but people using machetes to cut their way. Damn weather! How can we have rain and fog at the same damn time?"

François gestured everyone to be silent and listen. Several minutes passed.

François held his hand up and whispered, "There it is again. Someone's coming our way."

The soldiers froze, staring into the darkness, silent.

Chop. Chop. Chop.

"Alert everyone, but quietly; we have visitors," François whispered.

Several of his men set out, splashing across the village grounds, and sent out the word in hushed whispers.

Except for the rain pounding against the leaves, it grew quiet again, as though something out there had heard or caught sight of them. The stirrings settled, and then they heard no more movement.

Everyone stayed at their stations, weapons ready. The rain dumped, almost as though the heavens wanted to wash away all evidence of what had happened in this village so all could forget.

François wondered if the shallow graves they'd dug so recently would be adequate. He had visions of those limbless, decomposing corpses washing up in the mud to haunt them in the darkness. His boots splashed as he paced, as though trying to walk away from the horrifying images of the massacre.

"Where in the hell is Lester?" he asked no one in particular.

"Right here, you crazy Belgian!" Lester yelled from out of the darkness.

François jumped, startling everyone standing around him. "Christ! You scared the hell out of me, you old coot."

"Who you calling an old coot?" Lester asked, releasing Girlie's grip so she could race to greet François and his men.

"Lower your voice. We've company coming our way." François pointed in the direction in which they'd heard the chopping.

"We've been followed, too. Ever since you left us on the trail," Lester said quietly.

"Are you sure?" asked François.

"Something has been shadowing us, if that's what you can call it in this pitch." Lester looked out into the darkness in the direction from which they'd come. "I tell you, we had someone dogging us the whole way here. So who's our company?"

"Not sure, but they're humans, not creatures," François replied.

"How the hell can you tell in this soup?"

"Someone has been chopping their way through the jungle. I mean chopping toward us here in the village. Creatures don't use machetes."

"At least we don't think they do. What's our plan?" Lester asked.

"We'll stay on alert through the night and head out at first light to the caves tomorrow morning," François said.

Lester smiled. "Tomorrow is another day."

"You're beginning to talk like a Belgian, my friend." François smiled back. "You'd better get out of the rain and get some rest. There's no lack of empty huts here."

A chill passed over them as they thought of the reason the village was vacant.

Lester nodded knowingly. He took Girlie's hand and limped into the darkness toward one of the huts.

François thought they looked tired and wondered if they'd ever make it back to their little trailer in California. For that matter, he wondered if he would ever make it back to the vineyards of his youth in Flanders. He couldn't remember how long it had been since he'd seen the sunny fields of the Limburg countryside. He'd have to push those thoughts away. He was a soldier and would follow this mission to its end, even if it meant his end.

François and his French Foreign Legion unit had come across the research compound while escaping the mess in Algeria after the failed coup in 1961. The scientists had needed security, and François and his men had needed a new mission and a place to hide from the Algerian government, and so they'd stayed and become a security force. Now, while he couldn't explain it,

François somehow knew they were racing toward the end of their journey here in this dark place.

***

"They're military, and in force," Bauer said. He'd gone out with Gabriel at first light to scout the village.

"It's those damn Belgians." Vandusen got up from the mud and shook out his poncho. "It's no secret why they're all the way out here, but I don't think we have the force to attack them."

"I say let's bypass them and head straight to the caves," Gabriel said. He started to say more but stopped.

Vandusen noticed his hesitation and that he seemed to be holding something back. Scowling, he asked, "What is it?"

"My men think they heard something in the trees heading toward the caves," Gabriel replied, looking up into the jungle canopy, "something big."

Vandusen shook his head. "Well, I'd say we've lost the element of surprise, again." He buried his machete deep into a branch. "So what do we do now?"

"Use this to our advantage," Gabriel replied. "Let's head to the caves and trap the first ones we come across."

"Easier said than done," Bauer said. "We've been on the business end of those monsters."

"But you didn't have us along." Gabriel smiled and opened his arms, encompassing his men.

Vandusen and Bauer huddled with Gabriel and some of his men while others cleaned and dried out their weapons. Some looked back in the direction they had come.

"I think Gabriel is right," Vandusen said. "They're not worth the effort. Let's bypass the village. We're less than a half a day's march from our objective." He snapped his compass shut and handed a soggy, wrinkled map back to Gabriel.

"But that puts them to our rear," Bauer said, shaking his head. "I don't like it. If it's the Belgians, they're armed and trained and could cut us off."

"They're a bunch of do-gooders. I don't think they have the stomach to fight us again," Vandusen said.

"So why don't we just attack them at the village right now?" Bauer asked.

Vandusen scowled. "I just said, they're not worth the effort, and besides what do they have that we need? We can't afford another delay if we're ever going to get out of this godforsaken country before the rain shuts everything down—besides I'm on a timetable." He realized he'd have to share his whole plan if he was to get everyone to buy into it. "If we leave now, we can be in and out of the caves by tomorrow morning. They'll probably still be sitting in the village with their thumbs up their asses." Vandusen gazed up the trail in the direction of the village.

"But sir, as I said, they'll be able to cut us off if we need to retreat from the caves and come this way," Bauer said in a strained voice. He nudged Gabriel and reached for the map again.

"Not if we call in air support." Vandusen looked at both of them with a slight glint in his eyes. "With air support we don't need to come this way again."

"What are you talking about? Air support?" Bauer asked. He wiped drips off his face as he looked up through an opening in the trees.

Vandusen thought he half expected a Huey to drop a basket where they stood. "We're back in touch with Fort Devens—and Langley. If we find an appropriate airfield, we can be in Germany in twelve hours." Vandusen laughed at the surprise on Bauer's face.

"Where will we fly out of?" Bauer asked, his usually simple face wishful.

"Well, since you've asked, we have two choices. Clear a runway or commandeer the one the Belgians so conveniently made." Vandusen's dark eyes darted from Bauer to Gabriel, observing and assessing their reaction.

"I like the idea of a little payback," Bauer said, his eyes smoldering. "Let's retake their compound." He paused, thinking before continuing, "It should be easy now that we're resupplied, especially if we move before they can make it back from the field. They can't have left many back there to hold the fort. We could catch them with their pants down."

Vandusen was relieved he wasn't going to have trouble with this simpleton. He guessed his men would be of the same mind when they learned retaking the compound was their ticket home. They'd not signed up for how this mission had degenerated into some kind of Frankenstein experiment. They much preferred the simple pleasures of war, battling with other human beings. That was what they were trained for.

"So that's settled," Vandusen said, motioning his men to gather around. He could see they were tired from more than a night in the rain and guessed their failed ambush and the horror of the fighting hand-to-hand with the creatures was still vivid in their minds. He was sure that, like him, they feared ending up dead, deep in this rotting jungle, or worse, writhing in agony, limbless. The creatures had unnerved them. He was sure the men would've deserted by now if they'd had a way out. He was giving them that way out. A way out within their means, both physically and psychologically. Gabriel would capture the creatures and they'd attack the Belgians. He felt pleased with himself.

Gabriel interrupted his thoughts. "I'm a tracker, not a soldier. I didn't sign up to go to war with the Belgians. I have to live here."

Vandusen's hard eyes held the tracker's gaze until he looked away. "You just help us capture the creatures and guide us out of this shithole and we'll part ways—and don't forget your bonus." He'd deal with this crafty Portuguese and his men when he no longer needed them.

He tried to modulate his voice to sound as sympathetic as he could and softly said, "Let's deal with retaking the compound. Fighting is what we do best," he paused, surveying his men and not liking the look of them. They were tired and demoralized. "Our friend, Gabriel, will help us capture some of these things, these wild animals, and we'll deal with the Belgians. Then, we'll go home."

He was relieved when his men nodded, almost in unison. He'd given them a mission they could handle and a goal they could wrap their minds around: fighting men, not the creatures, and going home.

Vandusen had his plan in place. Gabriel and his men would set out to the caves with the dart guns to capture the creatures. He and his men would provide security. He'd split his force and send some back to attack and retake the compound before the Belgians could return. It was a complicated and desperate plan, but he deemed it could work. But only if they acted immediately and timed it perfectly. They might actually be going home soon.

***

Lester woke to the glare of the tropical sun. The rain had ceased, leaving puddles the size of ponds. Everything and everyone was drenched, and they busied themselves shaking the dampness from their ponchos. He could see the sentries stretching and stomping away the stiffness caused by waiting and watching all night.

The rainy season was coming, and Lester knew they were running out of time to even travel in the jungle, let alone find Mike. Soon the river would swell and jump its banks, flooding the whole valley that opened to the caves and making it impossible to reach them. They'd have to act quickly if they were going to beat the rains.

But, worse, they weren't alone. They'd heard stirrings in the jungle the whole way to the village. And every time they'd stopped to listen, they'd heard what sounded like footsteps continue for a few seconds before ceasing. As tired as they were, they'd quickened their pace to no avail. They'd been followed all the way to the village, and then nothing.

And then there was the chopping François and his sentries had heard. Lester and Girlie had been relieved upon arriving at the safety of the village the night before, only to find out that someone was closing in on them from the other side. It felt like a noose was tightening around them. They were surrounded.

François had doubled the guards and had stayed up all night. The men were jumpy and spoke in low, strained voices. Those lucky enough to have been able to sleep, slept with their weapons beside them.

But now, in the early morning sunrise, they heard only the jungle waking to another day. No more thumps, or bumps, or chopping. A flock of African grey parrots settled in the trees above, waking the rest of the soldiers. Someone piled wood to add to the cooking fires. The aroma of fried spam brought Lester and Girlie out of their hut.

"*Bonjour*!" François said as he stirred a hash of spam in a large, cast-iron skillet over a glowing bed of coals.

"I bet you didn't hump that skillet all the way here," Lester said, smiling at the thought of some poor private struggling and cursing all the way here so his leader could enjoy fried spam.

"One of the simple pleasures of command, my friend," François said.

"You seem in a good mood this morning." Lester picked a small piece out of the skillet and gingerly tossed it from one hand to the other before continuing, "The company seems to be making little effort to hide, considering we have someone at our gates."

François nodded. "Our first scouts are in and report that our visitors had a very wet and sleepless night. It looks like they've decided to bypass our little bivouac here and have struck a line directly to the caves."

Lester stretched his legs out on the rocks surrounding the campfire. "Who are they?"

"Why, Vandusen, of course." François waved Lester off before he could speak. "It would seem they have more pressing matters than us. Beside they're not of very great force."

"What pressing matters?" Lester asked, mimicking François' accent.

"Well, it would seem they're being led away from us by something—or so our scouts report." François attended to his cooking for a moment, then looked up, smiling.

Lester opened his mouth to speak but said nothing when he saw what walked toward them.

François stood up, laughing. "It seems we have friends in mysterious places."

Chapter Twenty-three

Detective Sandy frowned and signed off his radio. Something just didn't add up. The DMV report was puzzling. The black Buick, license Mapes 1, belonged to the owner of the Mapes, Charles Mapes, Jr., but he had an ironclad alibi. He'd been the master of ceremony for a fundraiser the night before, and, even better, had held a press conference at about the time Deputy Johnston went missing. Besides, he was one of the most well-known and upstanding citizens in Reno. In fact, the Mapes family was one of the most respected in Nevada. The casino-hotel they'd built served as a model for the high-rise gambling establishments in the American West. He couldn't believe any of the Mapes family had been in that black sedan. He needed to find out who'd driven it.

Pulling up in front of the Mapes was always difficult. The traffic on North Virginia Street at noon was so congested he had to light up his cruiser and push his way into the drive. As he approached the entrance, he turned off his lights and siren. The parking attendant stood confused, not sure if he should open the door and greet him or inform management. Sandy smiled at his dilemma and didn't give him time to decide. He asked for his boss, the valet parking manager.

While he waited, he noticed an expensive facelift had been done to the entrance of the casino. New glass doors and lights brightened and modernized this old standby. But he approved since it'd been done with taste and in keeping with the original design.

Expensive but necessary. While the Mapes was an original, it had new competition—new casinos with modern marketing plans. The Mapes was where the elite came, especially if you were old money. Sandy hadn't been downtown for some time as his new position had kept him out of the field and stuck in his office. Looking around, he could see there'd been a lot of changes.

Mapes management is spending a lot of money on the facelift of this old girl. Wonder where it's coming from? Everyone knows business is down.

He'd read an article in the paper, only this morning, about how the whole downtown area was struggling to compete with the new casinos opening at the edge of town. The amount of remodeling going on all over and the new construction struck him, but it wasn't the only thing he noticed. New faces were showing up everywhere. While he recognized some of these faces, others had a different look, an out-of-town look, a mob look. He didn't like what he saw.

I need to get out more, he thought as he followed the attendant into a small kiosk.

The manager stood in front of a wall of keys. When Sandy entered, he hesitated, stroking his pencil mustache, then said in a tentative tone, "Can I help you?"

"I'm looking for the whereabouts of a black Buick, license Mapes 1," Sandy said.

"It's a company vehicle. Let me see who has it this month." The manager fumbled through a set of cards in a small wooden file box. Eventually, he clapped the lid shut, handed an index card to Sandy and said, "It's not back yet—went out yesterday morning. It's not assigned to anyone right now. Our owner, Mr. Charles Mapes, Jr., lets VIPs use it when they're staying upstairs."

"Upstairs?"

"Yes, the luxury suites. They're mainly reserved for the big stars performing in the Sky Room on the top floor or other celebs or the suits—you know, the bosses."

The Mapes had a long history of ups and downs over the years. In fact, Sandy had spent time in it during one of its downs when the department received a complaint from a disgruntled employee. According to the employee, Joe Conforte of the Mustang Ranch—the famed house of prostitution a few miles outside of town—had been tipping the bellhops to send him clients. Detective Sandy had gone undercover, posing as a high roller, and learned how the other half lived—the half that was taking over his town.

"Who did he lend the sedan to?" Sandy asked.

"I don't know his name—everyone here calls him the General," the manager replied.

"He's a guest here?"

"He's been up there for months." The manager pointed to the top of the building.

Sandy looked up and couldn't help but admire the building's design with its graceful, rounded corners and towering presence. Art Deco; he recalled reading about it in the paper. The place had a reputation for elegance and luxury.

Who could afford to stay for months? He smelled big money from out of town.

"Did 'the General' say where he was going?" Sandy asked.

"I overheard him saying something about going to the airport. Look, I think you'd better talk to management if you want to know more." He picked up the phone.

"It's okay. You've been very helpful, and thanks." Sandy hastened out the door, but the manager kept dialing.

"A sheriff has been asking about one of our clients," he said when his boss Lu Gamboa answered.

"Who?"

"A sheriff named—just a minute." The manager grabbed Detective Sandy's card. "He gave me his card; it's Lieutenant Detective John Sandy of the Washoe County Sheriff's Department. He's a detective."

"A detective; no kidding. Who's he asking about?" Gamboa asked.

"The General." The manager grew worried now that he was thinking about it. He should've called his boss right away, but the sheriff had caught him off guard.

"What did you tell him?" Gamboa asked.

"Nothing, boss—just when he checked out the sedan and that he mentioned going to the airport. "Boss? You there?"

"Nothing, you say? Don't talk to anyone, and get your skinny ass upstairs. You understand? You sorry piece of shit!" Gamboa slammed the phone down.

***

Sandy drove out of the parking lot and headed towards the airport. *The General; who the fuck is he?*

He passed the newly completed MGM Grand and smiled as he read the marquee, *The White Horse Show*. He wondered when was the last time he'd done anything not work related. *I'll have to take in that show sometime—in my spare time. Yeah, right! I need to take some time off.* He frowned when he realized he didn't have anyone to take. He couldn't remember the last time he'd been on a real date. Since his promotion, it'd been hard to meet people in a social setting. It seemed every time he planned something, he had to cancel. Something always seemed to come up. He couldn't be sure if his work was tough on relationships or it was just him.

He'd noticed a girl in dispatch who'd shown some interest. Despite being gorgeous, she had a sweet innocence about her. Being so new, she'd not developed the hard edge most of his colleagues had from working in law enforcement too long. All the guys talked about her in the locker room. It sometimes made him angry.

He'd talked to her a few times, just small talk, but he could tell she liked him. Dating inside the department wasn't good, though—he'd seen it many times—but he needed to do something. Even his parents, of all people, said his personal life was shit.

He didn't like thinking along those lines, so he pulled himself out of those thoughts and was surprised to see he'd reached the staff entrance to the airport without even noticing how he got there. Disgusted with himself, he swore to get back in the game and pay attention. He was on duty, after all. Inattention was what got you killed in his business.

The airport was busy. Air traffic had become congested and noisy since the boom in development, bringing in tourists chasing the package deals the new casinos offered. They arrived, all smiles, believing that what happens in Reno stays in Reno, only to find out it that didn't for very long. They stepped off airplanes stirred by their dreams, and a few days later, they called home asking for forgiveness and money. Sandy was getting cynical, but in his line of work the hard edge was an occupational hazard.

He made his way through the milling crowds of the main terminal to reach the Reno Airport Police, which was protocol. Just a couple of weeks ago, a group of the guys in his department had transferred over. The airport was hiring after their recent expansion. It seemed everyone was hiring as his hometown grew into a bustling city.

Besides the airport, all the casinos needed more security, and most paid better than the Sheriff's Department. The hours were better, and it was less demanding.

Ex-Washoe County law enforcement was scattered all over town, which made his job easier. There always seemed to be someone he knew, which was especially the case at the airport. He figured he knew about half the little airport force. If this so-called General had been at the airport, there was a good chance he'd find out what was going on and get help cornering him.

The station facilities surprised him when he entered. The county had spent some money expanding and modernizing the facilities to a state-of-the-art complex. While smaller than the Sheriff's Department, it was well appointed. It even had small holding cells and the latest in electronics and communication. He thought how much easier his job would be with all this equipment.

"John Sandy!" yelled the desk sergeant.

"Trevor, looking good! Boy, your new digs are great," he said.

"Thinking of coming over to the dark side?" Trevor asked, chuckling.

"Why, is the position of chief open?" Sandy asked. He was glad to see an old friend and colleague. They laughed until the chief strolled up.

"Hi, Chief," Sandy said. His posture straightened as the chief looked him up and down, clearly not amused with his joke. He thought of apologizing, then thought better of it. "I'm here on department business, sir."

The desk sergeant retreated to his desk and faked a phone call.

"State your business, Lieutenant," the chief said, his face expressionless. A short, solidly-built man just making the height regulation for law enforcement, he wore a pressed uniform tailored with a large name badge that made his name clear to all—Chief Thompson.

Sandy had been promoted to fill Thompson's position at the sheriff's department when the position became vacant. Thompson had refused to recommend him for the position, stating that he was too young and inexperienced. Sandy had been vocal about his displeasure and what he thought about the new airport chief, so he picked his words carefully. "First of all, sir, congratulations on your new appointment."

The chief interrupted: "Actually, I wasn't appointed to the position but interviewed and selected out of a field of several hundred."

"And a good selection on their part, sir," Sandy said.

They both stood for several seconds before the chief broke the silence. "So what brings you over here, Lieutenant?"

"I'm looking for a man who may be connected to two missing persons' cases I'm working on, sir. Both occurred in the last year." Sandy hated the politics of his job but needed the chief's approval to carry his investigation into his realm. He had to swallow his pride.

"Do you have a name, Lieutenant?" the chief asked.

I have a name, asshole, Sandy thought.

"Only a moniker; he's referred to as the General," Sandy replied.

The chief's manner stiffened. He looked around and lowered his voice. "That's a 10-35. Let's go to my office." He motioned Sandy to follow, then paused and whispered something to the desk sergeant who nodded and picked up the phone.

Only Thompson would use a ten code instead of just saying confidential, Sandy thought, smirking as he followed the chief. He was surprised that just the name of this mysterious character had caused such a reaction. His heart raced as he entered the chief's office. The hunt was on.

The chief motioned him to a plush winged chair. "Please have a seat, John," he said, then took a seat behind an enormous, oak desk that engulfed his small frame.

Sandy felt suspicious at the chief's sudden change in manner, especially the use of his first name, and he found the plush office and its expensive appointments overwhelming. "Wow, sir! The county has sure taken care of you and your department." He didn't believe all this expensive remodel came from Washoe County, though.

The chief smiled. "I see you have an eye for expensive things, Lieutenant, but, actually, the county only rigged us up with the basics." Sweeping his arm around the room, he smiled and continued, "The rest of this was purchased from a federal grant I received."

Where have I heard that before? Sandy couldn't help but notice the expensive furnishings and art, but what really caught his interest was a whole wall of electronics. Apart from the usual monitors and radio equipment—all new and state of the art— he noticed a row of unusual equipment with brass labels embossed with D.O.D.

Of course, Department of Defense—Vandusen.

The monitors glowed green, highlighting maps of the Pacific Northwest with arrows pointing to various locations marked with longitude and latitudes. *Looks like some of the new global positioning technology the government is developing—secret stuff.*

The chief got up and pulled down a projector screen, blocking the monitors from view. "We're working with the Feds on their War on Drugs. Apparently, there are lot of pot farms up in the Pacific Northwest. One of the conditions of the grant was to allow them to set up a terminal and warehouse complex at the airport. They've been great to work with, sharing equipment and funding our facility in return."

"How about information?" Sandy asked, frowning.

The chief furrowed his brow. "Unfortunately, their work is way above our pay grade and, more importantly, classified."

"So I can't go over there and get some answers?" Sandy pointed out the bay window at the new gated facility.

"My advice to you, young man … John, is drop this right now and follow another trail."

They both stared at each other in silence before Sandy answered, hardly holding his temper, "I can't, sir. One of our own is missing, and the trail, as you call it, leads right to your backyard."

The chief took his seat again, rocked back as he looked up at the ceiling, and exhaled. Closing his eyes, he said, "Find another backyard, Lieutenant, and find it like yesterday."

***

Lieutenant Detective Sandy returned to the parking area next to the airport police station and found it almost empty. He groped for his keys in the fading light of approaching evening, then leaned against the open door of his cruiser and stared at the new facade of the entrance. Shaking his head, he said to no one, "The whole place is a fucking façade. Hell, this whole city is headed that way with this so-called outside help."

He climbed into his cruiser and leafed through his worn address book before turning the key. Time to call that young woman in dispatch. He smiled and headed back to his office.

Chapter Twenty-four

Girlie jerked her hand from Lester's grip and, hooting a loud greeting, raced across the clearing to Mike.

"Girlie, Girlie," shouted Lester as he followed.

Girlie embraced Mike, and they panted in each other's ears, leaning together, upright, not moving.

Lester finally caught up. "Mike, is that you?"

Mike had grown taller by a foot in the short time they'd been apart, and his upper body had become muscular, hinting that he was leaving adolescence and becoming an adult. Lester noticed that his panting and hooting were hoarse and low-pitched. Mike had matured in his time in the jungle. He jumped into Lester's arms, almost knocking him over. Panting, he opened his mouth, exposing two large canines, and covered all of Lester's neck, leaving indentations.

"Easy, boy, you're too heavy. Now leave it," Lester said in a calm but commanding voice.

Mike dropped from his arms, and Lester knelt down to Mike's level. Mike presented the back of his hand to Lester as he curled back his lips, showing his teeth. Lester kissed his hand, and they both embraced again.

François stood back smiling. "So … two friends are reunited." He knelt, opened his arms to Mike, and they embraced. Girlie ran up to Mike, tapped him on the back, then ran off on all fours. Laughter broke out as the men watched the two play a short-but-lively game of chase.

"Well, my friend, I believe we've gathered up what we came here for," François said as he watched the two chimps finally settle down to share a pile of mangoes.

"Almost everything—we still have no word of Oliver and Danny." Lester paused, watching Girlie reach out to Mike with an open hand as Mike grunted and bit into a plump fruit. Juice dripped onto Girlie's fingers, which she licked between begging.

"Mike, come here," Lester said.

Mike sauntered over to him, carrying a mango, and Girlie followed. Lester had to wait for Mike to settle and drop the seed and remains of the fruit before continuing, "Where's Oliver and Danny?"

Upon hearing their names, Mike stopped grunting and looked up at Lester, tilting his head to one side.

Lester asked again, "Where's Oliver and Danny?"

Mike looked from François to Lester. His lips puckered together, and he breathed in heaves through his nose.

Girlie turned to Mike and signed, "Where?"

Mike jumped up, his legs slapping on the soft clay, and in an awkward motion, pointed toward the caves.

"So that's the sounds we've been hearing. They've been trailing us," François said.

Mike pointed again and signed, "Chase, over there."

"Our scouts reported our visitors left this morning in the direction of the caves," François said.

Mike pointed several times in the direction of the caves.

"They're leading them in that direction," Lester said.

"I believe so—a dangerous prospect, but yes," François said.

Lester sighed. "At least we now know where Vandusen has gone, and maybe, Oliver and Danny."

Mike watched them stare in the direction of the caves, then signed, "Home now. Go home, hurry, now."

François nodded. "You heard Mike. Let's get out of here. I don't like the idea of being out here with Vandusen roaming around, and, worse, he's headed to the caves. God knows what he'll stir up. We'll have to leave Oliver and Danny to chance. We can't continue any further with Vandusen breathing down our necks. We have Mike at least. Let's leg it home, men."

The soldiers looked confused but relieved when François gave the order to pull out of the village and head back to the compound. It didn't take them long to pack up and head back the way they'd come. The going was easier as they'd cut a path the day before. But François felt uneasy—taking a clear path was an open invitation to being ambushed.

Dark billowing clouds threatened rain, so they moved at a brisk pace. François noticed that Lester and Girlie moved with renewed energy now they had Mike with them. They were keeping up, much to his relief.

They heard no stirrings in the shadows. The jungle seemed to tolerate their passing with a growing sense of foreboding.

Chapter Twenty-five

Vandusen hated the jungle. He couldn't abide the mysteries of this place. You could never see anything under the canopy, just hear stirrings deep in the dense and clinging vegetation, and it was hard to even tell what time of day it was. It always seemed to be twilight. Then there was the feeding of the insects and spiders. Gabriel had told him that more people died from insect bites than any other denizen in the Congo. Rot and infection were everywhere. He'd had several men die from the infection of simply scratching bites. And there were the dangers of war and, of course, the creatures. He was beginning to believe that life in the jungle was about odds. The longer he stayed in this nightmare place, the less the odds of ever coming out.

He'd toyed with the idea of just pulling the plug and going home, but the agency had a swift and decisive way of dealing with quitters. There'd be no part of the world where the General wouldn't find him. He had only two ways out of this situation: complete the mission or die trying. The sound of Bauer's voice stirred him from his thoughts.

"Gabriel's on his way. He thinks he's on the trail of the creatures. His men are tracking movement in the canopy leading to the caves—I think we're finally onto something." Bauer's voice quivered. Vandusen couldn't be sure if he was afraid or excited.

"But what are we onto?" Vandusen asked as he gathered up his pack and shouldered his rifle. "Make sure the men are armed and ready."

"They are, and Gabriel seems to know his business," Bauer said.

A loud crack sounded ahead of them on the trail. They both jumped. Everyone was on edge. The least sound or movement in the shadows put them in a panic. They'd been following a trail of sounds leading them directly to the caves. He'd warned Gabriel that the creatures were wily and not to under-estimate them. He couldn't shake a sense of foreboding, but knew this was their last chance to accomplish their mission. His throat was dry from fear more than thirst. His tongue stuck to the roof of his mouth as he spoke: "Stay alert. Make sure the darts are loaded and ready."

Bauer nodded, and they headed down the trail, looking from side to side. They paused often at the sound of something above them in the canopy moving heavily ahead and always toward the caves. Vandusen couldn't help but think they were being led purposefully, but he had to trust in the skill of his tracker, Gabriel. Hours went by as they trudged on. If it hadn't been for his watch, he wouldn't have known how long they'd been hiking or what the hour was. He found the stillness of the bush suffocating, and the heat sapped everyone's energy. Their damp clothes clung to their sweating bodies.

Just as Vandusen and his men thought they couldn't take another step, they felt a light breeze and saw light breaking just ahead, illuminating the dark patches of the trail. They must be reaching the edge of the open valley. It would give a clear view across to the caves.

"Make sure everyone stays under cover. Pass the word," Vandusen whispered. He craned his body, trying to get a better view through the vines that tangled their way.

Bauer nodded and jogged up the trail. The men knelt down, heaving from exhaustion. Soon he returned and began fanning the men out along the edge of the trees.

Vandusen adjusted his binoculars, but had to look away. His eyes were slow to adjust to the intense light of the valley after so long in the dim twilight under the canopy. Finally, he made out the dark mouths of the caves and spied movement in a clearing that skirted the cliffs. His body stiffened. He counted at least twenty large creatures hunched around one of the openings.

"We're going to wait until dark to make our move," Gabriel said. He'd slipped back through the tall grass of the valley after positioning his men.

"Did you see any signs of what we'd been following?" Vandusen asked. He leaned back, looking up into the towering canopy.

Gabriel shook his head. "The noises are gone now." He arched his back and swayed, looking from tree to tree. "But something has been with us all the way here."

"But did you see anything?" Vandusen asked.

"That's just it, from the noise in the treetops, you'd think we were on the trail of a whole troop of apes, but nothing. We've seen nothing."

"Are they the creatures?" Bauer asked, tightening his grip on his rifle.

"They're big for sure, but if they're creatures, why can't we see them heading across the valley toward those caves?" Gabriel pointed to the clearing.

"How the fuck do I know? You're supposed to be the goddamn guide," Vandusen said, his fists tightening.

"Let's get those dart guns ready," Gabriel said.

As Gabriel and his men prepared to head for the caves, Vandusen made ready to pay the Belgians a visit back at their compound. Handing Gabriel a box of syringes, he said, "If you do your part, we'll meet tomorrow afternoon at the airfield, and settle up before we all fly out of this shithole. We'll have the cages and runway ready, and, of course, you'll get what's coming to you."

"Don't worry about us," Gabriel said. Pointing at his men, he continued, "Just have our money ready."

Vandusen nodded and turned back down the trail. He planned to keep both his money and the creatures, and leave Gabriel holding the bag. The prospect warmed him.

Chapter Twenty-six

When Dr. Melon came to in the back of the car, he heard the roar of a jet passing low overhead, and even with his head throbbing and vision blurred, he realized they must be somewhere near the Reno Airport. They pulled up next to a Lear jet being loaded with cargo. The high-pitched scream of its two engines worsened his already aching head.

He caught sight of a female silhouette switch with the driver of the patrol cruiser ahead of them and drive it into a nearby hanger, while the driver ran back towards them and slid into the back seat beside Melon. *Very efficient,* Melon thought, when he recognized him as the one who shot the trooper.

So it wasn't all a bad dream. It really was happening. He moaned, as much from desperation as from pain.

The driver looked back and said, "Ah, the little prince is waking up, and just in time."

He wondered what they were going to do with the trooper's body they'd stuffed in the trunk of the patrol cruiser like so much baggage. For that matter, how do you get rid of a police patrol car? Then, he thought about himself; surely the police would be looking for him. It'd been several hours since they'd kidnapped him at the university and driven to the country, where they'd been intercepted by the trooper. It sickened him to think it was most likely his fault that these thugs killed the poor man in the first place. He didn't want to think about that right now.

He wondered if anyone would find his business cards on the roadside. It'd been a feeble effort, perhaps even stupid, considering the circumstances of his predicament. However, it'd been the only way he could think of at the time to leave some trace of his whereabouts. The more he thought about it, the more feeble he realized it had been. How would anyone connect his cards to what had happened to him and that poor trooper?

He found it difficult to think of anything but the throbbing in his head, and he had trouble focusing on his surroundings as his vision remained blurred. He wasn't sure if that was due to the recent blow to his head or the fact that he'd lost his glasses in his recent scuffle with his kidnappers. Despite seeing double, however, he could make out that they were in some kind of private commercial section of the airport, a part he'd never seen before. The jet warming up its engines must be one of the private ones only the rich and famous could afford.

Of more concern to Melon was what was going to happen to him now. He didn't like the idea of getting on a jet with these gangsters. He wondered where Vandusen had disappeared to and how his abduction connected to him.

The driver muttered something into the car phone, then hung up, knelt on the front seat, and poked Melon. "Looks like you're going to take a little plane ride." He smirked. "It'll be fun to see where and how you land." He chuckled to himself at his cleverness.

The other men joined in, and one said, "A fifty says he takes flight at forty thousand feet without a chute."

"You're on!" the driver said, sharing in the laughter.

Melon's stomach churned, and his broken wrist throbbed. He fought another wave of nausea and swallowed several times, knowing what would happen if he vomited in the backseat again. After the incident on the road with the trooper, his abductors had gagged and cuffed him despite his broken wrist. The driver had wanted to sap him again, but the other man had talked him out of it. It seemed that at least someone wanted him alive and in one piece. But that gave him little comfort at the moment. What were his prospects when riding in a Lear jet at several thousand feet with a bunch of criminals?

A young woman came out of the hanger and walked to the car. Her elegant appearance and age—the same as some of his grad students—surprised Melon. She didn't seem to fit with these thugs—until she spoke through the driver's open window. "Okay, now. At least one loose end is cleared up," she said in a hard voice with a hint of an East Coast accent. "Now, let's get this little piece of shit cleaned up and ready for his trip. The General likes people to be presentable when he interviews them."

They chuckled as they busied themselves removing his cuffs and gag. The woman patted down his ruffled suit and wiped his face with a moist towel. In a final flurry of activity, she stood him up and brushed him off with a whiskbroom.

They had to steady him at first as his knees buckled when he tried to stand. Melon wasn't sure if his weakness was from his injuries or blind fear. It took him several steps to stand on his own.

Finally, the woman stepped back with her hands on her hips, took a final look, and nudged him toward the waiting jet.

164

Melon had to shade his eyes from the bright lights shining from the windows in the fuselage. The running lights blinked in readiness.

Melon wondered who was taking him to God-knows-where in a private jet in the dead of the night. As they approached the steps, the door opened, silhouetting a trim, uniformed stewardess. She disappeared back into the jet as they climbed the steep steps.

He heard one of the thugs say, "Excellent! The General picked the cute one for this ride."

The young woman shook her head and, laughing, said, "Pigs."

Melon was the only one not laughing. His mouth was so dry he couldn't say anything.

Once inside, one of the thugs shoved him into a plush leather seat across from a thin, well-dressed man in his sixties. He had cropped hair and an athletic, medium build, and sat with one leg crossed, exposing a small pistol holstered near his ankle. The leg of his well-tailored slacks had pulled up, exposing a tan, muscular calf with a faded tattoo of oriental inscriptions. Even before he spoke, Melon knew he must be the General. Melon took furtive glances, trying to take in his surroundings while the General looked him up and down.

"Well, not much worse for wear I see, Dr. Melon," the General said and motioned the stewardess over. "I understand you had a bit of an ordeal on your way over here."

Melon nodded.

"It's a shame about the trooper. I'm a big supporter of our local law enforcement." The General flashed a smile. "It might surprise you to know, many of my contractors were peace officers of some sort before they joined our organization." He paused and waited for Melon to react, but continued when Melon remained silent. "We'll have to make sure the poor man's family is well taken care of." He smirked. "We can also offer our help in the investigation of his disappearance."

The two thugs beamed with admiration.

The General glanced at the stewardess, who stood a little distance away. "Ah, here we are—a dram of scotch, Dr. Melon?"

Melon couldn't speak. His body shook with the mixed emotions of fear and rage. A menacing presence in the General's hard voice and eyes defied his outward appearance of a wealthy, well-dressed businessman and indicated a raw savagery lurking just beneath the surface. Terrified, Melon could only nod.

"Excellent! Nothing like a rich dram of Glenfiddich eighteen to loosen things up—you know, put things right. We have a lot to discuss concerning your future prospects and employment."

Surprised by this remark, Melon opened his mouth to speak, but the General interrupted, holding up his hand: "A moment please, Dr. Melon. Let's have a toast first." He took two glasses from the stewardess, handed one to Melon, and held his tumbler out. "To plain talking with open minds and making it out of this safely."

Melon's trembling hand rattled the ice in the glass, but he managed to hold out his glass. The clink as the General's glass touched his startled him. He took a gulp, and before the burn had ended, took another longer gulp.

The General waited for Melon to settle and the scotch to relax him a little before he began, "You see, Dr. Melon, there's a problem I need you to help me with. Or, at least, I am hoping you can help, for your sake."

Melon took another gulp and hesitated, gathering his thoughts before he spoke. "I think there is some kind of mistake. I can't see how I can be of any assistance."

The General shook his head and, appearing sympathetic, asked, "You've been accepting some sizable ... stipends, shall we say, from one of my colleagues, a Mr. Vandusen, correct?"

"Well, yes, but—"

"You were very helpful informing us on the activities of Dr. Turner, and for that we're very grateful. I think we've shown that with the stipends we've given you," The General paused and picked up a phone. "We can take off now."

Melon panicked as the jet engines roared and they began to taxi down the runway. "Where are we going?" he asked in a strained voice. He leaned forward in his seat and tried to stand up.

The two thugs stepped toward him, but the General waved them off, his voice barely discernable above the engines. "I would be more concerned with how you're going to end up than where we're going." Despite all his previous pleasantries, the General's tone held a deadly threat.

Melon realized he needed to use another tactic. "Well, of course, the money has been very helpful for my research, but I didn't know you were connected to Mr. Vandusen. I haven't heard from him for some time. I just assumed our relationship had been terminated."

"We don't use that word much around here; it has, shall we say, such an ominous sound to it. Mr. Vandusen has been taking care of some loose ends for us out of the country. In fact, the information you're supplying us has been very helpful in that endeavor. But enough about these adventures. All these plots and plans are tiring." He picked up the phone and ordered two more drams. "Let's talk about how you fit into all this."

Before Melon could speak, the stewardess interrupted them by scurrying around helping everyone get ready for takeoff. The passengers obviously knew the routine as they busied themselves clicking their seat belts and storing their gear.

The jet taxied, making a slow turn at the end of the runway, and, within seconds, started down the tarmac, picking up speed and lifting off in a steep climb that pinned Melon in his seat. Clouds streaked by the window, compounding the sensation of high speed, and the interior pressurizing made Melon feel as if he'd been hermetically sealed. The engines made a faint roar that could just be heard over the hum of the motor lifting the landing gear.

"Now, back to business," the General said as they leveled off.

"Where are you taking me?" Melon asked.

"To your new facility, of course."

"My new what?"

"You're about to make a career move, Dr. Melon." The General's menacing tone unnerved Melon. He waited for him to continue, but the man took several sips before holding his tumbler up to the light and saying, "Ah, that's good, don't you think? We're building a facility in the Pacific Northwest to house some special animals the government is interested in studying. Animals your information helped us find. Mr. Vandusen is in Africa, working on that mission as we speak. Your services will be indispensable in designing the facility and conducting research for their practical uses. You'll be paid very well, of course—double what you're making now. And, of course, you need to think of the welfare of your little family."

Melon's blood chilled at the mention of his family. "What's my family have to do with all this?"

"Absolutely nothing," the General replied. "We just like to keep all our people in one place. It's easier to keep an eye on things. The company doesn't like loose ends."

"I can't just leave the NSF. They'll ask questions."

"You let us worry about that. You're about to join a top-secret Department of Defense project. We're used to taking care of these sorts of details."

"What do I tell my friends and colleagues?"

"Nothing; your research is classified."

Melon opened his mouth to speak, but realizing it was pointless, exhaled instead.

"I know it's a lot to take in all at once. Just relax and let us arrange everything." The General handed Melon a folder. "We have some papers for you to sign. Also, here are some pictures and floor plans of your new home for you to share with the missus. I think she's really going to love her new digs and the household allowance we provide our special people."

"What's all this have to with Dr. Turner and his group?"

"Interesting you should ask. We want to know the same thing. According to Mr. Vandusen, the good doctor and his wife have been moonlighting, so to speak," the General replied.

"Moonlighting?"

"They've been investigating the very creatures we're after, and have even been in Africa seeking them out. As you found out, they're very uncooperative."

"Uncooperative, to say the least. Is this about the whereabouts of his signing chimps and the fact he won't cooperate with any of us in using them for practical work?"

"Only in part. It turns out Dr. Turner and his colleague, Dr. Savage, have stumbled onto some creatures in Africa who could be hybrids of humans and chimpanzees. But we can't seem to get them to work with us, so we've had to do it on our own."

"My God, that can't be true."

"We have Vandusen there right now with orders to find and capture some specimens at all cost. That's where you come in. We'll need you, as you can guess, to help us use them for our purposes."

Melon wasn't sure what that meant, but he began to relax a little and saw some advantages to working with these people. "How do I fit into this?" *As if I have a choice.*

"It's very simple, actually, the D.O.D. ..." Seeing the quizzical expression on Melon's face, the General clarified. "Sorry, all these initials the government uses can be confusing. The Department of Defense, or D.O.D., as we say, has been interested in supporting research to see if signing chimpanzees could be used on the battlefield. But as you found out, in spite of offering a sizable stipend, Dr. Turner is not receptive. Very unpatriotic, I'd say. Now, with the possibility of these larger and more intelligent creatures being discovered, we may have hit a goldmine!" The General paused, then as if he thought better of his word choice, added, "Scientifically speaking, that is."

Melon nodded, thinking he could gain both financially and professionally from this partnership, but the real icing on the cake would be taking revenge on Dr. Turner and his cronies. He'd destroy him and his darling little chimps. And revenge would be especially painful with the General in the mix.

Dr. Melon stood, tried to straighten his jacket with his good hand, and emptied his glass. Looking around as though for the first time, he smiled and said, "So where are we headed?"

The General patted Melon lightly on his shoulder. "Now that's the spirit. We've purchased some property near a little town in the Pacific Northwest called Willow Creek. It's remote, undeveloped. With your design, it should suit us very well."

"I'd like to call my wife."

"All in good time, but first, let's celebrate our partnership." The General motioned everyone over to share in a toast. Melon felt a chill pass over him. He turned, noticed the two thugs glaring at him, and quickly looked away.

The General leaned over to the young woman who'd so efficiently dispatched the trooper and his cruiser and whispered, "Work some of your magic on the little professor."

She nodded without expression and glided over to Melon. Slipping her arm under his, she smiled and said in a provocative, syrupy voice, "No hard feelings?"

Chapter Twenty-seven

Vandusen peered into the shadows, but could see nothing. The humidity made his clothes sticky and lank with sweat, and the insects bit relentlessly. He absentmindedly swatted the back of his neck. Repellant was useless in the sweltering heat, as the sweat washed it away in rivers. It seemed that everything with pincers or claws was feasting. The air felt thick and smelled sweet with rot, making him labor to breathe. He wondered how much longer they'd be stuck in this shithole part of the world and dreamed of air conditioning and the bright lights of the casinos. These days, the closest he could get to a smile was a sneer, so he sneered, realizing he'd found a place that was crueler than he was.

Time dragged on under the canopy of this endless jungle of perpetual twilight, where they could hear stirrings in the shadows but never see anything. They hid just off a trail that led to the caves, waiting to be sure that Gabriel and his men made it to their destination. They'd set up an ambush for any of the creatures that might come their way should Gabriel miss some. He and Bauer were hoping to put the dart guns into use and had held back a couple from Gabriel. But so far, they saw no sign of any living creature except the feeding insects. The trail was empty and the jungle unusually quiet, too quiet. Something didn't seem right.

Vandusen stiffened and stood, jarring the men closest to him out of their musings. "Something's wrong," he whispered. "The jungle's never this quiet. Nothing's moving—listen." He hissed his final words. All they heard was an ominous stillness. The jungle remained still, as though hiding from some unspeakable menace. His men stirred and clicked off their safeties. Bauer and Vandusen checked their dart guns, making sure they were locked and loaded.

The men looked at one another, then dispersed into defensive positions and waited for something to happen. Tension grew with each heartbeat for what seemed an eternity, but nothing happened. Vandusen thought that perhaps they'd been detected, and the creatures wouldn't be passing this way. He hated the jungle.

Just as they began to relax, the silence broke—a racket of breaking branches and shrill cries from behind them. Several creatures broke out from the cover of the trees and charged. They turned to meet the threat, but dark shadows surrounded them and jumped onto their backs from the trees above. They were being attacked from all directions. Large beasts overran them before they could react, downing some before they could raise their weapons, while others stood frozen, unable to engage. The cries from man and beast were deafening. Their fortunes quickly turned from ambushers to ambushed.

Vandusen was first to react. "Close ranks; back to back!" Vandusen shouted. He motioned to Bauer. "Get those automatics going. Cover our flanks!"

Bauer grabbed several men and pushed toward the creatures. A large creature—its rank smell making him gag—raced past him, ripped off one of his men's arms, and began beating the screaming man with it, while hooting in glee. For the first time on the battlefield, Bauer froze. He'd never experienced this kind of terror. The first rounds being fired by his men finally drowned out the shrill screams of the dying man. Bauer sprang back into action.

At first, the fire rang out in ragged shots as the creatures bore down on them. The screams of the wounded, both human and animal, were deafening. Only when Bauer got their automatic weapons going did the creatures retreat at last. The remaining men watched in horror as the last of them disappeared into the shadows of the bush.

"Hold your position. Reload and make ready for a counterattack," Vandusen ordered.

"From us or them?" Bauer asked, shaking.

"Just stand ready." Vandusen stood in shock, surveying what remained of his tattered crew. Almost half his men lay at his feet, dying. Though they'd shot many of the creatures, none were to be found. It was unnerving. They'd retreated as quickly as they'd charged, dragging their wounded and vanishing like ghosts.

A blood-chilling scream pierced the quiet of the jungle, followed by a deafening chorus of deep-throated howls that sounded almost like a challenge. The screams of what they made out to be their comrades-in-arms jolted them into action. Several of the men grabbed their weapons and moved in the direction of the cries, eyes flaming.

"Hold on!" Vandusen yelled.

The men turned, frightened and confused.

"We can't do any good here. We've lost the advantage of surprise. Let's get the hell out of here before we have to fight our way back. Gather your gear and let's move out."

"What do we do about the wounded and captured?" Bauer asked. "We need to warn Gabriel." He knelt over a man who was screaming in pain while staring in horror at his arm twitching next to him.

Saying nothing, Vandusen pulled out his sidearm, and to the horror of all, shot the man in the head. The screams stopped.

Vandusen's men stood frozen in disbelief.

Pointing his weapon, Vandusen motioned them down the trail. "I said, get moving."

Several more shots rang out as they retreated down the trail, and the screams from deeper in the jungle grew fainter behind them.

***

Oliver watched as humans retreated back down the trail in panic. He was puzzled but pleased that they'd left their dead and wounded. He nodded to the other creatures, and they took little time in making a feast. The screams soon died out.

They worked their way through the dead, gathering many treasures. Danny danced nervously around a fire stick that lay still on the ground. The humans had used the odd-shaped things to kill or wound many of Oliver's group. Though frightened of its power, Oliver couldn't show that fear to the others—his apparent lack of fear of mysterious things was what made him their leader.

He picked it up cautiously, handling it with care, ready to drop it and run if more fire came out of it. It was warm and smelled like the smoke from the hot pits at the base of the mountain that burned. He touched the metal tip and dropped it instantly, screaming from the burning pain.

Several creatures ran around it, hooting and kicking dirt over it. Oliver knew that if he was to stay the leader, he'd have to pick it up again, so he stepped closer and kicked it. Startled, the creatures scattered, then grew silent when he picked it up. He motioned to the others to do the same with the many others lying around the dead. He'd have to watch those who picked up the fire sticks, especially the younger ones.

He opened his mouth, the blood-red interior contrasting with his large ivory canines, and hooted in triumph, sending even the insects off in flight.

When the creatures faded into the jungle this time, many carried fire sticks instead of their usual clubs.

Chapter Twenty-eight

"Our objective is the runway. We must hold it long enough for that Portuguese to arrive with our special cargo from the caves. Understood?" The men nodded and readied their gear, simpering at him calling the creatures *special cargo*. "Okay, let's move out. Lock and load!" Vandusen waved his men toward the runway.

He watched as they faded into the growing darkness. He'd timed their arrival to coincide with dusk, hoping to surprise what he thought would be a small contingent of soldiers left behind. Part of him regretted not engaging the Belgians at the abandoned village when their forces were divided, but timing was everything, and taking and securing the runway would be doable with most of them out in the jungle far from their compound. They'd doubled-timed it back out of the bush to get positioned before the rest of the Belgians returned.

"If Gabriel and his men capture some of these creatures, and get them back while we still hold the runway, we can be out of this shithole and back in the States in days. I want to end this operation once and for all." Though he didn't want to say anything to Bauer, Vandusen was growing nervous at the time this mission was taking to complete. The General would be getting impatient, and he'd seen firsthand how unhealthy it was to keep him waiting.

He couldn't help but wonder why such a large patrol of Belgians had been on bivouac at the abandoned village so close to the caves. This part of the jungle was getting too crowded, and he didn't like the changes he saw: too much was happening; everything was on the move and out of his control; and it was happening way too fast for his liking. He needed to wrap this whole mess up and pull out. *Time is running out.*

"I can't tell how much of a force they have left at the compound," Vandusen said to Bauer as they moved forward, "but they can't spare many, if any, to guard this runway. If we can just hold it for a few hours, we'll be clear."

Bauer nodded and gestured to his men to gather around. "We'll hold the strip. Let's just hope our ride makes it."

"It'll be here." Vandusen motioned the radioman to give them space and whispered, "I just got off the network the General set up. The radio's reaching out pretty well. He's scheduled more COM flights over us, and he's got them loaded with long-range, relay radio equipment that can reach Ramstein in Germany. They'll make a pass over us at 10,000 feet, every morning at 0800 hours, until we get out of this shithole. He's sparing no expense and guarantees a transport is headed our way. I gave them our coordinates. You just hold the field long enough for us to be in and out as quickly as it takes us to load, and for me to take care of a few loose ends."

Vandusen debated if he'd need the Portuguese guide after he delivered the creatures. He didn't trust him or his men. A plan had been turning in his mind to take care of any dead weight or loose ends. If he played his cards right, he could leave him on the runway holding the bag. *Let him be a guest of the Belgians.*

Just thinking about it warmed his heart and kept his mind off the oppressive heat and relentless bugs.

***

Bauer frowned. He guessed his boss had only ordered one C-140—not big enough to carry all the men as well as the creatures. Obviously, Vandusen's plan didn't include all the men going home. And as for Gabriel, at best, he figured the Portuguese wouldn't be getting paid.

But first things first, he needed to secure the runway. His heart raced, realizing that everything was in motion. If he did his job, they'd be on that plane and out of this nightmare before daybreak, headed for Europe, most likely Ramstein, Germany. Any military installation would work, but Ramstein was huge, and they'd hardly notice a single plane coming in from Africa. It would be easy to make a transfer to the States. Bauer smiled, taking little notice of the men waiting for him to get on the move. The plan made sense to him, and it was finally coming together.

He'd been on several missions that had flown in under a number of different convenient covers. Lately, the CIA was fond of using the cover of the UN, or other *feed-the-hungry* organizations, when coming out of Africa. All it took was a call to Langley to requisition believable paperwork and a quick paint job. *Thank God Africa's still the Wild West, and money can buy almost anything.*

Corruption was the fire that forged the CIA's agenda. Nevertheless, Bauer felt that this operation, even for the CIA, had crossed the line, or was at least blurring it. He realized, however, that when it came to that mysterious spook, the General, there were no lines. It was best not to ask too many questions if you wanted to contract for him and live to do another job. That was true of his boss as well. Vandusen wasn't loyal to anyone or anything but money, and people had a way of disappearing when their usefulness had ended. He admired Vandusen's attention to detail. He'd leave no loose ends in this engagement if all went the way he planned. When it came to deviousness, Vandusen was a genius. And when it came to cruelty, he was an artist.

Bauer would have to pay close attention if he didn't want to become a loose end. *Those who snooze, will lose.*

He stirred into action as the last of their force worked their way toward the edge of the runway. The strip was empty except for a stack of barrels and crates backed by two ransacked hangers that hadn't been repaired since their previous raid.

It didn't take long to discover there were no guards, allowing for a quick exercise in setting a perimeter around the strip. He took special precautions by ordering his men to dig in at the edge facing the road that connected their position to the compound. That was where he expected an attack to come from if they were detected. So far, they'd been lucky. It seemed the Belgians had been so preoccupied in repairing and fortifying the compound after the raid, they'd not spent any time or resources on the runway.

His men took cover and attended to their weapons. Bauer almost felt saddened when he realized the waste of trained mercenaries this operation was going to cost if he was correct about Vandusen's plan. He noticed they'd affected considerable damage to the landing strip in their last raid. They'd have to make some repairs before a large transport plane could land safely. At the very least, they'd have to fill the larger craters made by stray mortars. He sent a patrol to make repairs with instructions to do it as quietly as possible while it was still dark.

Bauer knew they'd have to secure the tower, but at least it wasn't damaged, and, better, he suspected it was empty. He sent a squad to the tower with his radioman. In less than thirty minutes his men had the runway secure and defendable. They just needed Gabriel and the transport to arrive before daylight, which would be no easy task as they were working independently of one another with no communication between them. Luck and force would have to carry them through. He wasn't sure about luck, but force they had, and they were ready to use it.

***

"Let's see that fancy scope of yours," Vandusen whispered, tapping Bauer on the shoulder.

Bauer stiffened to his touch and hesitated before answering, "Sure thing, boss." He handed over his Starburst scope.

Vandusen peered through the scope and grinned. "There are guards on the wall, but, fortunately, none here near us. I'd say the Belgians are asleep at the switch." He handed back the scope. "Tell the men to lay low for now. I don't think they're onto us yet, but it's gonna get interesting when our transport buzzes over and makes an approach. Make sure the radio's ready. We need to figure their ETA. I don't want them landing before Gabriel gets here if we can help it. Timing is everything in this operation. I don't want any surprises unless they come from us."

Bauer nodded. "We've set it up in the tower with one of the *prick 77s*. It will have the range we need. I'll see if we can raise the plane."

Even with everything that was happening, Vandusen couldn't help smiling at the nickname these 'Nam vets gave the portable AN/PRC 77 transceivers. The ones the General had given them had worked well in contacting the airborne flights that flew over the Congo every few nights at 10,000 feet. But tonight was not going to be a problem as the cargo plane would be equipped with the latest in communication devices. The General would see to that. It had been worth humping these large and heavy manpacks through the jungle for engagements just like this. *Everything was falling into place*, he thought.

Bauer worked his way toward the tower as the remaining men reinforced the positions around the runway. He could just make out the bush antenna projecting out the window. All eyes looked to the night sky, longing for a ride home.

That is, all except the ones behind them in the shadows of the jungle.

***

Oliver's upper lip curled in a snarl, revealing two large canines, as he watched the humans below on the runway. Many of the creatures grimaced and pulled back, on the verge of running into the forest. He growled them into submission. They knew that these humans were a vicious tribe who'd killed many of them. They carried the fire sticks that killed with a deafening crack. He'd been patient, stalking these humans for days, waiting for an opportunity to attack again. Hatred brewed in him as he built up his nerve. The last ambush hadn't gone well for his clan.

They'd retreated, carrying off many of their dead. It was time to get revenge. He wanted to feed on these humans before the sun took the night away.

These humans were different from the ones they preyed on in the villages along the river. The villagers were timid and put up a weak fight. But these humans were dangerous. They traveled in hunting parties with no females, were well organized, and did not frighten. The fire sticks they carried maimed and killed when flames came out of them. Worse, they threw stones that made the earth shake and burn with deafening blasts.

The purpose of this clan of humans confused him. They attacked, but didn't eat the dead. To kill to eat or capture to breed made sense, but this did not. He didn't understand why they pursued his clan, but he did know that for his clan to survive, they'd have to kill all of them.

The humans inside the walls were different. While they had fire sticks, they didn't harm the clan, leaving them alone in their caves. And Lester and the little chimp, Mike, were their friends. Oliver knew they watched them in the forest, but they left these humans alone. The villagers were easier and had many females.

He'd been captured by these different humans and taken inside the walls. But for all of his fear, they'd not harmed him. They'd kept him in a cage with a lock for a long time, but they'd given him plenty of food and water.

He remembered the day of the fighting inside the walls. The humans with the fire sticks attacked and killed many of the humans inside the walls, and they put some of the friendly humans in a cage next to them. He knew they were friends because they shared their food and water.

The little ape, Mike, had visited him. He'd brought gifts of fruit and taught Oliver hand signals that represent thoughts. Mike had been put with the friendly humans in the cage next to the creatures but later had helped them all.

When Oliver had killed the mean human who'd taunted and teased, the small ape had helped them all escape. He'd had to protect the humans once they were all free. His clan would have killed them all if he hadn't stopped them and led the way out. The humans had followed him and his clan and scattered when the fire sticks started killing. There'd been so much smoke and fire when they came outside that no one had noticed their escape.

After his escape, he'd taught these signals to all his clan. The signals allowed him to share his thoughts and improved how they hunted. The friendly humans also used these signals, but not those down on the runway below.

Oliver fingered a large ring of keys. He'd learned other things during his captivity. These metal pieces had great power. They opened locks which held doors closed even to his strength. The small ape had dropped them when he helped them escape, and Oliver had picked them up and hidden them under a rock. In their haste, no one in his clan had noticed the treasure. He'd retrieved them now, thinking their magic might be useful again.

He couldn't work out in the clouds of his mind why the little ape had helped them escape, but he had, and he'd used the magic Oliver now held in his hand.

Once under the cover of the jungle, he and Danny had made it to the caves, and then fought their way back to the top of the clan. Now they could signal each other, and had even taught themselves to use the fire sticks they'd taken from the humans who killed. It was time to kill all the humans, except for any females; they gave great sport and were fun to breed.

His eyes smoldered as he watched the humans sneak in the darkness. It seemed that the killing humans were planning to attack the ones behind the walls. The ones behind the walls had not harmed them, only the ones down below.

Suddenly, a clear idea came to him. He would help the friendly humans, the ones who had not harmed them, the ones behind the walls who gave good food and taught helpful signs. The keys jingled in his hand. One of the other creatures tried to touch them, but he shoved him back and signed, "Stay."

His mind pictured the gate below the wall that they'd once spied men sneaking through. They could open the gate and warn the humans inside. They might use their fire sticks to kill the bad humans or make them run away.

He tucked the keys under his arm and picked up one of the fire sticks they'd taken from the dead in the jungle. He'd learned that when he pulled the small part in the ring, it exploded sometimes, but not always. All the creatures feared to touch them. He did as well, but he overcame his fear. That's why he was the leader.

He signaled his clan to come near. They moved toward him, looking from one to the other. Some hovered and held back. He slowly signed, "Quiet. Now, go there, under." He waved his arm toward the compound below and added, "Quiet."

The creatures moved ahead of their leader, eyes smoldering. Like Oliver, some of the braver ones carried a fire stick.

Chapter Twenty-nine

"We'll wait until dark when they're sleeping—that is, if they ever do," Gabriel whispered.

He and his team lay in the tall grass at the edge of the clearing in front of the caves. The breeze carried a stench that assaulted their senses.

He motioned to one of his men to bring up the cases that contained the dart guns. The man handed one of the rifles to Gabriel and blew in the chamber to insure it was clean. A man next to him measured out what they'd decided would be a proper dose of the tranquilizer to knock down a creature but not kill it and poured it into a syringe, then he held the syringe at eye level and tapped out the bubbles. The rest of his men gathered around to watch the loading of the dart guns.

The creatures varied in size and Gabriel had never darted one before, so the amount was no more than an educated guess. Worse, he didn't know how they'd react to ketamine, and he feared it could have the opposite effect of sedating them. He'd observed that in some chimpanzees and gorillas, and it'd been frightening to watch. The drug could cause unpredictable and aggressive behavior in some animals when first taking effect. He didn't want to think about what that would be like in one of the creatures.

"Besides the darts, I want everyone to be ready with a round in the chamber," Gabriel said quietly to his men. "We want to take some of these freaks of nature alive, but don't hesitate to shoot to kill if you have to." He grabbed an AK-47 from one of his men and charged it for effect. Several flinched as a round slammed home. "I want everyone to come back alive and in one piece, if you take my meaning—one piece." He knew his men had all seen the remains left after encounters with the creatures. Limbless corpses still visited many of them in their sleep, disturbing their dreams.

The scouts returned with encouraging news: the creatures seemed to be asleep without guards. Even so, Gabriel dreaded leading his men into the darkness of the caves. He wasn't sure how many they'd engage, but he knew they were outnumbered. Then there was the question of their size and savageness. Many of the men cast furtive glances at the trail back into the jungle, clearly having second thoughts about going in.

"Okay, now. Let's move in," Gabriel whispered. "Remember that we need to capture as many alive as we can and kill the rest." He handed off the four loaded dart guns to his most dependable men and paired them with an armed backup. "I want this black pit cleaned out of these vermin so we can have peace in this part of the jungle again." He nodded to the teams with darts. "There'll be an extra bonus for each creature we take alive."

The men nodded but said nothing.

Gabriel looked at each of his men, then gave the command to move in.

They dashed across the clearing in front of the mouth of the cave, but, guards or not, Gabriel still felt vulnerable. The moonlight cast long moving shadows on the ground as they neared the darkness of the opening. While the full moon aided their progress, he wasn't sure if it was a good omen.

It took several heartbeats for his eyes to adjust to the blackness upon entering the chamber. He could just make out a smaller opening that led into a lava tunnel that plunged down deep into the bowels of the mountain. With a gesture, Gabriel led them on. The damp, stuffy tunnel had barely enough room for his men to tread two abreast, and their footfalls echoed off the walls, unnerving them. Their progress in the darkness was slow until they made out a faint glow ahead. Gabriel halted them and put his finger up to his lips, but thought better of shushing them for fear of the noise carrying.

After what seemed like an eternity, the tunnel opened into a large volcanic gallery. Gabriel froze. The moon above shone through a hole in the ceiling that gave enough light to see creatures sleeping all around them. He could hear their deep, rhythmic breathing. The hair on the back of Gabriel's neck stood up. The creatures' strong, musky stench choked his lungs, and he felt as if they'd entered the lair of something evil and menacing. He felt an urge to retreat and fly for his life, but it was too late. A piercing cry of alarm came from across the chamber, and several huge forms rushed at them out of the darkness. The men barely had time to react, but an instant later, blinding flashes from automatic weapons illuminated the dark gallery, and deafening blasts shook the walls. The creatures' screeches added to the cacophony.

Gabriel shot his dart gun at a rushing giant, sending it retreating, screaming, as it pulled at the dart hanging from its shoulder. Someone lit a torch, and Gabriel saw men and creatures writhing all around them on a floor slippery with blood. His eyes and nose stung from the pungent smoke of gunpowder. Barely able to breathe, he retched from the acid smell of urine and excrement. Many of his men vomited as they fired their weapons. Even with the light of the torches, it was hard to see through the choking smoke.

He had just enough time to load another dart and shoot an advancing creature before he had to draw his side arm and empty a full magazine of his 1911 service revolver into another coming from behind. It dropped, screaming, to the floor, still grasping a bloody twitching arm—a human arm. He reloaded his pistol and called for another dart. He had to call several times before one of his men made it to his side and helped him reload, while he kept the creatures away with his pistol. Working in pairs, his men darted or shot to kill as they slowly made ground against what many would later say was like fighting demons in hell.

Finally, no creatures remained alive or conscious. The smoke cleared and daylight illuminated the cavern, revealing the horror of what had transpired. Gabriel examined the bodies. There were no wounded, only dead. He and his men stared at their dead comrades. They had only lost five, and he knew it could've been worse. Surprise had been in their favor. But still the stat of the bodies was sickening. They'd bled out from hideous bites or separated limbs. Gabriel felt thankful that none had survived as he wasn't sure what he could have done for them.

Despite fighting for their lives, his men had managed to dart nine creatures—six males and three females. This was the first time anyone had seen one close up, and they stared in horror, tightly grasping their weapons and keeping them pointed at the sleeping giants.

Gabriel thought them grotesque, as if someone had experimented with making a human and failed—huge, at least seven feet tall, muscular, and proportioned more like a human than an ape. Most had little hair, revealing a creamy flesh. The eyes unnerved him the most—deep amber with specks of gold rimmed in red, they had a cruel, menacing cast to them. Close up, their musky stench became overwhelming.

Gabriel counted the dead creatures and realized that not all of them had been in the caves. There were more than half not accounted for, and, worse, they had no idea where they were.

"We need to get out of here as quickly as possible," Gabriel said. "We didn't get them all." He looked up the lava tube and realized that, going two abreast, they'd not be able to get out if the other creatures returned.

The men looked around, some sizing up the tunnel, others looking at each other, but they said nothing. The vast cavern became silent—except for the creatures they'd darted, who lay, breathing rapidly, their eyes twitching.

Gabriel, a master in transporting large primates, sent most of his men out of the caves to gather nine branches that they could use to carry the unconscious creatures. They'd tie the wrists and ankles of the creatures to the tree limbs so two men could shoulder the limb at each end and the creature would swing in the middle. This had worked when capturing large apes like chimpanzees and gorillas.

The trick was to keep them sleeping, if that was what you called it. Some of the creatures were already having emergence reactions which look frighteningly like they were waking up.

Gabriel and his men could only hope they'd brought enough ketamine. He didn't want to think what would happen if one awoke while they were transporting them back to the runway.

Gabriel had only one more chore to do before they set out to meet Vandusen. He split his remaining men into two groups, leaving five to guard the creatures and organize getting them out of the caves when the others came back with the tree limbs, and four to stay with him. "Let's do a quick once-over of these chambers before we move out of here," he said to the four men he'd assigned to himself.

A labyrinth of lava tubes ran out in all directions from the chamber where Gabriel and his men stood. The sun rose above the jungle canopy outside, illuminating many of the tubes through openings in their ceilings, making it appear like an ancient gallery of sculptures. Despite everything they'd experienced, Gabriel was struck by the beauty of the walls of multicolored lava flows that had frozen far back in time. The light streaming through the holes far up in the ceiling cast a soft and eerie glow on these subterranean paths. Veins of quartz speckled with what looked like gold sparkled in the shifting light.

Armed and alert, he led the way into several of the wider tubes but found no other creatures, only dead ends to vacant chambers. Evidence of leaves and soiled human clothes revealed that they'd been recently occupied.

Gabriel was about to turn back to the central cavern when he felt a strong, cool breeze blowing out of a larger tube that pitched upward. In contrast to the stench that permeated the lower caverns, it had a clear, refreshing smell. He followed its freshness until they stood on the shoulder of the volcano above the caves. He squinted at the brightness of the sun. The air was clean, filled with the fragrance of the grasslands below. He looked down on the clearing and the jungle canopy stretching out to the horizon. The sun was burning off the mist that rose from the jungle. Morning was passing.

Gabriel led the way down a worn path. "I should've guessed there was more than one way out of these caves. Did anyone notice what was absent?"

One of his men nodded and said, "Where are the village women they captured?"

"Exactly! And there were no younger ones. No babies or children." Gabriel swept his arm in an arc, pointing at the vastness of the jungle. "They're somewhere out there, though. Most likely, they herded their captives out at the first hint of us." He stood, not moving or speaking, while the wind blew in gusts high up on the pathway. "Poor devils."

His men walked past, not wanting to disturb him from his thoughts. He heard them whispering to each other as they followed the path down through the boulders of the spent volcano.

As if waking from a dream, Gabriel collected himself and hurried to catch up. It didn't seem like a good idea to remain in this place alone, and it was a long way across the jungle to deliver his cargo to Vandusen, and the creatures would certainly slow them down.

Where are the rest of them?

His men regrouped in the clearing and redistributed the gear from the fallen. The men kept looking up the trail. While it led them out of this place, it might also lead them into an ambush. They unfastened the safeties on their weapons.

The men gathered around to listen as Gabriel spoke. "We've a long haul back to deliver these abominations, these freaks." He kicked the one closest to him as it slept in fits. "Let's double time and get our pay. After last night, I think the price has just gone up. If they want these things alive, they're going to have to pay a lot more." His face grew hard. "After we get what's coming to us, we're coming back to finish this and bury our dead." Though smaller by half, his crew hoisted the creatures and moved down the jungle trail with purpose.

Payback's a motherfucker, Gabriel thought.

Chapter Thirty

"Listen!" Vandusen whispered in the kind of hush used for a voice to carry but not too far.

His men stared up into the night sky, hoping to hear the familiar drone of the engines of a C-130 Hercules, their ride home. The roar of those engines would be music to the ears of these mercenaries anxiously waiting for a lift out of the landing zone, the LZ. The moon sat overhead, casting ample light for the men to work. It was so bright they feared being detected from the walled compound just a few kilometers away. The Southern Cross glimmered on the distant horizon just above the canopy of the trees, reminding them how far they were from home. But listen as hard as they could, they only heard the evening sounds of the jungle. A troop of monkeys sent up a chorus of howls, drowning out everything else.

But Vandusen had been in this part of the world long enough to know something or someone had stirred the monkeys to make such a racket.

"Stay alert," Vandusen said louder than he liked, and immediately lowered his voice before continuing, "Something's out there at the edge of the strip."

The men looked out in that direction, and then back to the sky. They had been busy preparing the LZ in the darkness and had everything ready for any large transport plane to set down on the repaired airstrip and lift them out. Everyone was ready to go home.

Where in the hell is that goddamn Portuguese? Vandusen scanned the darkness in all directions.

Bauer appeared out of the darkness. "Gabriel is here. He made it, boss."

So that was what all the racket was in the jungle, Vandusen thought. "Send some men out and bring them in. See if they have any of the creatures alive."

If the Portuguese arrived empty-handed, he wouldn't need him anymore. But he'd have to wait until the end of this operation. The most expedient way to handle him would be to leave him stranded for the Belgians to deal with.

Vandusen looked up from under the stairs of the tower. The distinct sound of a plane finally could be heard coming out of the northern sky. The radio in the tower came to life as the transport made a low pass over them.

So much for remaining under the radar.

"This is Easy Six requesting clearance for landing, over." The radio echoed across the strip and sent a flock of sleeping birds screeching as they flew into the night.

Search lights suddenly blazed out from the walls of the compound, cutting through the darkness where they hid and blinding them. Small weapons fire followed.

"Return fire!" Bauer shouted.

Their M-60 machine gun opened in bursts, setting Vandusen's ears ringing. Well-placed fire soon extinguished the search lights and the battle continued in the dark, except for the streams of tracer rounds arcing toward them, and the blinding blasts from mortar fire that dropped behind them, hitting the airstrip.

"We're under fire, so you have to make your approach dark, over."

"Roger that. It looks like the Fourth of July down there. Our ETA is five minutes, repeat five minutes, on my mark. Easy Six out."

"Okay, men, let's get cracking," Vandusen ordered, then, lowering his voice, he said to Bauer, "We need to load and be in the air double-time. We're sitting ducks out here. No one is to board until we retreat into the plane."

"Those Belgians sure know how to lay down fire," Bauer shouted, trying to be heard over the din.

Vandusen nodded and ducked as a man standing near them dropped. The pilot obviously knew his business. After making a low approach under heavy fire, the transport dropped a wing, making a slow turn, then came out of the darkness and touched down for a landing. The props blew dust, blinding them as it turned and made ready for takeoff as quickly as it had landed.

Vandusen ordered some men to set a perimeter around the plane as the rear loading door opened, its ramp lowering to the humming of the hydraulics. Rounds buzzed all around, some finding the fuselage in loud thuds.

The men knew their business, helping Gabriel and his men load the creatures on the plane first. Two hadn't survived the transport through the jungle and were dumped unceremoniously.

Vandusen beckoned Bauer and whispered, "I repeat. No one is to board until I say, understand?"

Bauer nodded, and raced off to deliver orders.

After Gabriel's men had loaded the creatures, Vandusen's men turned their guns on them, disarmed them, and marched them out of the plane and into increasing fire and confusion. The Belgians moved steadily toward their position on the airstrip with increasing force and frightening accuracy. Several men fell, and time was quickly running out for them to get the transport out in one piece. Mortar blasts fell all around them, exploding too close to the plane.

In a prearranged signal, the perimeter of men around the plane dissolved and filed into the plane. The loading ramp slowly lifted, and the plane began to move. To the surprise of the men remaining outside, Vandusen and Bauer raced up the closing loading ramp and the transport taxied up the air strip. Despite the confusion, it didn't take them long to realize they'd been abandoned, so they divided their fire between the advancing Belgians and the retreating plane.

*****

Oliver and his clan hadn't gone far when the night sky lit up with bursts of fire. He cowed under the ear-piercing blasts that shook the ground under his feet while streaks of fire shot above them from the walls where the humans lived. The streaks were like the flames that sometimes burst from the mountain of fire near their caves. His eyes stung from the smoke that settled in the tops of the trees and sifted down making it hard to breathe. He couldn't see the stars, only a pink glow illuminating the jungle.

Oliver realized there was no reason to warn the humans behind the walls as the fight had already begun, but, even so, the powerful urge to contact them remained. He kept to his purpose and started down the small creek that led to the gate under the wall. Many of his clan crouched in fear and hesitated to follow. Clearly, the noise frightened them, but entering through the walls scared them even more. In the end, he prodded his clan forward by pointing the fire stick at them. He was relieved not to have to pull the trigger. Just pointing it caused enough terror to get them back on their feet. He'd have to remember the power the sticks gave him by just carrying one. Just the same, he walked behind them to make sure that none disappeared into the bush.

A clear idea to help the friendly humans emerged from his murky thoughts. Help them attack the bad humans on the clearing where the loud bird landed. The conflicting instincts that stirred in him, confused him, but he kept to his direction. Helping the friendly humans would get the dangerous humans out of their forest, and that was a good thing.

He felt the wall loom up before he saw it and hesitated down in the shadows of the ravine near the opening under the stone wall. Peering into the darkness, he could just make out a path leading beyond the rusted gate. If he could open the gate, they could make it under the wall and inside. The secret gate was out of sight from above, where the humans were firing the sticks, making piercing noises and raining down sparks that burned them.

He picked up a smoking piece of shiny metal but quickly dropped it as it burned his fingers. The other creatures jumped back from where it landed on the ground and grimaced in fear.

He licked his fingertips, then moved down to the gate, keys in hand.

He fumbled with the metal pieces on the ring, trying each one with care. His fingers, tender from the burns, were clumsier than usual, making it difficult to insert the keys into the jagged hole on the lock. The others gathered around him and watched, tilting their heads in concentration. Some smacked their lips and others pressed in for a closer look. Oliver elbowed one who stood too close and grunted, exposing his teeth. But he quickly thought better of it and instead signed, "Stay." The others backed away. Oliver felt pleased with the power of these signals the little ape had taught him. They gave him more power and, more importantly, more status. He was the leader.

He tried several times before he found the key that fit and racked his brain as he worked on the lock, trying to remember an important sign the little ape had taught him. It was a special sign, a sign to use with the humans inside the walls. The lock clicked open. Oliver paused, unmoving, trying to pull the image of the sign up from the clouds of his mind. The special signal. The little ape had taught it to him, and it was very powerful. He'd only used it a few times, but he'd learned that it could change the flow of fear and rage if its meaning was understood, and if used before the rage took over.

He thought back to when he'd been in the cage and the little ape had come in to visit him and the humans in the other cages. It was long ago, and it was hard to see the images now. He hardly noticed when Danny bumped into him as he stood thinking, trying to remember. He grunted, but didn't turn in his concentration.

Ignoring the noise of the fighting humans, he closed his eyes and followed the images in his mind. He saw the little ape, Mike, signing and remembered the change in his feelings upon learning the special sign. In a flash, he remembered, seeing it in the depths of his mind. He held his fists in front of him, pointing his index fingers, and touched the pads of his two fingers, then rotated them, touching them again, signing, "Friend."

The creatures surrounding him immediately signed it, and placed their hands out to him, palms down. He signed, "Friend," again, and the creatures hooted and signed it back as they looked down, careful not to make eye contact.

Oliver panted in loud grunts and signed, "Good. Follow."

The others hooted and followed, casting furtive glances from side to side.

They passed through the gate and hugged the wall as they made their way along in the darkness. Oliver knew that if the humans discovered them, even the good humans would be afraid and might attack. But he knew the power of the sign. He would use it with the humans, and maybe they would not attack, but he was afraid they might.

He turned to the others and signed, "Stay," then left them in the darkness, huddled together against the wall. Each blast startled them as projectiles hit the wall, coming closer. They pushed up against the wall, feeling vulnerable at being left alone without their leader. Danny glared as he watched Oliver disappear in the darkness. He didn't understand the signs very well, so he growled the others into submission.

Oliver crept up some stone stairs leading to the top of the wall, being careful not to come out of the shadows and stopping often to watch and wait. Just below the crest of the wall, he stopped to gather his courage. He felt conflicting urges; one to fight and the other to run. But something deep inside him stirred an urge to keep going. Finally, he built the courage to go on, and a few steps later, he reached a large, open parapet on the top of the wall. Several humans stood with their backs to him.

It was brighter at the top, and he could feel a strong breeze, but he had trouble breathing in the dense, swirling smoke. He froze, staring through the haze at the humans, but they were so intent on using the fire sticks, they didn't notice him standing so near. He wasn't sure what to do. He only knew how to attack humans or chase them when they ran. This was different for him. He took a step out of the darkness toward them and hesitated.

A rage welled up inside him at the sight of the fire sticks in the men's hands, and his hair bristled, but his mind fought against the instinct to attack. He signed "Friend" to himself and kept signing it, trying to convince himself, hoping the power of the sign would work against his urges. He kept signing, "Friend, friend, friend."

One of the men turned and his eyes widened at the sight of Oliver standing only a few yards away.

***

"Do you see what I see?" the young captain asked.

The group of soldiers turned and froze in fear behind their captain. Some blinked, not believing their eyes. One of the soldiers raised his rifle and took aim at the creature standing so near. Upon seeing him take aim, the creature bristled and grimaced, showing his teeth. All the soldiers followed, their rifles shaking, but they hesitated to use them. The presence of a creature in their midst, inside the compound, surprised and unnerved them. And he wasn't attacking. Just standing, watching them.

For several heartbeats, they and the creature stood, unmoving, staring at each other. And in that pause, the captain realized what the creature had been doing with his hands. He lowered his rifle and ordered his men to hold their fire. Then he stepped forward and signed, "Friend."

He couldn't explain later exactly why he didn't order his men to shoot, only that the sign, "Friend," made by Oliver had registered in him deeply, making him hold back a moment, just long enough for the meaning to register.

A play of emotions crossed the creature's face before he returned the sign, "Friend."

The captain signed back, "Friend." And to his men, he said, "He's telling us he's our friend. I think this might be the one called Oliver."

The soldiers lowered their weapons.

In a beckoning gesture familiar even to the soldiers, Oliver signed, "Follow," and turned down the steps the way he'd come.

Hardly believing his own words, the captain ordered, "Let's follow him, but stay ready." His men hesitated for only a moment, then followed their captain as he trailed after Oliver and into the darkness.

Chapter Thirty-one

"Hello, this is Dr. Turner. As per your request, we're contacting you before leaving town." Ken held his hand over the receiver, smiled at Fred, and said, "Well, Fred, he said to contact him—he didn't say in person." He put the phone back to his ear and continued, "Dr. Savage and I will be leaving town for a few weeks to finish up our technical advising. I hope your investigation is going well. Goodbye." Ken hung up the phone, and they laughed as they headed for the suburban.

Once settled in the car, Ken paused, both hands on the steering wheel, and said, "So, north or south?"

"South," Fred replied. He said nothing more, just sat looking up the drive toward the chimp cabins. Ken waited, not wanting to disturb his thoughts. Finally, Fred continued, "I think it's better to drive. The airport has cameras and lots of people monitoring the coming and goings. Plus, we need to meet up with Bobby and Hunt. They've been in contact with Africa. The Circus Luncheon Club meets tomorrow. We can hook up with them there. After that, we'll meet Chris at the WATC and then—"

"Germany, I'm thinking," Ken interrupted. "We need to check out that circus where Oliver was kept before he landed here. If he was there, others could've passed through or could be coming."

They sat deep in their own thoughts, silent, both wondering what would happen next.

Mary tapped on the window, startling them. "You're not going to get very far if you don't start the engine," she said, standing with her hands on her hips.

"Can you hold the fort again?" Ken asked. He dreaded leaving her again and wondered if she'd be there when he returned.

She smiled, sensing his concern, and looked at Fred. "Is he having one of his red alerts again?"

Fred laughed, amazed at how she could break the tension. He decided she had a gift. "No, actually, he's been very good. He hasn't hyperventilated in days. He just may become normal."

"Excellent, though I doubt our good professor will ever see the right side of normal. Of course I can take care of things—that's what I do." She brushed a strand of her red hair from her forehead.

"I'm worried about you being alone here. What if Vandusen or some of his cronies show up?" Ken asked as he looked down the road.

"Don't worry about me. Plus, I have Consuelo and Mark. If I can be really blunt, I don't want to hurt your feelings, but I think I'm in more danger with you guys hanging around here than when you're gone. So get your asses out of here. What could go wrong?"

Fred looked away as Ken and Mary said their goodbyes. It seemed like that's what they were always doing these days—

saying goodbye. He wondered if they'd ever get their normal lives back. Hopefully, they could wrap things up in Germany and go to Africa, but how? They'd become caught up in events out of their control and would just have to play things out day by day—minute by minute, actually.

Ken turned the key. "Well, let's go." They bumped into motion down the gravel drive and onto Holcomb Lane, headed toward Highway 395 south.

***

The agents watched Mary walk back to the main house, then ducked under the dashboard as the professors turned out of the drive. "Well, that was sure touching," one agent said to his partner. "Call the General. We need to let him know they're on the move."

His partner picked up the phone. "If he orders us to pick them up, we need to do it cleaner. No mistakes this time."

"What the fuck do you mean?" The first agent glared at his partner, slipped on his leather driving gloves, then drove after the professors.

"No mistakes like last time with that little prince, Melon," his partner replied. "The General wasn't happy, and that could be very unhealthy for us."

"Are you saying it was my fault?" The driver looked at his partner more than the road and had to swerve to avoid an irrigation curb.

"Relax and watch the road! I'm just fucking saying we need to be more careful." The second agent now wished he hadn't brought up the subject, but the General wouldn't tolerate another screw-up.

"So now you think I'm a bad driver," the first agent said, slowing the vehicle.

His partner pointed at the car ahead. "Look, they're turning onto 395. Let's just drop this. I'll make the goddamn call. Can we get going before we lose their asses?"

The driver accelerated to make the light onto the highway. "It wasn't my fault the heat pulled up on us."

"Yah, Yah, just drive," his partner said and picked up the transmitter of the AN/PRC-77.

Chapter Thirty-two

Bauer leaned out the side door of the transport as it labored under the weight of its cargo to gain altitude. "It looks like we're clear, boss." He could just make out the tracers dying in the blackness below. The engines emitted a high-pitched whine as they continued to climb. He wondered why the engines were working so hard.

"Not quite," Vandusen said, pointing out a window. "Look."

Flames streaked across one of the windows fed by a spray of fuel leaking from one of the engines. Several holes pockmarked the skin of the left wing. Some of the bullets had hit a fuel tank.

Bauer shouted to an airman who was just finishing securing the rear loading bay, "An engine's on fire!"

Shaking his head, the airman sighed and said, "Again?" Without bothering to look out the windows, he walked toward the cockpit, where the silhouettes of the pilot and copilot could just be made out against the glow of the instruments. He no sooner leaned in between them when they heard the engine being feathered, and blasts of foam covered the windows where they stood. They felt the fuselage vibrate and pitch over, throwing the men over the rumble seats under the windows.

Another airman came out of the cockpit and made his way toward them, using a line of straps that hung from the ceiling for support as they pitched side to side. "It'd be a good idea if your men secured your special cargo and got seated."

Vandusen couldn't believe he hadn't attended to the creatures—the whole purpose of the mission. He swore to no one in particular, "Christ!" Several of the men followed him to where the creatures still lay, securely tied, while others assisted the airmen in lashing weapons and gear to the netting that hung from a bulkhead.

The two airmen seemed to take everything in their stride including the engine fire and the "special cargo" as they called it. As Vandusen's remaining men cleared the floor of debris and gear, he realized that the transport had sustained considerable damage. Air blew through holes where shrapnel had blown completely through then stuck in the ceiling.

Smiling, one of the airmen poked his head out a door opening from a side bulkhead and said, "Good news! The shitter still works."

For the moment, the tension broke and several men laughed. One even replied, "Hell, I don't need one. I shit my pants on takeoff!"

Laughter filled the plane, contrasting with the strain of the evening's events. To their relief, the plane appeared to be a workhorse. In spite of the damage, it leveled and kept flying.

The mood changed when one of the creatures let out a piercing cry.

Vandusen knelt down for a closer look at one of the sleeping creatures and reeled from the rank smell of urine and bile. A soldier beside him squatted back, covering his nose with a bandana. The creature slept in fits, his eyes blinking in rhythm to his shallow breathing. Despite being tied to a large limb by its wrists and ankles, it suddenly tried to sit up, startling the men.

Vandusen realized that the creatures lay bound—hastily tied to thick tree limbs—and huddled together at the back of the plane. "Why in the hell are these things not in cages?" He looked around and realized there were no cages.

"This is the way they were brought to us, sir," the soldier replied.

"I want guards posted with every one of these animals." Vandusen motioned Bauer to step out of earshot and whispered, "Pump them full of ketamine. I don't care if we OD them. Just keep them out."

The ten-hour flight would be little time to arrange everything at the other end for the transportation of the animals to the States. He'd first have to arrange the offloading at Ramstein Air Force Base without drawing too much attention to their operation, then find a place to hold them under wraps off the base until they could get them to a facility in the States. He knew of a place in the countryside that might work. A little rundown circus where, for the right sum, no questions would be asked. He'd have to radio the General as soon as possible and let him know their status. Complicated logistics would be required to get the creatures there without clearing customs and the like.

He surveyed the plane and felt encouraged. Things were getting back in order, and the hideous freaks of nature were still sleeping. He wanted to kill them where they slept. Now that he could get a closer look at them, he realized that they were the product of some very unnatural experiments. He couldn't tell the males from the females. They'd lost two before loading, and he tried to figure how many of each he had. Their proportions were much like a human, not having the long, protruding arms of an ape or at least what he thought an ape would look like. Their heads were small in relation to the rest of their bodies, reminding him of the big, brute character in Popeye, and they had huge muscular arms and legs. It was easy to see how they could pull a limb off a human body. Their flat faces lacked hair, and they had high cheekbones and heavy brows. The lack of hair made it easy to see the scars evidencing a violent life. Vandusen thought them abominable, possessing the worse traits of both apes and human.

Abominable is the perfect word to describe these mistakes of life. It'll be fitting to take them to Pacific Northwest—the land of Sasquatch. They'll fit in perfectly in a place rumored to have giants roaming the forests. The General's a true genius.

Bauer tapped him on the shoulder, startling him out of his thoughts.

"What now?" Vandusen asked.

Bauer hesitated, looking down at one of the creatures as it tossed in its drugged state.

"Come on, spill it," Vandusen said.

"We're out of ketamine," Bauer whispered.

"Damn that Portuguese for loading these things without cages!" Vandusen lowered his voice before continuing, "Don't let the rest know about this, but be ready to shoot any one of these sons-of-bitches if they start to work their way loose from the ropes."

Bauer nodded and realized, for the first time, that his boss was frightened. The prospect of one of these creatures getting loose among them while flying at ten thousand feet with one engine down was enough to sober the most battle-hardened veterans. He surveyed the gear and luggage they'd packed and tied down and whispered, "I wonder if there're any parachutes aboard?"

Chapter Thirty-three

"Yes, sir! I can have a crew on standby all evening." The master sergeant wondered what was so important that a full bird colonel would need to reserve a whole hanger just to receive one single flight.

"I want this whole operation on the down low. Understood?" the colonel said.

Must be some kind of black ops horseshit, or worse, the sergeant thought. His suspicions grew when he learned the flight was coming in from Africa, and wasn't on any of the manifests he'd received from HQ. Something was up, for sure.

"I'll handle it personally, sir," the master sergeant said and sharply saluted.

"Very good, Sarge." The colonel returned the salute and barked, "Carry on!" His footsteps echoed across the empty warehouse as he made his way to the door.

The sergeant picked up the phone as he surveyed his surroundings. He had much to prepare to get a whole hangar ready for whatever was coming their way. And he didn't have much time, just a few hours. He'd have to keep the number of his crew down to the bare minimum, but it'd be difficult to plan, not knowing the nature of the operation.

He'd been in the service long enough to know that when a high-ranking, military intelligence officer gave an order to keep the mission on the down low, you didn't ask questions. You simply followed orders, and the sergeant was good at keeping his mouth shut and minding his own business. Especially in a world of top-secret clearances and the "need to know." These MI types gave him the woolies, and it seemed there were a lot more of them turning up here in Ramstein lately.

He wondered what kind of mission was going on down there that required so many secret flights out of this one part of Africa, the Congo. Hell, he didn't even know where that was. Probably, some armpit the Army had no business even being in. This was at least the third flight he'd heard about. They may have their secrets, but he had his sources. You had to, if you didn't want to get sucked into whatever these guys were up to and end up in the brig. Six months more and he'd be clear of all the shit. He had to play it cool.

Right off, he'd noticed the patch on the colonel's shoulder. Eagle talons grasping two lightning bolts, the A.S.A.—Army Security Agency. So, one thing was for sure, he'd need to make space for some really sophisticated communication equipment. He'd worked with these spooks in 'Nam. They didn't say much but carried a shitload of radios and crap.

A.S.A? Something's definitely up.

The sergeant pushed his men well into the evening, frantically trying to set up for any contingency.

"I need plenty of stingers to plug in their equipment, and make sure you light up this whole area. We need to be ready this evening to support a bunch of long-range communication. Oh, and set up plenty of benches and tables. And we're going to need

213

to partition off that whole corner over there, for … for, let's just say, privacy."

The sergeant had no sooner stepped out for a smoke break with his men when the first unmarked trucks began rolling in full of large crates. What caught his attention the most was his men struggling to offload several large, steel-barred panels.

The makings of holding cells; now this is really off the radar.

As the trucks continued to roll in and the equipment piled up, it became clear that live cargo was headed their way. Recently, the sergeant had been on a couple of operations coming in from Africa that imported chimpanzees for the Army research centers. These operations were becoming more secret as government restrictions made it more difficult to import these animals into the States. But the Army and the Department of Defense still needed them for research. That wasn't a popular topic, and the Army didn't like bad PR, so the powers that be just classified these operations as Top Secret, which put them off limits to any pain-in-the-ass politicians or civilian animal rights groups.

But tonight seemed different. The whole operation was especially secret, even for the Army and its MI types. The place was soon crawling with plainclothes types with CI badges. The presence of Counter Intelligence Agents, or spooks as he called them, always made him uncomfortable. He began to suspect this was more than just a routine, clandestine intake of live animals.

One of his men called his attention to the arrival of the colonel, who stood at the door waiting.

Here we go, thought the sergeant as he walked towards the man.

"Well done, Sarge," the colonel said as he oversaw the assembly of the steel cages. "Check the bolts—I mean every bolt, and shoot the cages down to the floor. They need to be solidly locked down."

"Yes, sir," the sergeant answered as he kept in step. A series of sharp reports rang out. The sergeant jumped, then realized that it was just a soldier shooting rams into the concrete. He looked up apologetically.

The colonel nodded. "Carry on, Private."

They continued to inspect the hanger as the men wrapped up their preparations. It was getting late and darkness wrapped the runway outside.

"Finish setting up and dismiss your men," the colonel ordered. He powered up a large transceiver and motioned a radioman over. "But I need you to remain, sergeant. A flight is inbound, due at 0300 hours." He held the sergeant's eyes. "I want you to personally take care of the manifest, if you take my meaning."

"Do you have a particular list of cargo, sir?"

"Yes, Sergeant—nothing."

"Nothing?"

"You heard me. Nothing is arriving."

Well, now, everything is becoming clear as mud, the sergeant thought.

Once the work had been completed, the sergeant dismissed all his men, but it left him feeling uncomfortable. He might as well be invisible for all the attention he was being paid. Even though they were all in the same army, he was a stranger in this crowd of spooks, and he could tell they were only going to tolerate him around for as long as they needed him. He'd have to be very careful; he was quickly getting in way over his head.

As regular army, he liked everything upfront and in the open. It seemed that every time he got wound up with these people and their world of secrets, something bad happened.

The colonel's men took charge. They'd ignore him until they needed him to fill out the manifest, which was fine by him. He figured his job was to stay out of the way, and when the time came, do whatever he was told. He decided the best place to wait was over by the radio, where he'd be able to hear what the hell was actually coming their way, his way. So he stood by and watched the specs finish installing everything. Everyone standing by the radio kept looking at their watches and then back at each other. They seemed reluctant to talk as long as he was around. He was probably the only one who didn't know what was going on.

The radio remained silent except for background static until the radioman, after checking his watch one final time, glanced at the colonel, picked up the microphone and said, "Easy One. This is Base, over."

The colonel took a chair next to the operator.

All activity stopped as everyone clustered around the table behind the colonel and the operator. No one even looked at the sergeant.

"Easy One, Easy One, this is Base. Do you copy? Over."

A low hum resonated out of the speakers, but nothing more than a crackle broke the silence.

"Are you sure you're on the right frequency?" the colonel asked.

The radioman gingerly adjusted several large, illuminated dials, and a series of high-pitched pops and whistles came out of the speakers, causing many to cover their ears. He hunched over his equipment, cast in an eerie glow, holding one side of his earphones tightly against his ear while the other dangled loose. Ignoring the colonel, he continued, "Easy One, Easy One, this is Base, over."

The minutes ticked away and still nothing but static filled the hanger. Soldiers started walking away in twos and threes, whispering as they headed for the snack table.

The colonel left for a smoke break and paced outside, looking out into the darkness of the adjoining runway. All was calm and quiet outside, contrasting to the bustle inside the hanger. It began to drizzle, making the faint breeze chilly. Just as he was about to light another cigarette, the first transmissions startled everyone into action.

"Base. This is Easy One, over."

The runway suddenly lit up and everyone stirred into action.

"Goddamnit!" yelled the radioman while trying to soak up hot coffee from his crotch and grab the microphone at the same time. "Easy One, come back, over."

"Base, this is Easy One. We're inbound on 240 at 4000 feet, over."

"Easy One, you're cleared for landing on 224, over."

"Roger that, Base, cleared on 224. Be advised, we're on three engines and losing altitude. We're coming in heavy, over."

"Easy One, repeat."

"I repeat, we're coming in heavy. We have a situation on board. Little busy right now."

"Copy that, Easy One. We have your six. Good luck. Base standing by, over."

Everyone jumped into action. The radioman grabbed the phone, clicked it several times, and said, "Tower, prepare for a crash landing of a priority flight coming in on 224."

The flashing red lights of firetrucks pierced the darkness as they converged on the runway from every direction. The deafening screech of a siren wailed across the airfield in undulating tones.

Shaking his head, the colonel said, "So much for secrecy." He motioned to several of his men carrying M16s to gather around. "They're not to escape from that plane." He paused. "Understand?"

Cocking their weapons, the men nodded, then ran to the field.

The colonel, noticing the sergeant as though for the first time, said, "We won't be needing you anymore tonight, Sarge."

"And the manifest, sir?"

"As I said. Nothing is coming in tonight."

"Yes, sir!" the sergeant saluted and marched away as quickly as his legs would work. At least for tonight, he'd dodged a real clusterfuck, a fubar.

He practically ran to his jeep, wanting to put some distance between him and the place before he was dragged back into this shit show. The ominous roar of the Hercules' engines came overhead, the whistle of the struggling engines, deafening, drowning everything else out as it limped its way in.

He looked up, wanting to get a glimpse of what had been so damn secret as to highjack most of his evening. But he saw nothing. It was hidden in the night, landing without lights.

Chapter Thirty-four

The lieutenant pointed toward the edge of the jungle. "If it hadn't been for them, we'd all be dead."

Smoke still hovered in the valley from the firefight of the previous night. A medic attended to the bodies strewn across the field. After the transport had lifted off and turned to the north, Vandusen's remaining men, realizing that they'd been abandoned and then that creatures fought alongside the Belgians, had soon dropped their weapons and raised their hands.

François froze when he saw what the lieutenant indicated. Several of the creatures stood in the shade at the edge of the tree line across the field from them. He opened his mouth to speak but could only point, his hand shaking. He unbuttoned his holster and took a step backwards.

The lieutenant took his arm and said, "As crazy as it may sound, there's nothing to fear. They helped us last night."

Lester, Mike and Girlie walked up. Lester stopped in his tracks, his eyes wide. Mike, hooting, raced across the field toward the creatures. Girlie ambled, lagging behind, stiff from the trek back from the caves. A small group of soldiers stood looking at each other, confused, as the creatures and chimps greeted and began signing. It seemed that the largest of the creatures knew Mike. They ignored the men and some began to gather their dead and pick up rifles.

"I don't understand," François said. He'd been defending the compound, not on the airfield.

The lieutenant nodded gravely. "It was the damnedest thing. They appeared out of nowhere last night and helped us repulse the attack. That dirt bag, Vandusen, got away with some of his men, but, with those creatures' help, we took care of the rest."

"How?" François asked.

"They led us out the back gate, under the wall, and we attacked them from the rear. Apparently, there was a disagreement between some of Vandusen's men. They were so busy fighting each other they never saw us coming."

"Fighting each other?" François asked.

"Yes, it looks like Vandusen took off and left most of his men in the field, our field. The ones left behind didn't like that very much." The lieutenant smiled.

François shook his head. "So Vandusen got away."

"He abandoned most of his men and flew out with some of the creatures—they must've captured them at the caves. It looked like they had them sedated."

"They flew out of here?" François asked, looking above the treetops.

"Yes, in a big ass cargo plane—a Hercules, I think." The lieutenant pointed in the direction of the airstrip. "Vandusen surprised us and took control of the field, holding it just long enough to escape."

François stared at him in disbelief. "They must have had some serious backing. Think of the logistics it would take to get a large transport plane down here."

François and the lieutenant nodded and looked up in the sky. Their eyes followed the imaginary path of an aircraft taking off. "Where's Vandusen taking them, and why?" François asked.

The lieutenant pointed at the chimps and creatures standing across the field, docile now. "Takes some getting used to, doesn't it?"

"It sure as hell does," François replied.

"We had to intervene, or this would've turned into a killing field. We have one of the guys who was working for them. I think you know him, a Portuguese named Gabriel. He's been a guide and tracker along the river for years. He was lucky we got to him before the creatures." The lieutenant grimaced. "We couldn't help the rest lying out there." He looked at the bodies on the field. "Their handiwork is all over, but you've seen it before."

"This all happened last night?" François asked.

"I think their battle plan changed when Vandusen ran out on them. At first, when they attacked, they seemed only interested in holding the airstrip long enough to fly out. But when they were abandoned, their objective changed to taking our compound."

The lieutenant looked at the creatures. They stared back at him. "They showed up just in time and helped us tip the scales. We were outnumbered and outgunned; barely holding on. I think the creatures were the last thing they expected. As it was for us."

"So what now?" François whispered.

"Let's try to thank them," Lester said as he began walking across the field toward the creatures. The lieutenant followed.

"Christ!" François exclaimed, throwing up his hands.

***

A current of emotions welled up inside Oliver when the humans walked toward him. He gripped the fire stick and gnashed his teeth, but then he recognized Lester. Lester, his old friend, didn't hesitate. Something in the slow, deliberate approach of Lester, even with the other human, calmed him. His thoughts cleared and relaxed; he didn't feel threatened.

The sign he used the night before came back to him, and he laid the fire stick down and signed, "Friend."

Lester stopped and smiled before signing back, "Friend." The other humans waited behind him.

Oliver found something comforting in the signing. It felt good to have human friends.

They stood, hybrid and humans, looking at each other at the edge of the jungle. Mike tapped Oliver on the leg, then ran over to Lester and jumped into his arms. Oliver looked back at the rest of his clan, who watched with mixed emotions, then he followed Mike. He was the leader; it was up to him to lead the way, to show they would benefit from having human friends.

***

Lester stood still as Oliver neared, his long strides swooshing in the tall grass. Oliver stopped an arm's length away and tilted his head from side to side, his strong, musky scent filling the air around him. Lester had to lean back to look into his deep-set

223

eyes—piercing and intelligent, but very different from an ape, with a striking dark-chestnut color speckled with blood red. The red speckles gave the impression of cruelty, but Oliver's eyes seemed calm at the moment, almost sorrowful.

The other creatures held back in the shadows not far away. Lester, standing in the bright sun, could barely make out their forms, but he counted ten. His experience working with wild animals would have to carry him now. Lester took a step forward.

Oliver stiffened, and a rustling came from the edge of the jungle where the others waited.

Lester reached out his hand, palm down.

Oliver leaned back but hesitated.

They stood without moving, staring at one another, as though they were the only beings left on earth. Oliver broke the spell by holding out his hand and touching Lester's, back to back—a classic gesture of friendship among most of the apes Lester had ever worked with. He marveled that this hybrid creature would use this universal symbol of an open hand positioned not to grab.

Mike stepped up, gripped both their hands with his and held them for a moment. He panted hoarsely, let go, and signed, "Friend."

Oliver looked at them, tilting his head, then pulled back his hand and signed, "Friend."

The other creatures hooted so loudly that a flock of birds flew out of the treetops, blocking the sunlight. The whole jungle came alive with a chorus of hoots, howls, and growls. The humans froze in wonder, knowing they'd just observed something rare and special in the story of living things.

Oliver turned back to rejoin his troop, but before he'd taken a step, a rustle came from the trees and a dark form stepped out into the open. Danny stood in the sunlight across from Lester. He paused, squinting in the brightness of the open field. The creatures' primeval cries drowned out all other sounds.

Mike ran through the tall grass and jumped into Danny's arms. After a greeting, Mike climbed down, and they walked up to Lester. The rest of the creatures faded into the shadows, disappearing like ghosts.

Even larger than Oliver, Danny towered over Lester, his huge frame making Lester appear frail and vulnerable. One of the soldiers raised his rifle to take aim, but François motioned him to lower it and signaled all his men to stand down.

"Well, old friend, we meet again," Lester said quietly. "Come, it's time to go home." He signed, "Home."

Danny looked from Oliver to Mike and signed, "Home."

Lester smiled, took Mike's hand and they led the way across the field toward the compound.

Oliver and Danny followed, headed home.

***

Lester had to move back into a corner to get out of the way of all the activity as the soldiers packed equipment into crates and destroyed documents. "Thank God for radios," he said.

The radioman laid his earphones on the table and, turning to Lester, asked, "So are we done here?" He held up his hand, signaling the soldier who began disconnecting the tangle of wires behind his equipment to wait.

225

"Yes, the *Si Como No* will be waiting for us in the cove," Lester replied.

The radioman nodded to the man at the typewriter. "Okay, let's sign off and start packing up all this shit." He beckoned Lester to come out of his corner. "I don't know where we're headed next, but wherever it is, we'll need this equipment. Let the captain know we'll be wrapped up and ready to move out by dark."

The compound became a flurry of activity. The few remaining scientists carefully packed their notes and instruments, and the soldiers boxed weapons and rations. None knew where they were going, but orders were orders. Some of these men had spent most of their lives isolated in this part of the world—the only place they'd ever known as home. But it struck Lester how they were still packing up and getting ready to leave.

In his short time in their company, Lester had learned that these soldiers were a special breed. While most were Belgian by nationality, they were French Foreign Legion above all else. Their military customs and the secrecy surrounding them fascinated him.

In a moment of insight, he realized what a perfect match the Foreign Legion was for the protection of this secret place. He wondered how the unlikely marriage had occurred between the Soviet experiments and the French Foreign Legion. François had only hinted.

But once when asking about a banner in François's quarters, Lester had learned that he and many of his soldiers had escaped to the Congo after the failed coup, or *putsch* as they called it, in Algeria in 1961. Factions of the Legion took part in this *putsch*, and later, when it failed, joined an underground insurgency called the Organization de l'Armee Secrete or O.A.S. In English it was called Secret Army Organization, and in time it also failed.

Being loyal to their generals instead of France, they had few options or safe places to escape to, and so found themselves in one of the most isolated and dangerous places in the world. The timing had been perfect, as was the location. They'd arrived just after the old Belgian Congo had been overthrown and while the new government and reformed army were in disarray. They'd been able to disappear in this distant place far up the Congo River and assimilate as members of the research compound. It had worked.

A perfect home for a legionnaire, Lester thought.

Sadly, now it was time to move—to close this chapter in the history surrounding the creatures. Not for the first time, it bothered Lester that he'd been a part of the events leading to their downfall. Their search for the creatures had led Vandusen right to this place that had previously remained secret for over forty years.

Girlie tugged on his arm and signed, "Go, now."

Lester followed the technicians as they carried out the last of the boxes. All their work had paid off. They'd been able to reach Bobby and Hunt and arrange a way out. And, better, a way out with everyone including Oliver and Danny. He wasn't sure what would happen to the soldiers and scientists, but they'd figure that out. He'd make sure they didn't abandon François and his men.

"So here you are," François said, smiling, when Lester joined him in the radio shack. "And so our next adventure begins. We need to get a move on. I don't want to reach that beach and find the *Si Como No* gone and the creatures at our backs."

"Didn't they just help us?" Lester asked.

François nodded, but said, "I'm thinking there are plenty of stragglers both animal and human wandering around this jungle that we don't want to meet. Gabriel took advantage of our kindness and managed to slip away, and we're going set all the captives free. They'll have more than us to worry about. There are rumors of a company of soldiers of the D.R.C. coming upriver headed our way. Knowledge of the creatures' work is spreading, my friend. We need to quit this place."

"The D.R.C?" Lester asked.

"The Democratic Republic of the Congo—the government which took over about the time we arrived here in the sixties. They don't have much of a standing army, but it would be better to not make contact if we can avoid it." François opened a window. A warm breeze scattered some loose papers off the table, which François hastily tried to gather. Seeing the difficulty he was having trying to gather and hold them with one arm, Lester came to his aid.

"How long before we leave?" Lester asked.

François eyes welled up. "Tonight," he said, trying to keep his voice level.

"Tonight! How will we get rid of all the evidence?" Lester asked.

"We'll burn it down—our time here is over," François said, then left the room.

Chapter Thirty-five

GuGu's mind spun as Omar piloted the *Si Como No* through the jagged rocks protecting the mouth of the bay. His friend, this quiet Arab, had prowled this coastline for most of his life, so he felt safe with him, though they'd never talked about what had brought him to the Congo, or what trade he'd practiced before they'd met. He saw Dr. Raven on the foredeck readying the dinghies for landing and remembered their last visit to this distant part of the world. The events of that last day still haunted his dreams: their frantic retreat out of the jungle with the creatures pursuing them down the beach to the very edge of the breaking waves; the screams of the dying creatures as they shot them, and the sand stained with blood. The images in his mind were so frightening that they overshadowed even those from his French Foreign Legion days.

He could just make out the rusting wreck of the *Orion* on the beach, covered by verdant tentacles of jungle vines. It lay in the shadows, harboring dark secrets deep in its bowels. It seemed to GuGu that they'd awakened a sleeping demon that would've been better left dormant as it had for the last sixty years.

GuGu frowned and stepped out of the wheelhouse, squinting in the bright tropical sun. The creases in his weathered face wrinkled with concern as he leaned on the rail, deep in thought. He watched the wake ripple out from the bow, colliding with the line of swells that rolled toward the distant white sands of the beach, and wondered what he was doing here so far from his home in Belgium. If he had one fault, at least one fault for a mercenary, it was loyalty and friendship. That was what had brought him back to this hidden bay without a name. He'd made few friends during his life as a soldier for hire, but Chris Raven was one. They'd met long ago when the Congo was different. It had been less crowded then and full of promise. They'd become fast friends, bonded by adventures they shared with no one else. Just the same, it had taken all his will to come back to this place. A place he hoped to never see again. A place he hoped to forget.

Chris had radioed him to meet at this spot. GuGu had asked no questions but guessed they'd be picking up the last remnants of the complex the Belgians had kept secret for so many years. So far they'd seen no one. The steep beach leading up to the edge of the jungle was vacant. He could just hear the sounds of the birds and monkeys over the distant roar of the beach break—the usual racket as evening approached. The trail into the jungle looked like a gaping hole into the darkness of the dense vegetation lining the beach. For humans it was the only way out of the jungle and onto the beach, so he kept an eye on it.

He wondered if Vandusen and his men were still on the move and if the creatures were still on the loose. He'd heard rumors of atrocities happening in the distant villages upriver and wondered if he and his doings had any part to unleashing this terror on this lonely part of the world. He wondered about many things when it came to this adventure.

"This is as far as we can come in," Omar said as he spun the wheel, bringing the ship around to point into the current. "We'll lay to until we get the flood tide."

GuGu nodded. "We can put the dingy in then and do some scouting." The anchor chain rattled. He flinched and looked around. "Keep an axe on deck. We may have to slip anchor real fast."

Omar nodded and motioned to one of his men to go below. The *Si Como No* swung anchor in the current since there was no wind. It was so still that it was hard to breathe and an effort to move in the oppressive heat. All the air seemed sucked out of the bay, the stillness surrounding them only interrupted by the distant roar of the beach break.

GuGu sensed a growing watchfulness from the crew. They'd wait until evening before venturing through the surf to set foot back on that forsaken beach. Until then, they'd watch and wait as patiently as they could.

GuGu called to the wheelhouse, "Let's set a watch rotation. We need to get some rest. It could be a busy night."

***

GuGu woke when the *Si Como No* swung its anchor to the changing tide. The breeze freshened with the coming of evening but didn't stay the heat. Despite his nap, he awoke tired. He'd slept in fits, disturbed by recurring dreams, nightmares of the creatures attacking.

His tunic stuck to his body with sweat. Did his awful dreams or the sweltering humidity cause it? He didn't know. He thought of changing to something clean and dry but realized it would be damp again in minutes. He licked his forearm and

231

found it salty. He needed to make sure the crew drank plenty of water and not their usual preference if they were to stay healthy and on their game.

An ominous atmosphere permeated the ship. The crew had become sober as they worked their way down the coast toward where they now lay anchor and engaged in little chatter as they busied themselves rigging the dinghy for landing on the beach. GuGu dreaded going back there, but they needed to scout the beach and be ready to help Chris.

Before long, GuGu climbed into the dinghy and they set off, him marveling at Omar's seamanship as he steered toward the beach—a tricky business. The small Johnson Seahorse outboard motor could barely be heard over the roar of the breaking combers. The captain picked the last of a set of waves and kept the bow on its back. The last rays of the setting sun shone, glimmering prisms off the spray that engulfed them, and the backlit silhouette of a large shark darted under them in the depths of the green, clear swell.

If they slowed too much, the huge wave behind them would run up on them, broaching and swamping the dingy. But at the same time, they had to be careful not to overrun the wave they followed or they'd find themselves cascading over it as it broke on the reef. It was amazing how calm the seamen were, having trust in the ability of their captain.

Without a word, as though on cue, the crew jumped out of the dinghy as the wave broke under them in a cauldron of frothing foam and set the dinghy high and dry on the beach— but only until the next set of waves broke. They raced to pull the boat up the steep beach before the sea dragged it back. GuGu jumped out to help.

They began unloading gear, and when the next set of waves rushed up the slope, they had to hold the dinghy steady in ankle-deep, surging water. When they finally emptied it, they carried it up the beach, setting it well above what they figured was the high tide line. GuGu wondered how they'd navigate back through the line of huge breakers. They seemed to be getting larger with the receding tide. It wouldn't be an easy task, especially if they had to do it in a hurry and couldn't wait for enough water to flood the bay.

GuGu looked up at the twinkling stars that pierced the dark sky. Stars so bright and clear you could see their different colors. They'd be entering the canopy of the jungle, a place always cloaked in twilight, where day and night were often measured by the illuminated dial of a wristwatch.

Without a word everyone checked their weapons, making ready for the next step in the mission. They left two armed crew members to guard the dingy, their ride home, and headed towards the hole in the dense jungle foliage, the start of the trail. GuGu thought how forlorn the guards looked standing by the dingy on that lonely beach. Obviously they didn't relish being separated from their comrades.

GuGu followed the others up the trail, feeling as if the jungle were a giant beast swallowing him alive. He thought—and not for the last time—that if he ever left this place, he wouldn't miss the jungle.

Chapter Thirty-six

They'd been loading all day and Lester was exhausted. It seemed that everything in the jungle had conspired against them on their journey to the bay where the *Si Como No* had anchored. The long, dark, uneven trail, which wound through the dense vegetation, was so narrow that it forced them to carry or drag everything single file, and when they reached the soft sand of the beach where GuGu and his men waited, carrying the heavy crates and boxes was torture. They sometimes sank to their calves in the soft sand while trying to traverse to the waiting dinghies. The shore break they had to cross to reach the ship had pitched up and broken in steep lines of combers. When they finally reached the ship, the sun beat down, torturing them as they hoisted their gear to the decks.

They'd been unmolested in their journey so far, but François kept sentries posted at the edge of the jungle. Many remembered their hasty retreat on that very beach when they'd been pursued by the creatures. Now, they weren't sure who or what might show. All was in a flux in this lonely part of the world. The world as François and his men knew it was changing. Everything had seemed so certain a few days ago as all their efforts had been put into helping their friends reach and board the *Si Como No*. But now that he stood on the deck of the ship,

François felt uncertain. If they went ahead with their plan, they'd be heading to an uncertain and hazy future. He could see his men were having doubts as well.

"We need to come up with a way of keeping the chimps and creatures safely housed," Dr. Chris Raven said as he looked down from the decks to the dinghies offloading. He'd used the wrapping of the movie to make a final trip to Africa to help his friends make their retreat. They'd use the *Si Como No* to take them back to the movie location, where they could fly out with Chris's film crew, posing as trainers and animal actors.

It would still be touchy to enter at any port of entry back into the States. But Chris was a genius at passing his crew and animals through borders and airports. Then, there was GuGu, the fixer. He had contacts all over Africa. But getting out of the Congo would be the easy part. They'd be reentering through LAX, the very place from which they'd departed almost a year before. According to Chris, as long as they kept their numbers right and held their nerve, they'd be fine. He was well known by custom officials all over the world as it seemed he was always working on a film somewhere. They'd just have to trust in his expertise.

The chimps balked at being caged. Their time free in the jungle had made them reluctant to be locked up again. The situation became tense, right in the middle of all the loading activity on deck.

"I can tell you right now, they're not going back in cages. I don't care what the men think," Lester said as he gripped Girlie's hand.

Mike whimpered at the sight of the cages sitting behind them on the foredeck, and Oliver and Danny bristled. Lester looked frail and Chris exasperated as he tried to broker a solution.

"What if we set up some den boxes that are unlocked and cluster some of the crates around them?" Chris suggested. "We could lock down a little compound below decks for them but leave hatches above them open."

Lester nodded. "That just might work." He set some men to swing crates down into the hold below the foredecks. The chimps, along with Oliver and Danny, watched with interest. They appeared to understand what was happening.

The *Si Como No* had to reset anchor several times as the tide receded. The swell started breaking on the reefs, putting the *Si Como No* at risk as she lay in the narrowing channel. But the crew stayed at their work, and, in time, GuGu and Omar stood on the deck gazing at the distant shore as the sun set, casting long shadows on the sea.

"We're ready. Let's weigh anchor and leave this place," GuGu said. Followed by Chris and Lester, he and Omar headed toward the wheelhouse.

"Not just yet, my friends," François said.

The group stopped, their attention caught by something in François' tone.

"What is it, François? Are we forgetting something?" Chris asked.

"Yes, my duty," François replied. His whole manner changed. He stood erect and spoke with purpose.

"Your duty? I think we're done here," Lester said.

"You are, but we're not." François looked back toward the jungle. "We have some creatures to look after." He motioned his men to leave the ship. They seemed almost relieved at the change of events as they ambled down the webbing to the dinghies below. François smiled at Omar and said, "If we could trouble your crew for a return trip back to the beach, we'd be most grateful."

Omar nodded without saying a word. The legionnaires fell silent as they waited for their turn in the dinghies back to the beach. Even the most seasoned wiped tears from their leathered cheeks as they said their goodbyes to Lester and the remains of the research team.

When the last of his men were off the deck, François turned and simply said, "Many thanks."

"But the compound is destroyed—where will you go?" Chris asked.

"To our destiny, my good friend." He paused, looking at his men, and added, "We've some captured women and girls to rescue." François stepped onto the dinghy and disappeared into the gathering darkness as the sun set once more in the Congo.

When the dinghy returned, empty of legionnaires, Lester nudged Omar and said, "If we're going, let's get going."

After weighing anchor for what he hoped would be the last time on this lonely beach, Omar set a course north.

Chapter Thirty-seven

Vandusen couldn't help staring. He'd seen midgets before, but never so many, so close, and all in one place. The grounds of this little amusement park were full of them. It seemed like everywhere he turned they popped up and scurried off. What made things even more bizarre was that some wore costumes. The whole situation felt surreal, especially after what they'd been through the night before. He felt tired and not sure of any of his decisions.

"Are you sure we're in the right place?" Vandusen asked as a group of midgets raced by dressed in green elf costumes, laughing and taking little notice of them. They wore buckskin moccasins with curled-up toes. Little brass bells on their toes jingled with each step. Vandusen watched them disappear through a round, wooden gate and heard them laughing from the dense thicket of pines and cedars on the other side.

Seeing one midget was strange enough, but Vandusen found a whole group of them really bizarre, almost revolting. He hated midgets. In a group, the similarities they had with regular people, big people, made their freakishness stand out all the more. It gave him the creeps.

He looked closer as a larger group passed. Seeing them up close reminded him of the different kinds: midgets and dwarves.

The midgets were well proportioned, looking like miniature big people, but the dwarves were hideous, grotesque. They had normal-sized heads and hands set on short, thick bodies and looked like the reflection from a distorted mirror you'd find in a funhouse in a carnival. And that's where they appeared to be— some kind of circus or carnival.

Young and old, male and female, and, even more disturbing, attractive and ugly midgets passed them by. It disturbed him to even think that some of them could be attractive. And some were taller than most, while others were shorter. He felt as though he'd awakened from a crazy dream where he was Gulliver in a Lilliputian-like fantasy world.

"Look at that young girl over there," Bauer said, waving at a group that walked past. "She's normal except for her size. She's no bigger than a little kid. But no kid has tits like that. She actually looks fuckable—I'd love to spin her like a top." The group smiled and waved back. "I've always wanted to fuck a midget."

"Keep your goddamn voice down," Vandusen ordered as he looked around. "They can hear you."

"Too late! Look, she's smiling at us." Bauer laughed and waved again. "What a fucking freak show," he whispered.

Vandusen figured this place was still some kind of amusement park, and all these midgets were part of some outlandish theme. "I'll ask you again. Are you sure we're in the right place?" he asked. "Is this the place the General told us about?"

"Yes, boss; this is the place," Bauer replied. "He said it's out of the way and hard to find. The Belgian who sold us the dart guns also knows about it. I guess this is a place many of the animal smugglers use when they come out of Africa. According to him, we can hide our cargo with no questions asked—and no one, at least no one we're worried about, is going to come around here." Lowering his voice in a conspiratorial tone, he added, "And if these freaks don't cooperate, we'll take the whole place over. What are they going to do about it? Squeak?" He laughed, thinking of the prospect.

Vandusen agreed he had a point. Besides a few groups of school kids and their chaperones, there was nobody around but these little people. He and his men could get everyone in line in no time. At least he hoped they could.

It was late in the afternoon, and he was tired. Once off the autobahn, it had taken several hours winding down country lanes just to get there, and in the fading light, the atmosphere of the park gave him an eerie feeling. He realized, though, that as tired as he was, they needed to get moving and get the creatures settled and hidden before dark. He didn't want them to die after all they'd been through to get them out of the Congo. The General would be waiting for them to radio, and his cooperation would be needed for the next leg of their journey. They'd have to transport themselves and the creatures to a new, secret complex in the Pacific Northwest without raising any suspicion.

They'd left Ramstein Air Base in a hurry—a big hurry. Their cover had been blown with the crash landing. His men had done their best to keep the rescue crews back from the plane until they got the creatures secured and hidden in the cages in the hanger. Plenty had seen enough, though, and would start talking.

He needed to make sure they disappeared for a while, and let everything die down before their next move. And he needed time to get everything ready to transport the creatures out of Germany. This looked like a good place to buy a little time, but for how long? While these midgets were little, there were a lot of them, and they looked crafty.

"Let's take a look around and find out who's in charge. How much money do you have on you?" Vandusen said as they followed a group of elves through a large, round gate. He jerked his hand back from the latch after catching a splinter off its weathered wood. It seemed everything in the park was falling apart. Obviously the decaying little park had seen better days. It looked like just the kind of place that would welcome an infusion of capital in exchange for a little privacy. If money didn't work, they had other means. Vandusen liked the thought of turning Bauer loose on these munchkins. It would be worth it just for a few laughs.

Steinwasen Park was a dying amusement park hidden in the shadows of the Black Forest of Germany, a perfect location for Vandusen's needs, tucked away about 292 klicks or kilometers from Ramstein Air Base.

In its glory days, it had been the home of all kinds of circus animals starring in feature acts. It had originally been decorated to look like a fairyland populated with elves, hence all the midgets and dwarves. But it was in such disrepair, it was hard to get into the spirit of fairyland anymore, especially with the broken gates, fallen-down fences, and peeling paint. You could hardly read the weathered signs anymore. The only thing keeping this little failure of a park from bankruptcy was the rent and other benefits received from its renters. The place was in much need of money, and money was an easy commodity for Vandusen to find.

The park had a dark history, known to circus people and animal traders as a place where you could layover with no questions asked. For almost two centuries, this decaying camp had been a stopover for Romas and other misfits passing through with circuses and carnivals on their way to bigger villages with more money to spend.

Over the years, a permanent staff of sorts had formed from the performers and runaways of bankrupted and broken-down acts. The park had become a hideout for pickpockets and petty thieves, and sometimes murderers. But, just the same, it might work as a place for Vandusen to hide out for a little R&R.

Behind the leaning cedar fence in front of them sat an encampment of fading banners and circus wagons housing a small settlement of circus has-beens turned thieves. Here was where the permanent staff lived.

"Who's in charge?" Bauer asked a group of midgets who were dividing up the proceeds of a purse.

They looked at each other but no one answered until a petite, fair-haired female midget broke the silence in a high-pitched voice that sounded like a bird. "Depends on what you're looking for, pinky—my wagon is back in the woods a ways. Believe me, I can be in charge if that's your preference." She slapped her hand on the round of her ass.

Bauer and Vandusen stared, both surprised at her perfect proportions. She lacked the large, coarse hands and head often attributed to little people. Her movements were graceful, body shapely, and her green shirt fell open enough to expose the round of her impressively sized breasts.

Vandusen smiled to himself. This was the midget Bauer had previously referred to with carnal desires. He took a closer look. "What's your name?"

"Susana. See something you like?" She spun gracefully and bowed.

"For now, we'd like you to show us to who's in charge of this place," Vandusen said, surprised that this midget had aroused him with her provocative manner. He almost felt embarrassed when he thought of the prospect of bedding her.

She smiled as though reading his thoughts, winked, and said, "Ah, business before pleasure. First things first, is it?" She wiggled her finger. "This way, pinky."

They followed her down a worn, slate pathway that wound through the trees toward an antique, wooden gypsy wagon. She glided gracefully, seeming to float in front of them like a wraith. When they reached the steps leading to the door, they heard soft violin music and subdued laughter drifting from inside.

She knocked on the door but paused before turning to leave and said, "My place is just over there." She pointed into a thick part of the woods where a faint glow of lantern light streamed out between the trees. "You're both welcome if you think you can hold up." She winked and disappeared into the shadows.

Vandusen and Bauer looked at each other, speechless. Before either could break the silence, the door popped opened and a coarse dwarf woman in her sixties stood blocking the light. The contrast between her and Susana amazed them.

"So here you are! I heard you were in camp," the dwarf said in a rough voice. "I was about to send someone to find you.

Come inside and let's talk some business." She eyed them slyly and led them inside, walking with a clumsy gait, a kind of waddle on stiff, bowed legs—a sight Vandusen found amusing.

"We'd like to layover here for a little while," he said. "We have some special cargo we want to keep safe and secret."

"I've heard about this special cargo of yours," the dwarf said, frowning. Upon seeing their surprise, she continued, "News, you will learn, travels fast around here. We're used to keeping things safe and secret, so for the right price there'll be nothing to worry about."

"Excellent!" Vandusen said and motioned Bauer to pull out a roll of bills.

"We had some cargo like yours here several years ago." The dwarf paused before continuing, "I believe it came in from the same part of the world in the same way, if you take my meaning." She watched them closely.

Vandusen's eyes narrowed. "What do you mean?" he asked as he watched the dwarf count and fold a wad of bills in her stubby hands.

"An animal dealer came through here with two large, apelike creatures he'd captured in the Congo. I think probably from the same place you've just come. He stayed here until he could arrange for a sale and transport them to the States."

"Exactly how long ago?"

"Well, now, let's get our business settled first—a little more money is like oil to the rusty gears of this old brain." The dwarf tapped her temple with a stub of a finger.

Vandusen nodded to Bauer, who began counting out gold *Krugerrand* coins. "Maybe a little gold will loosen those gears of yours."

"Wow. Seems like these little South African nuggets find their way from all parts of Africa," the old dwarf said as she scooped a pile across the table, letting them cascade off a worn Formica table into her velvet purse. Snapping the brass clip shut, she continued, "Now my memory seems to be improving."

An older male dwarf opened a door from the back of the wagon and limped in, balancing a tray holding a bottle and three greasy glasses.

Their host motioned him out of the room and filled a round. "A little Grappa and a toast to seal our partnership."

Vandusen and Bauer hesitated before picking up the dirty, overfilled glasses. The fiery liquor spilled, burning the back of their hands as they raised them.

"To well-kept secrets and everyone minding their own business," the dwarf said.

They threw them back and slammed the glasses down in unison, the Grappa burning their throats on its way down. She slopped out another round before they could refuse.

Vandusen and Bauer's heads spun when they staggered down the wooden steps of the wagon and wandered back to find their men. The shrieks of the creatures made it easy to find their way. Their men had been busy in their absence and had set up camp. They'd commandeered several wagons, to the dismay of the midgets who lived in them. But a little money and the fact they were armed soon set everything right. They left the cages with the creatures shut up in the vans to keep them out of sight. It muffled their cries to some degree.

Vandusen settled in one of the wagons to make plans for their next move, and as he went to close the curtains, noticed Bauer disappearing up the path leading into the forest toward the midget settlement. He smiled, figuring that Bauer was accepting Susana's invitation. He'd pay her a visit as well once it was completely dark. Several of the midgets circulated among his men, sharing drinks and God knows what else. He wondered if he should say something, but thought better of it and busied himself setting up his field radio. The General would be waiting.

**

The ceiling spun and his head throbbed as he came to his senses. The morning sun, streaming through a gap in the curtains, sent a stabbing pain to his temples. He searched for his clothes, having trouble moving around the tiny bedroom.

Susana's bedroom was little larger than his closet at home. Circus photographs adorned a tiny dresser that could've been part of a set of doll furniture. He tried to gather his thoughts and remember what had passed the night before. He checked his trouser pockets and was relieved to find his wallet and cash.

He steadied himself and waited for the room to stop spinning. How had he ended up in this little dollhouse with its walls covered with posters of circuses and carnivals from around the world? It seemed Susana had gotten around. Her diminutive size made her appear a child, but he wondered how old she really was. He realized that mystery was part of her attraction.

A large photo of Susana standing beside a colorfully painted circus wagon caught his attention. He could just make out the faint details of a form lurking behind the bars of the wagon. He leaned for a closer look and noticed a set of eyes glaring out of the haze of the soft focus. Those eyes were unmistakably those of one of the hybrid creatures. Susana stood smiling, as though unaware of the menace lurking behind her as she pointed at a painted sign tacked to the side, which read, *Wunder der Welt! Halb Mensch, Halb Schimpanse.*" He read it several times before his high-school German allowed him to discern the meaning. "Wonder of the World! Half Man, Half Chimpanzee," he whispered to himself.

He swore as he struggled to stand, swallowing against waves of nausea and bumping his head on the ceiling. He needed to get out and find that idiot Bauer and ask him again if he was sure they were in the right place. Of all the places they could've picked, they picked the very one that had knowledge of what they were trying to hide.

The door opened just as he reached for the knob. Susana stood there smiling as she looked at his naked legs hanging over the bed. "Well, you barely fit on my bed, but you fit in me just fine—actually you both do."

Taking the picture from his hand, she pushed him back into the folds of the bedspread and straddled him, pulling up her green elf tunic. He forgot about his headache as a wave of passion took over.

Chapter Thirty-eight

Phillippe's had been in business since before World War II, making it old by LA standards, and it was packed as usual. Rows of customers lined up all the way to the back of the large dining room, waiting to place their orders. Trays overflowing with steaming plates of French dips, piled high with pickles, coleslaw, potato salad, and cheesecake were carefully carried back to rows of red Formica tables that funneled the traffic to the back of the room.

Ken and Fred had just made it in time to catch the Circus Luncheon Club. They worked their way along the back wall and weaved through the crowd toward the back booths where several tables were reserved for the club meeting. Ken slipped in his haste on the sawdust floor. Fred followed as best he could through the growing crowd.

The Circus Luncheon Club had been meeting the third Wednesday of every month, rain or shine, since anyone could remember. If you worked in the circus and were in town, you came to the Luncheon Club. Anyone who was anyone, or thought they were anyone, didn't miss a meeting. It was the place to find out the gossip—the dirt, as Mary called it.

Fred thought back to the first time he'd been to Phillippe's. *How long had it been?* He'd just met Lester, Girlie, and Bobby at

Lester's trailer. It seemed so long ago, but the calendar on the wall—proudly displaying a photograph of Union Station just across the street—told him it hadn't even been a year ago. So much had happened since then, and he had a premonition that much more was about to happen.

The famous and the infamous of circus royalty greeted them as they neared the tables. Fred realized that nothing had really changed in this tight-knit culture since his last visit. In fact, when it came to circus culture, he remembered Bobby telling him that nothing had changed in centuries. These people endured by keeping to themselves and passing on their traditions, generation to generation, in the stories they told.

A perfect example of an oral tradition in an anthropological sense, Fred thought as he embraced Winnie McCay and Chester Cable.

"So you've finally made it back. Welcome!" Winnie said as she stepped back for a better look at Fred. Before he could introduce Ken, she took Ken's hand and said, "This must be Dr. Turner."

Fred whispered under his breath, "Isn't her smile hypnotic?"

Ken whispered back, "Stick to our business."

Though Winnie didn't hear, she guessed. "You're more handsome in person than Hunt described! But never trust a man, even a gay man, to tell the truth when describing another man to a woman." She smiled and led them to the head of the table, where she made room for them between her and Chester.

"Winnie and Chester are circus royalty and personalities in this club," Fred said to Ken as he held the chair for Winnie.

"Is Winnie his daughter?" Ken whispered.

"She's his wife. I wouldn't say that too loudly. He holds the record for tumbling the largest table on record. They're both in the Guinness Book of Records."

"What does she do?"

"She's a trapeze artist, a flyer as they say in the circus."

"She's beautiful. What's she in the record book for?"

"Luring men to their death, I think." Fred chuckled. "She flew before the largest audience ever at the World's Fair in Montreal."

The assortment of people seated around them fascinated Ken. Many wore some hint of their occupation. The animal trainers had small wire clippers, which they used to repair caging, attached to their belts. The clowns wore colorful jerseys and often placed red-nose pieces to accentuate a point in conversation. The jugglers carried balls they used for practice to fill the time. He saw acrobats, ringmasters, midgets, knife throwers, business agents, and for some he had no clue.

The primatologist in Ken found it interesting to watch their choice of seats. There seemed to be a hierarchy of sorts, but he couldn't put his finger on it and decided to just watch and enjoy. They were guests in a secret and exclusive world few outsiders ever observed.

Winnie settled next to Ken, taking his attention. He picked up the faint scent of jasmine as she leaned over and whispered, "We have much to talk about." She placed her hand on his arm, sending a thrill through his body. Sensing his reaction, she laughed. "I see even professors can be men under the right circumstances."

Embarrassed, Ken stammered to say something and was grateful when Fred interrupted, "Winnie, once again we're in need of your help."

"I'm at your service, Dr. Fred," she said.

Chester pressed in between them. "I spoke with Dusty the other day. Unfortunately, he couldn't make it today. He had a load of hay being delivered at the WATC. He has information on that little circus you're asking about."

Ken blinked, amazed at how quickly news traveled in this little world. He'd called Hunt less than a day before, asking about the *Steinwasen* Park, and already what appeared to be the whole circus world knew of his interest.

Amused at Ken's surprise, Chester chuckled, sending his large frame shaking. "We can take a drive out to Norco and pay a visit to the WATC. Dr. Raven should be there as well as Dusty."

Tall and muscular—in contrast to Winnie's petite, athletic frame—Chester had a big presence and always seemed to be around. He looked to be in his late sixties but fit. The two of them made an odd couple, though elegant in a way Ken found hard to explain. But one thing was certain, Chester was someone to keep on your good side.

"I was hoping to see Bobby and Hunt. I thought they'd be here," Ken said.

"Well, you can be sure Bobby always makes his call times." Chester nodded in the direction of the door.

Ken thought Bobby and Hunt must know everyone in LA. They worked their way through the crowd of customers, stopping often to hug and greet.

When they reached their table, Bobby said, "As the great Yogi Berra said, 'This is déjà vu all over again.' Let's get this meeting started."

With Winnie's help, Hunt called the meeting of the Paul Eagles Circus Luncheon Club to order. Ken and Fred watched in wonder.

The introduction of guests included such luminaries as Gunther Geble-Williams and Siegfried and Roy, among others. Ken found it amazing that such stars were so deferent to Winnie, Chester, Hunt, and Bobby. Apparently, the circus world had their own celebrities, and they had little correlation with the broader world of show business. At one point, Gunther even brought Winnie and Chester their lunch trays.

"And now a brief announcement from our good friend, Mr. Bobby Waiter, star of the center ring and screen," Hunt said.

Bobby jumped up and squeezed between the tables, making his way up front. "How many of you have played Europe in the past few years?" A sprinkling of hands rose. Bobby nodded and left the podium to stand in front.

"Stand up, Bobby!" a clown from Happy Time Circus yelled.

"Very funny, Happy," Bobby said, standing on his tiptoes. A ragged chorus of laughter rose from the back tables. "How many have played Germany, East or West, recently?" Most of the same hands rose again. "After the meeting, I'd like to talk with any who have knowledge or have visited a little amusement park in the Black Forest called *Steinwasen*."

The meeting continued as they shared performances, job openings, and gossip but finally wound down as people finished their lunches and wandered off to visit in small groups that mirrored their occupations.

"Leave me to this," Bobby said to Ken and Fred. "I'll do some circulating and find out about this circus of yours." He set off on his mission, and the dispersing crowd engulfed his little frame.

"Where do you suppose he gets his energy?" Ken asked Chester.

"You should've seen him when he was young and working in the clown act with his parents—he was hell on wheels," Chester said, laughing.

"He still is. You should've seen him in Africa," Fred said.

Chester put his index finger to his lips and whispered, "Shush! Not here. It's not safe to talk about your wanderings even here."

Some time later, Bobby rejoined Ken and Fred. "The park is still in business by all accounts," he said before being interrupted by some stragglers just leaving.

Though frustrated and eager to get more news, Ken and Fred knew they'd have to be patient. They waited and watched Winnie and Chester packing up.

Hunt strolled up and watched Bobby with amusement. "I think Bobby is more famous than even Gunther with this crowd. He loves this."

Ken watched as Bobby made his final partings. Clearly, Bobby had found a niche that worked for him—a perfect fit. He'd taken what many considered a handicap, made the most of it and made it pay. Ken remembered Hunt once sharing that Bobby was on the golden list of highest-paid stuntmen. His balanced proportions were a perfect fit to double for children on movies. The labor laws only allowed children to work a limited amount of time and precluded them from doing stunts; and that was where Bobby came in. He lived larger than his diminutive size.

He has the heart of a lion, Ken thought, remembering his exploits in the Congo.

"So here we are, together again!" Bobby exclaimed as he jumped on a chair to give Fred and Ken a hug.

Chester and Winnie stood smiling, watching old friends linger in their embrace.

"Let's sit for a while." Bobby slid into a corner booth and motioned them to follow.

Winnie squeezed in between, practically sitting on Fred's lap. They waited for Bobby to continue. He seemed to relish the attention and paused to pour a glass of iced tea.

"Bobby!" Winnie exclaimed.

Bobby raised an eyebrow in amusement. "All right, then. *Steinwasen* is still in business but is more a gypsy camp than an amusement park now. I can tell you from experience, it's an unsavory place. But it sounds like it's gotten worse." Bobby took a long sip.

"Do you think Oliver was there? And more importantly, do you think we should check it out?" Ken asked.

"Absolutely, we need to go there. It's a place where smugglers hide their animals. If any of the creatures came up, that's where they would've landed." Bobby waited for a waitress to clean their table before continuing, "Plus, I've a score to settle with some of the boarders there."

"So what's our next step?" Fred asked.

"Head to the WATC and have a talk with Dusty," Bobby replied.

"Dusty? What's he got to do with this?" Ken asked.

Bobby grinned. "He's going with us. He just doesn't know it yet."

"What do we need him for?" Ken asked.

"Nobody's going to talk to you guys. Dusty has the credibility even there."

"Okay," Ken said. "Let's go."

"Hold on. Not just yet; I need a word with Dr. Savage before we all get going." Winnie squeezed Fred's arm and leaned against him.

Chester made his way out.

Chapter Thirty-nine

"I know that little circus if that's what you want to call it," Dusty said as he unloaded bales of straw hay from a flatbed trailer.

"We saw a postcard of that park on the wall of a detective's office in Reno." Ken took a seat on a bale. "There was a group of little people posing with a tiger. They were all dressed in elf costumes, or maybe they were supposed to be Robin Hood and his merry band or something."

"The *Steinwasen* Park is really more of a camp than a circus," Dusty said. "It's where circuses used to layover in the off season. It's not much anymore. It's really just an old gypsy camp with a bad reputation. Bobby was there once, I think. By his own account, it was full of little people like him, which is what interested him at the time. I think he was doing a genealogy thing. If I remember right, they robbed him, and he just got away with his life." Dusty laughed and jabbed two large hay hooks into a bale next to him.

"I saw a newspaper clipping of Oliver with a banner behind him. I could just make out the name on it—*Steinwasen*," Ken said, nodding at Chris as he walked up. "I remember Lester saying Oliver was imported from Germany by a Belgian animal trader. I think we need to at least pay the place a visit and ask around."

"You guys will stand out and most likely be stonewalled." Dusty cut the wire on a bale and threw several flakes of hay to his elephants.

"What choice do we have?" Fred asked. "It sounds like Bobby didn't have much luck, and he's one of them."

"You need someone who's less of an outsider to go with you," Dusty replied. "You could ask around the Circus Luncheon Club."

"We need someone who's a world-famous circus performer and elephant trainer," Ken said. "Someone who trained the largest elephant act to ever be featured by a circus anywhere in the world. Someone who could drop his wallet in the middle of the shadiest little circus in the shittiest part of the world and it would be returned unmolested. Someone who is adored by every performer, roustabout, and trainer in the world, including the worst cons and grifters our industry can produce."

"Are you referring to the greatest elephant trainer who ever lived, Dusty Smith?" Fred asked him, smiling.

"I'm not going." Dusty frowned and waved them off. "You're way off on this one."

"Do you remember when you had that little problem with Fish and Game a few years back?" Ken said. "I believe you said that if there was anything you could do, Chris was just to ask. Well, we're asking for Chris. He's in this with us, as you know."

Dusty shifted his large, sturdy body from one foot to the other, his face reddening. He opened his mouth to speak several times but could just manage to exhale in loud puffs. Finally, he gathered his wits enough to speak. "I need to be way more careful with what I promise. Who would watch my babies while I'm gone?"

"I think I could manage, Dad," Sheri said as she joined the others. "Besides, it would do you good to get off the compound and see the world again."

"I don't have the money to make a trip like that." Dusty tapped his thick index finger across his palm as he added up costs. "At least five hundred and fifty for a ticket one-way, food, lodging, and—"

"The movie will pick up all the expenses, Dusty," Ken said. "And I'm sure I can convince Chris to throw in free rent for your whole herd for the rest of this year."

Dusty muttered something, looked from one to the other, then finally sighed. "He doesn't charge me rent now."

Ken smiled. "How soon can we leave?"

Everyone broke into laughter, including Dusty. Years in show business taught him to know when he'd been outmaneuvered and it was time to give in gracefully.

***

Lieutenant Detective John Sandy listened intently before saying, "You're sure? They've booked flights out of San Francisco to New York?"

"Yes, sir, that's affirmative. I checked the airlines at SFO and they both have connections to Heathrow—London on British Airways," the duty sergeant on the other end of the phone replied.

"Hell, that's an easy jump to Germany," Sandy said, half to himself.

"Sir?"

"Never mind. How did you get this information?" Sandy asked.

A pause, then, "Sir, you said to follow them day and night."

Sandy guessed they'd bugged Dr. Turner's ranch without a warrant, but thought better of asking for any details. "Is the captain in?"

"He's just back from lunch, sir." The sergeant paused longer than usual at the other end.

"Thanks, Sergeant, you did well. That'll be all." Sandy hung up and began leafing through two folders, both on missing persons: Gordon Childs and Deputy Johnston. He was going to have to give some really good reasons to get the captain to spring for a trip to New York, and an even better one for England.

Chapter Forty

Chris thought GuGu had earned his money chartering a direct cargo flight to LAX. Flying Tigers had had to fly out of Europe to meet them, but it was done, and they'd soon be loading. Chris watched as the jet touched down. He admired the bold letters, "Flying Tigers," printed across the fuselage. Those letters had always meant home to him. He couldn't count how many times Flying Tigers had safely carried him and his cargo to distant parts of the world, and then home.

GuGu hurried to meet the African officials headed out to meet the jet.

The voyage on the *Si Como No* had been uneventful but long. They'd remained away from the normal shipping lanes to avoid being detected. GuGu had arranged, or "fixed" as they called it, the offloading and transport to the airport. His contacts and some US dollars had smoothed the way.

He watched as the jet taxied to a stop in front of the warehouse where they were packing the last of the equipment for the trip home. GuGu huddled with a group of Africans who'd pulled up next to the jet. Their gestures indicated an animated conversation, but finally everyone shook hands, and GuGu headed their way.

"All is *bon*," he said. "While corruption make everything easier here, it's getting more expensive." GuGu shrugged.

"Do you need more money?" Chris reached into his pocket.

"No, you've been fair enough. This one's on me." GuGu smiled. "The jet is clear and legal. You just need to finish packing and clear customs. You remember what I said to do?"

"Yes, I have the 'tip' ready. Well, my good friend, I think we're about out of here." Chris embraced GuGu.

"See you on the next movie—or other adventure," GuGu said, being careful not to say too much.

Ken nodded, tapping his index finger to his nose. There were ears everywhere in this part of Africa these days. He turned to attend to their packing.

***

"Be careful where you're rolling the crate!" Chris shouted, throwing up his hands and staring at the animal handler. "That's a $120,000 Panavision camera you're banging into." Slamming his clipboard down, he motioned all his crew to gather around. He waited for everyone to settle before speaking. "Listen, people, when I say we're in a hurry, I don't mean you have carte blanc to destroy everything in sight. We need to work smart." He waited to let his words sink in. "I want all the transport cages loaded carefully and labeled properly—understand? We don't want some USDA agent asking us to take one of our special cargo out for a closer look." Then he motioned everyone to get back to work.

He called Lester over, held him by his shoulder, and lowered his voice. "Make sure you have someone stencil

'DANGER' on Oliver and Danny's boxes. It was hard enough to get them back into those boxes without the mayhem that would occur if we had to open them again."

Chris always hated the last-minute cleanup for the trip home from a location. It seemed all the little loose ends piled up, and it took far longer to wrap up than expected. But they were close. The last thing he always did was load the animals. And on this job, it hadn't been easy. Transporting animals on a jet required them to cage the animals. They weren't allowed to let their animals remain loose like they'd done on the *Si Como No*. It took some coaxing to get the animals back into cages, especially Oliver and Danny. Had it not been for Lester, they would've had to dart them. Once again Lester proved his prowess as an animal trainer.

A tall, lean African inspector checked the cages, and when satisfied, handed Chris a stack of passports. Chris walked the inspector out of the custom warehouse and looked around them before slipping him a wad of US dollars. The African smiled and signed their transfer papers. *It's the same the world over.*

Lester struggled to roll open the large steel door. He paused to catch his breath in his effort to push Girlie's cage toward the loading ramp of the waiting Flying Tigers cargo jet. Two trainers ran over to help him.

"Okay, people, let's load them up," Chris shouted above the din of the idling engines. Everyone scurried into action. They struggled to lift Oliver and Danny's cages and carry them across the heat-softened tarmac, while the hybrids hooted at each bump and shook their cages. The trainers were careful where they placed their fingers, but with some effort, they finally rolled them up the steep ramp and into the waiting jet.

It took several trips between the customs warehouse and the jet to get everything loaded. But the crew knew their job and were used to hard work. Lester and Chris stood at the top of the ramp, watching the activity below. As the last crewman made his way up with camera gear, Lester looked out at the dense jungle surrounding the airfield. Waves of heat distorted the tree line, and he could smell the rotting vegetation. He frowned and said, "Well, Chris, I'm not going to miss this place."

Chris nodded. "Then let's get battened down and take off before someone changes their mind."

Even in the tropical heat, a chill passed over Lester as he helped Chris close the hatch.

"We're finally headed home, Lester. But I wonder what will be waiting for us?" Chris said before turning to work his way up to the cockpit.

***

Chris's crew had spread out in the spacious Boeing 747 Flying Tigers cargo plane, or freighter as most in the business called it. It'd been a long and turbulent flight over the Atlantic. Fortunately, the chimps and Oliver and Danny had slept through most of it. Everything had calmed down after the bustle of loading the jet. So much so that Lester took Girlie out of her cage and played with her behind a stack of crates, being careful not to wake those sleeping. Those not asleep busied themselves at cards or other games.

Lester could see Chris leaning into the cockpit, talking with the pilots. The instruments cast an eerie, green glow. The high-pitched whirl of the engines suddenly changed to a stuttering moan followed by the squeal of the landing flaps.

Chris turned. "Okay, everyone, we're on the final descent. Get all this mess cleaned up," he said loud enough that they could all hear.

Knowing the drill, the trainers stirred into action. Most were veterans of many movies, and though their cargo was unusual this time, they'd do what they were told, especially if they wanted to work on another of Chris's movie gigs, and they all did.

Chris had learned from passing through countless ports of entry that first impressions were everything. LAX international cargo terminal was one of the toughest to clear. They needed to have all their paperwork in order and not give any reason for them to be subjected to a secondary inspection. Chris motioned Lester to cage Girlie. Mike started hooting and shaking his cage in excitement, setting off all the rest. But that was normal when transporting animals. In fact, it would be helpful. Inspectors often hastened their work when chimps started rocking the cages, pounding the bars, and screeching. Their piercing cries unnerved them. With a little nerve, and some luck, they might just get through this.

His watch showed two a.m., which could be good or bad depending on which inspector turned up. If it was someone new who decided they needed to call a vet or USDA or US Customs headquarters, they'd be sitting there until morning. But if they got someone they knew, they might just get waved through after a cursory inspection. You just never knew.

Chris pulled down a jump seat and buckled up with a loud click. "Let's get strapped in. We'll be on the ground in fifteen."

Customs at the cargo terminal at LAX was nothing like the international arrivals for commercial airlines. The sparse but spacious warehouse had a stark counter that served to partition passengers from the offloaded cargo in the back, and a wall blocked the view into the cargo storage and inspection area. A sterile place ready for government business, the cavernous warehouse with its metal walls and concrete floor caused even the slightest sound to echo and amplify. It seemed to most who passed through that the place was designed to catch smugglers. Quarantine animals lived in a separate building at the back.

Passengers usually filed off the cargo jets and queued up at the counter, separated from their cargo and luggage, but, fortunately, when live wild animals were involved, exceptions were occasionally made, and trainers were allowed to accompany their animals during off-loading and follow them into the cargo area.

Chris directed his trainers to stack and group the crates and water the animals. The door behind the counter slammed, making him turn. He shaded his eyes against the glare from banks of fluorescent lights. He frowned, trying to make out the two approaching figures. His frown soon changed to a broad grin when he recognized one of the two.

"Good morning, Lt. Davis," Chris said, extending his hand.

"I'm glad to see you, Dr. Raven." The agent took Chris's hand. "I understand this'll be your last trip out of the Congo, for this movie at least."

"Yes, indeed." Chris directed his attention to a young man standing next to the lieutenant. "And who do we have here?"

"Meet Jeff. He's a student from Cal State interning with our department."

Christ, all we need is a new guy whom Davis will want to impress and show the ropes to. It could be worse, though, they could've sent a coed this old leech would want to impress.

"I have your manifest. Shall we get started?"

"As you wish."

They sorted through the luggage, making their way toward the animal cages.

"I'm glad you guys made it out of there in one piece," the lieutenant said. "We've been getting some disturbing reports." He gave them a side glance before walking toward the animal crates.

"What kind of reports?" Chris asked.

"A massacre of a whole village upriver from the Port of Banana."

"We didn't hear anything, but that was way south of us." Chris tried to keep his voice from wavering.

"Oh, that's right. I was hoping you could give us some details," the lieutenant said.

"I'm glad we can't."

"I'm glad you're back safely, Doctor. Are these the same animals you left with?"

"Of course."

Turning to the student, the lieutenant said, "We'll just do a count and match it to the manifest. Hell, I wouldn't know one of these chimps from another."

"So as long as the same came in as went out we're okay?" the student asked.

"Yep, until we require tattoos or some kind of computer chip, that's all we do."

Shaking his head, the student asked, "I've learned quite a bit about chimps from school. Would you like me to take a closer look?"

Christ, Chris thought.

The lieutenant glanced up to the ceiling and sighed. "As you wish, young man." Smiling at Chris, he followed the boy towards the animal crates.

Shit. Chris got into step.

As the boy approached the animals, a chorus of hoots and screams echoed around the warehouse. Lester and the others watched the boy stride toward the cages and got up to intervene, but Chris waved them off. As the boy neared, all the cages shook and the doors rattled.

The lieutenant hesitated, looking at Chris.

In as serious a tone as Chris could muster, he said, "I sure hope those doors hold, for that kid's sake."

But before they could say or do anything, a cloud of feces engulfed the student, splattering him, head to toe. His clipboard dropped, ringing off the concrete floor, and the student's exclamations and gagging could just be heard above the laughter filling the warehouse.

"Enough!" Chris shouted, glaring at his team. "There's not a person in this room, the lieutenant excluded, who hasn't had this happen to them. It's not funny when he's just trying to do his job." Chris tried not to lay it on too thick or laugh himself.

Lester gave the boy a towel as he recovered the clipboard with the soiled manifest.

"I think we can sign off on this manifest," the lieutenant said. "Could someone please bring it over here?" He shook his head as he took the clipboard from the boy. "Now if I can just find a dry spot to initial."

"My apologies, Lieutenant," Chris said in the most apologetic tone he could manage.

The lieutenant waved him off. "No worries. You're free to go, Dr. Raven."

Chris caught the lieutenant's eye and could tell he was working as hard as he could not to laugh.

"All right, you heard the man. Let's pack up and head for home!" A roar of applause filled the warehouse, then they gathered their gear and loaded the animals onto the waiting trucks. They'd be home at the WATC in a few hours.

Lester stepped next to Chris and whispered, "Good old Mike." Chuckling, he added, "He always seems to know the right thing to do at the right time."

Chris laughed. "As we say in show business, timing is everything."

They both laughed until they lost their breath.

"It'll be a long time before that young man does that again," Chris said.

Chris breathed a sigh of relief as he jumped into a truck. He could feel the Santa Ana winds warming the morning as the sun rose. The San Bernardino Mountains glowed with a reddish, orange hue. He looked to the driver and asked, "What do they say? Red sky in the morning, sailor take warning. Red sky at night, sailor's delight."

The driver just shrugged and put the truck in gear.

Chris looked forward to getting back home to his compound. He wondered where the others were. He'd not been in touch with any of them since he'd left the ranch. He rolled down the window, stuck out his head, and shouted, "Fuck the red sky. I'm home!"

Chapter Forty-one

Ken found Kennedy Airport packed as usual. They'd hoped to get a direct flight from Reno to Berlin, but Reno wasn't quite that international, and they had to fly out of San Francisco. The best they could do on such short notice was book connections in New York and then in London and ending in Berlin. Already feeling tired, Ken waited in the boarding area of British Airways for their connection to London while Fred made a hasty retreat to the restroom to clean mustard off his best travel shirt. He'd dribbled it after his first bite into a New York pretzel.

Two stewardesses smiled at Ken as they passed by in black high heels. Their short cut mini-skirts revealed two sets of shapely legs.

No need for hose on those legs. He wondered how they could work dressed like that, then realized that when you looked like that, a passenger could be quite forgiving, at least the males.

Fred arrived back, still drying his shirt with a handful of paper towels. "What's so funny?"

"You missed it. I just saw two good reasons you'd want to take a job in New York," Ken replied, smiling.

"Well, I saw something that isn't as—how do you say?—humorous." Scowling, Fred looked across the aisle to the opposite waiting area.

"That can't be who I think it is, is it?" Ken asked, barely moving his lips.

"It is, and he's waving."

An announcement blared over the intercom: "Flight 1781 to Heathrow, now boarding at gate seventy-eight."

Lieutenant Sandy of the Reno Sheriff's Department approached, smiling from ear to ear. He almost bound across the aisle to meet them. "Well, well. How fortuitous!" Sandy exclaimed. His voice resounded above the din of the waiting area.

Several people smiled and looked in their direction, thinking it was a meeting of old friends.

The professors could only look at each other as Sandy continued, "I'm headed for Germany, and from the looks of it, I think we're sharing the same flight, at least to jolly ole England."

"Are you following us?" Ken asked, then cursed himself for giving away their plans.

"I'm on a case that takes me to a little amusement park in the Black Forest. Let's see—what was it called? *Steinwasen*, I believe." Sandy paused to catch their reactions before asking, "how 'bout you?"

"Perhaps we should cut the crap, Lieutenant," Ken said, his voice wavering.

"My sentiments exactly," he replied.

The professors stood speechless for several heartbeats, taking little notice of anything but Sandy. They felt trapped. Everything seemed to shrink around them. Before either could speak, an announcement blared over the intercom, "Flight 1781 to Heathrow is now boarding at gate seventy-eight."

"I believe that's us." Sandy stood and picked up his briefcase and some magazines. "After you, Professors."

Ken and Fred hesitated for a moment, both thinking about not boarding.

Sandy's eyes narrowed at their hesitation. "We can cooperate, or I can hold this flight long enough to call airport security and have you detained, or perhaps arrested on suspicion of being an accessory to kidnapping or worse." Sandy's voice turned hard, losing all the country bumpkin tone. "At the very least, I can hold you both as persons of interest in my investigation."

The final announcement echoing over the bustle of departing passengers stirred them into action: "Last call for boarding Flight 1781 to Heathrow, gate seventy-eight."

Ken and Fred joined the last of the passengers filing through the gate, boarding passes in hand. Sandy followed.

A man watched from a bank of pay phones as the last of the passengers disappeared through gate seventy-eight. He motioned to his colleague, who came from across the waiting area. "Get the car. I'll meet you as soon as I make this call."

The man nodded and, without saying anything, headed for the parking exit as the other man dialed. "The professors left for London with that detective, just as you thought they would, General." After hanging up, he waited until the plane for London took off, then left.

***

Lieutenant Detective Sandy flashed his badge and had their seating assignments rearranged so he could sit with Ken and Fred. They had plenty of time to "catch up," as Sandy called it, as they waited for clearance to taxi for takeoff.

Once they were in their seats, Sandy squatted in the aisle and asked Ken to start talking.

Fred, sitting beside him, listened and watched as Ken filled the detective in without mentioning Gordon Childs. He couldn't tell how much Sandy knew, so he gave him details of Vandusen and Melon and their attempts to force them to do government research that they felt was unethical.

Sandy seemed sympathetic to their cause, but though they found that encouraging, they couldn't be certain. The detective seemed especially interested in Vandusen's possible connection to covert government agencies, and Ken was relieved to learn that he wasn't a big fan of the CIA. He also made it quite clear that any events that happened in Africa were completely out of his jurisdiction. Ken almost felt guilty hiding what they knew about Childs, but he quickly got over it.

"I think our interests might be closer than you think," Sandy said. "I could be of some help, and you to me. My investigation is no longer seeking Mr. Childs, though it would be nice to know what happened to him. I'm seeking information on the disappearances and possible murders of Dr. Melon and one of our deputy sheriffs."

"What does that have to do with us?" Ken asked. Surprisingly, he felt sympathy for Melon.

"I think the people who are pursuing you and your chimps are connected with this case," Sandy replied.

"Vandusen and Melon are definitely connected," Ken said. "We figured that at the meeting at the university. There's a lot of money being thrown around, and I think it's been coming from Vandusen and whoever he's connected with."

Sandy thought back to his visit at the Reno Airport. "That just might make sense. Have you ever heard of someone they refer to as the General?"

"Yes, I think he's who Vandusen works for. He mentioned him when he tried to force us to go with them." Ken paused as a stewardess checked the overhead luggage compartments.

Fred finally couldn't contain himself any longer and asked, "So, please, tell me again. Why are we going to Germany?"

Before Ken could speak, Sandy broke in, "Everything in my investigation is pointing to that airbase and little amusement park as the route for smuggling animals out of Africa, and this Vandusen character is somehow part of it. If Vandusen is connected, like we think, with these shady government types, we should be able to find out a lot by poking around that park, and maybe even pay a visit to Ramstein Airforce Base." Sandy smiled as a trim stewardess checked their seat belts as they made ready for takeoff.

"Vandusen and his crew are the last people we want to run into," Ken said. "We just want to get more information on various aspects of our research and not end up guests of the government or worse." Ken purposely didn't get too specific as to what their research entailed, especially concerning the hybrids.

Sandy had been in the business of detecting long enough to know when someone was holding out on him, but he could wait. He picked his words carefully. "You leave Vandusen to me.

I have some experience dealing with his type. Nothing is going to happen to the both of you. I doubt very much we can get access to that airbase, so we'll have to do this on our own, and fill in the blanks if we can."

Ken wasn't so sure but felt they had no choice but to go along with this detective for now. "Just know that they appear to be working for some arm of the government, or a bunch of gangsters, or both."

"We'll do some poking around when we get there and take it from there," Sandy said.

Ken didn't know what that meant but decided not to press this young detective, who seemed so sure of himself. One thing was certain, he was resourceful. In a short time, he'd managed to find them and had learned much about their problem.

Sensing their concern, Sandy continued, "I think you're caught up in events beyond your control. It'll be best if you leave this to the professionals."

The professors had wanted to come clean about this whole matter and now everything seemed to be racing in that direction. They both wondered how much of their secret would remain just that, a secret.

The captain's announcement to prepare for takeoff jarred them out of their thoughts, and the passengers busied themselves securing their belongings and taking their seats. The spell had been broken.

"Let's take a break for a while," Sandy said, and then stared at them for a moment before adding, "but I still have more questions." He took his seat across the aisle.

The cabin lights dimmed as they leveled off for the long crossing over the Atlantic. Fred had to ask their stewardess twice to bring them blankets and pillows, but she looked so provocative as her miniskirt hiked up when she stretched to reach one of the overhead luggage compartments that he didn't feel like complaining about the service.

He felt ready to get some sleep, though, and wasn't sure if the travel or the tension of meeting Lieutenant Sandy had exhausted him—probably both. He'd have to think about their new partner and talk to Ken later.

They'd meet Dusty and Bobby in Berlin and head for the Black Forest, wherever that was, but that would be later. Everything seemed to be racing to an end, but an end he didn't understand.

Ken drifted off and Sandy scribbled notes. Fortunately, the Scotch whiskey the stewardess brought Fred, as an apology for her tardiness, did its job. He felt sleep approaching and gave in to it.

Chapter Forty-two

Ken thought the Berlin Zoo looked more like a research facility than a zoo, at least the zoos in which he was used to working. The apes were housed in sterile enclosures of bright lights, glass, and stainless steel, which must have cost a fortune to build, and were very different from the enclosures Ken and Fred had helped design at the San Diego Zoo. They'd worked hard to give the primates as natural an enclosure as possible, while keeping the fine balance between a natural environment and accessibility to the public. The cages at this zoo, however, prioritized accessibility, and it showed in the listless behavior of the animals.

Ken had suggested the zoo as a cover for their trip to Germany, so they needed to make a visit before they headed to *Steinwasen*. He and the director were colleagues, but the welcome by the zoo personnel had been less than enthusiastic, which was uncharacteristic and concerning. It had been at least an hour, and they still waited for the director to receive them.

"Something's wrong," Ken said.

Fred nodded. "Our reception is different than last time, for sure."

Sandy looked down a long hallway. "I see the reason."

Ken and Fred stood and joined him. They all watched as the director and several uniformed police approached.

277

"I hope this isn't because I'm double parked?" Fred whispered.

"Very funny," Ken said under his breath.

The director hung back as a tall officer looked at Ken and said, "Herr Doctor Turner, I believe?"

"What do I owe the honor of such an official reception?" Ken asked, looking from one policeman to another.

"Please make yourselves at ease. We have a few questions if you don't mind, but I think it will be more comfortable in the Herr Director's office."

The director stepped up and shook Ken's hand. "I'm sorry for this, Ken. They just showed up this morning and seemed to know you'd be dropping by." He led them up a flight of stairs to his office.

"Sandy, do something. You're a cop," Fred whispered out the side of his mouth.

"I don't think that's going to carry much weight over here," Sandy said.

The director's office was well appointed. Photographs, diplomas, and certificates filled the wall behind a large, walnut desk. Ken waited as the director settled into a plush leather chair behind the desk.

Ignoring the police, Ken caught the director's eye and asked, "Gunter, what's this all about?"

The director opened his mouth, but before he could speak, a German police officer interrupted, "Our station received information that you are planning on importing some primates into our country illegally."

This has got to be Melon's work, that asshole, Ken thought. "I'm sorry, but you're mistaken. We're here on holiday, and thought we'd pay a courtesy visit to the zoo."

"Is that the case, detective?" the officer asked, looking at Sandy.

Sandy's eyes widened, shocked that this policeman knew who he was, but before he could answer, the officer continued, "It's our understanding that you're investigating a missing person and the professors here are suspects."

"I'm not sure who you've been talking to," Sandy replied, "but I assure you they are merely people of interest in my investigation. I know nothing about any intention to import any primates. That, of course, would be out of my jurisdiction."

"Precisely! You have no jurisdiction in our country and would be dealt with in an expedient manner should you be found meddling in our affairs."

Sandy and the officer stared at each other for several heartbeats before the director broke in. "I received word that there was a crash landing at Ramstein Airbase of a cargo transport coming in from Africa. Everyone seemed to vanish into thin air, but not before several witnesses observed some large primates being off-loaded and whisked away in trucks." The director paused, looking at Ken. "And then I received a call and visit from the police inquiring about you and your visit."

"We know nothing about any crash. We're simply here on holiday."

The police officer interrupted. "Really? So your visit here has nothing to do with this incident?"

"Nothing, I assure you," Ken said.

"Let me say this again; we will deal with any meddling in our investigation of this incident harshly." The police officer paused as an assistant whispered something in his ear, then, looking at Sandy, he continued, "We've been in touch with your captain, Detective."

Sandy just stared at him.

"Good day to you. Do not forget what I have said." He left the room with his officers following.

"What's all this about?" the director asked as they watched the last of the police officers leave the room.

"Close the door," Ken said.

"There are rumors floating around about you, Ken." The director's voice sounded strained.

"I can only say that we've had inquiries by several agents of the US government offering large sums of money for us to cooperate with them, but there are strings," Ken replied, being careful not to reveal too much. Though he knew the director professionally, he didn't trust him. He didn't trust any of his colleagues anymore, not since Africa.

The director nodded and said nothing more.

Ken wasn't sure what that meant, but he let the conversation die, and they said their goodbyes.

Visitors crowded the zoo by the time they got out of the administration building.

"So where do we go from here?" Fred asked as they crossed the parking lot.

"That's easy; let's pick up Bobby and Dusty and make for *Steinwasen*," Ken replied. "It's close to Ramstein. Word may have gotten out about the crash."

"Yeah, but Vandusen may be there, and I don't like the idea of running into him." Fred stopped and looked around.

"What's wrong?" Ken asked.

"I don't like how everyone seems to know our business. I have the feeling we're being followed."

The three men turned and took in their surroundings, but all they saw were families making their way to the zoo. Children raced ahead, their mothers calling them back. The sun broke out of the clouds, and another day at the zoo began for the happy Berliners. The contrast between the joy of those around them and their own feelings wasn't lost on them.

"We'll just have to risk a visit, or what's the point of this whole trip?" Ken said.

"True; if the crash was related to Vandusen, word will spread to that little circus. It's been a haven for smugglers for years. Someone there will know. But what about the police?" Fred asked.

"I doubt the police have any knowledge of what goes on there. Most likely it's just another gypsy camp to them," Sandy said.

"I'm more worried about running into Vandusen than the police," Ken said, setting off towards their rented van. "Let's go. We can pick up Bobby and Dusty on the way."

Chapter Forty-three

Vandusen woke to someone pounding on the door. His head throbbed and the whole trailer shook. He groped around in the dark, but Susana wasn't there. Everything seemed to be spinning, making it hard to work the door knob, but he finally got it open.

Bauer stood at the door holding a handkerchief on his forehead and his revolver in the other hand. "Something's wrong," he said.

Vandusen pushed the revolver aside as he stepped past him into the open. "Where is everyone?" As his eyes adjusted to the faint moonlight, he made out some of his men staggering toward them, rubbing their heads.

"That's just it, they were still in their racks when the shit hit the fan. The lucky ones are just waking up. I think we've been drugged. That little princess woke me up, fortunately, or we'd all have our throats slit by these little shits."

Gathering himself, Vandusen picked up his rifle and motioned Bauer to follow him down the pathway leading to where they had the creatures caged. He jumped back as one of them lunged at him, jarring the bars. *Too close for comfort.* He felt reassured to find them still there, but realized they'd been double-crossed by the crafty little people. The old lady had offered them the use of several large cages to house the creatures. With him and his men out of the way, she could've sold them to the highest bidder.

"Find that old bitch," Vandusen said.

Bauer nodded and disappeared into the darkness just as it began to rain.

***

When Bauer returned, he found Vandusen finishing up a conversation on the radio. "I can't find her," he said.

Vandusen handed the microphone back to the radioman and turned to him. "The General is not happy."

"How so, sir?" Bauer asked.

"We're on the radar now. The word is out since the crash. We're truly fucked." Vandusen looked around as the men gathered their gear and continued searching for stragglers. "Even the German police are mobilized, and apparently Turner and some cop have been talking to them."

Bauer raised an eyebrow, amazed, as always, at how good the General's intelligence was. "What now?"

"Complete our mission. We need to get to Rotterdam and book a cargo vessel to the States."

"The States! Where?"

"The General is setting up a new cover in the Pacific Northwest. It should be ready by the time we get there. We can't fly now—it'll be safer by ship."

"What are your orders?"

"Dart and load the animals," Vandusen said as he surveyed the park in the morning light. "Kill everyone you find and burn this place down. I don't want anyone to find a trace of us."

Bauer broke into a wide smile. "With pleasure."

Bauer sure loves his work.

***

Susana hid in the shadows in a thicket of cedars near her burning wagon and watched the big people at their work. The boss lay next to her. She wanted to give the old lady away, but that would've meant giving herself up. Their eyes smoldered when they met, but they lay as quiet as they could, fearing even the sound of their breathing would give them away. She watched in horror as Vandusen's men set fire to the wagons and ran down the last of the midgets. They loaded the dead in the trucks along with their gear. Susana covered her ears to the screams as the men made sport of the killing.

The two midgets wept as they watched from the shadows. There was nothing they could do, but wait until this horror passed out of their camp.

***

Vandusen was amazed at how loudly the midgets could scream.

Bauer returned when silence finally descended on the park. "We didn't get them all. Some are hiding in the forest," he said.

Vandusen frowned. "We don't have time to hunt them down. Who's going to believe these little bandits, anyway? Let's wrap this up and move out." He walked over to get a closer look at the drugged creatures. Once again, their rank smell assaulted him, and he winced as one of his men turned one over; their grotesque features disgusted him. "Are they alive?"

The men nodded as they struggled to load them into the transfer cages.

"Has anyone fed these things?" Vandusen asked.

"Not since yesterday," Bauer answered.

"We need to keep them alive," Vandusen said.

Smiling, Bauer said, "I have an idea." He dashed away and returned soon after with a struggling midget. Laughing, he threw him into the cage. "That will give one of these freaks something to play with and eat when it wakes up."

A chorus of laughter broke out, and several more midgets, dead or barely alive, were found and thrown into the cages.

Chapter Forty-four

Steinwasen lay in ruins. Smoking piles of debris littered the charred grounds, and dwarves and midgets lay scattered like so many broken and discarded dolls. Death had come to visit this black little settlement, and only a few were left to tell the horror of what had happened. Never in his career in law enforcement had Sandy witnessed such a bizarre scene. Dusty, Ken, Bobby, and Fred stood beside him looking justifiably horrified at the sight of the massacre.

"This has the smell and feel of Vandusen and his cronies," Bobby said, his expression turning to anger.

Sandy stepped forward. "Let's find out what happened here."

Bobby pulled Sandy back and whispered, "It'll be better if we let Dusty do the talking here. They don't trust outsiders much."

Dusty headed off towards a group of midgets who were looking through the rubble. Sandy noticed how his large frame contrasted bizarrely with the petite little people. "And he's not an outsider?"

Bobby gestured in Dusty's direction. "He's famous in the circus world, this world. Hell, that's why we asked him to come along. He's respected and trusted by them. If you hang around with us very long, you'll learn that circus people, especially gypsies, keep their secrets close to them. If anyone's going to get to the bottom of this, it'll be Dusty. Besides, do you speak Romani?"

"Do I speak what?" Sandy asked. Taking a back seat was frustrating, but he knew Bobby was right, besides the German authorities had made it quite clear that he was out of his jurisdiction in this part of the world.

"Romani, it's the language of the gypsies," Ken replied. "He'll get more out of them speaking their language than us trying English or our freshman German."

Bobby followed Dusty, and the professors found an old park bench on which to wait.

Realizing that no one was going to speak with him, Sandy decided to busy himself by sifting through the smoking debris of what was left of the park. He could at least look for clues before the whole site was disturbed.

Dusty sat on the tongue of a splintered circus wagon and the group of little people gathered around him. Some stood close to him whispering and gesturing emphatically while others remained silent, hugging each other and weeping. The group parted, making way for a woman not much larger than a doll. They closed in around her as she settled next to Dusty.

"What happened here?" Dusty asked.

"Evil came to collect from us," she said. Her voice wavered and she seemed dazed.

Bobby looked at Dusty and whispered, "Is she going into shock?"

"Yes, I think so." Dusty called for someone to bring a blanket.

"Can you tell us more?" Dusty covered her with the blanket and massaged her as she sat trembling.

"The Pinkies seemed okay when they first arrived, but I think those creatures they brought poisoned their minds," she replied, then took a sip from a flask Dusty handed her. "I think they poisoned us all—they're unnatural." She broke into sobs.

"I think we all know who's behind this mess," Bobby said.

Dusty nodded. "Just the same, I'd like to hear her out."

Bobby started to say something but thought better of it when Dusty glared.

The crowd of little people waited while Dusty watched Sandy pick his way through the ruins. Directing his attention back to the midget, he asked, "What's your name?"

After gathering herself, she answered, "Susana."

A crowd of midgets pushed in around her and Dusty.

"She brought this on us," an old midget shouted in a low, gravelly voice. "She's a little whore. She caused this! She spent the night with the big people."

Several of the midgets lunged in to grab Susana. Dusty had to bat them away. "Back off!" he yelled. "What happened here was a violent crime—a crime. Do you understand? No one can be blamed for this but those who committed it."

Susana pointed at the old midget and shouted, "You lie. She's the one. She took gold from the Pinkies but then double crossed them."

The old woman's gaze darted around the group. She opened her mouth to speak, but Dusty held up his hand and stopped her. He looked back at Susana and said, "Go on."

The crowd waited for Susana to continue. "She made a deal with traders to steal their creatures. She tried to drug the Pinkies last night." Susana fought to hold back her sobs. "You were all in on it!" she screamed, glaring at the group.

Embarrassed, many of the little people dropped their heads and avoided eye contact. They dispersed, muttering amongst themselves and casting hateful stares at Susana. They busied themselves by picking up what was left of their belongings and hitching the wagons that could still roll. In one way or another, the camp began to empty.

"We're not going to get much more from this group, and if we don't hurry they're all going to be gone," Dusty said.

"I'll show you the cages," Susana said.

Bobby waved the others over, and Susana led them through the shattered remains of a round gate towards her trailer and the cages beyond, sticking close to Ken's group. They figured she didn't feel safe out of their protection amongst the clusters of little people gathering what was left of their belongings.

"We keep the cages back here behind what's left of this fence," Susana said.

They followed her along a winding stone path into a thick stand of cedars. She pointed to a smoking pile of charred wood and said, "That used to be my wagon," then led them on to a large clearing. Several stone cages with iron bars clustered around the charred remains of another wagon. "That used to be the boss's—the bitch. As I said, she sold us out."

"Let's have a closer look." Bobby bounded ahead. The rusted door to a cage squeaked as he opened it.

Sandy sifted through the remains. "There's not much left here," he said, shaking his head. "Whoever was here last night did a thorough job of burning all evidence."

"Not quite all of it," Bobby's soft voice echoed out from inside a cage.

The group gathered around the cage and looked through the bars at Bobby. When everyone settled, he pointed at the wall. "I've seen this artwork before."

Ken and Fred knelt next to a set of markings that reminded them of pictographs from an ancient Paleolithic cave. The red pigment contrasted with the white limestone of the caging floor.

Ken touched the markings with his fingertips, careful not to mar the artwork. "I can't be sure, but I think this pigment is blood."

Bobby slid in front of them for a closer look. "Two lines above six. This is the same as we found on the trail in Africa."

"Someone or something put a lot of effort, and pain, I'd guess, to leave this behind."

"But why?" Ken asked.

Fred shrugged. "Maybe for us to find."

"Looks like we're running out of time," Bobby said, pointing down the path to a flurry of activity.

"From those flashing blue lights, I'm guessing the local constabulary is on the scene," Sandy said. He pulled a small Instamatic camera out of his coat and took several shots.

"I think it's time for us to take a hint from our gypsy friends," Bobby said.

Sandy nodded. "The police made it quite clear from our last meeting that they didn't want our help. I suggest we leave." Looking at Susana, he asked, "Is there another way out of here?"

She smiled. "Yes; I'll show you if you take me with you."

Sandy frowned. "I'm sorry, but that's out of the question."

"I know where Vandusen is headed." She tapped her wristwatch and looked back at the police.

Sandy looked up the path as they approached. "Fine. Lead the way."

She led them on a circuitous route back to the van. They climbed in, and with Dusty behind the wheel, headed away from the park.

The clouds that had been thickening all day released their load, and rain pelted down.

"I don't think anyone saw us leave; at least, no one's following us," Ken said as he peered out the windscreen. The sheets of rain made it hard to see.

"So what'll we do now?" Fred asked. Cuffing his sleeve in his hand, he tried wiping the windscreen.

"Get the hell outa here," Bobby said from the back seat. "I sure don't want to cool my heels in a German jail." He tapped Dusty on the back. "Slow down."

Dusty ignored Bobby. He seemed more preoccupied with the knobs on the dashboard than the road, and he had to correct several times to keep the van in his lane.

"Well, we know one thing for sure," Fred said. "Vandusen, and his thugs, were around last night, and according to Susana, they had four creatures with them."

Susana slept with her head on Bobby's shoulder, but her eyes fluttered open at the mention of her name.

"Yeah," Dusty said, "and I bet they still have them and are taking them somewhere. If they're anything like Oliver or Danny, there's going to be a shitload of trouble wherever they land." He kept fiddling with the switches on the dashboard. "Christ, does anyone know how to turn on the damn wipers?"

"Yes, pull the white knob that says *schreibenwisher*," Susana said, smirking between yawns.

Dusty, catching her smirk in the rear-vision mirror said, "Smart ass."

Susana smiled. "*Bette schön*, you're welcome. By the way, I'd like something to eat."

"She's right," Sandy said. "We should all grab something. Let's find a place. That'll give us time to figure out our next move, especially with the help of our new friend, Susana." He smiled at her. Though he wasn't sure about the little midget, she was the only person who might be able to tell them where Vandusen had gone.

Dusty nodded. "I agree with the lieutenant. Let's find a truck stop or something and talk. Susana, do you know of a place?"

"I might." She grinned.

Dusty glared at her in the mirror, brow furrowed.

Susana laughed. "A couple of kilometers on the left."

Once they'd put some miles between them and the park, the tension eased and the group began to relax. They found themselves racing down the autobahn, which lived up to its reputation for speed with cars passing them at ninety-five miles per hour in the pouring rain.

"Look for a sign that says, *autohof.* The exit should be coming up soon," Susana said.

An *autohof* or German truck stop was nothing like what they were used to in the States. The food was fresh and good, and the place had a homey feeling.

Dusty sighed as he finished a plate of *weisswurst.* "God, that was good." Pushing his chair back to make room for his expanded waist, he placed his hands on the shelf of his belly, laced his fingers together and twirled his thumbs.

Bobby laughed. "Dusty, I believe that's becoming your trademark."

Dusty ignored him, closing his eyes, and smiled.

Ken lowered his voice. "And now down to business, please."

He waited for a waitress to clear their table before he began, "We need to figure out our next steps."

"That's simple," Bobby said. "As I said, let's get the hell out of here. I'm sorry to say, but we're burned."

Sandy looked at Susana. "I agree we can't do much more over here, but I think you had something about Vandusen to share with us."

"I overheard him tell his friend they'd be going to Rotterdam. They're booked on a cargo steamer headed for the States."

"You're sure of that?" Sandy asked.

"Yes."

Bobby shook his head. "That's not good for us."

Ken nodded. "Worse, it sounds like they have some of the creatures."

"They do, four of them," Susana said. "They're frightening."

"Do you know the name of the ship?" Sandy asked.

"No, but I know someone in Berlin who will know."

"They could land anywhere," Ken said. "But it'll not be easy to keep the creatures on the down low for very long. Someone will talk."

"What caused the fight, anyway?" Sandy asked.

"They found out the boss was going to double-cross them," Susana said. "She tried to drug them. My people were all in on it. They were going to sell the things to an animal trader we know named Gabriel. It would've worked had they not been tipped off."

"Tipped off? By whom?" Sandy asked.

"Me."

The group stared at her in silence.

Susana glared back at them. "They promised to give me gold if I looked out for them. I thought they'd be my ticket out, but I was wrong."

"Apparently we are instead," Bobby said, shaking his head.

Susana smiled and winked at him.

Bobby ignored her. "Let's go home."

Dusty sighed. "I'm sure we can book a flight out of Amsterdam."

Chapter Forty-five

"So why Rotterdam?" Sandy asked.

They'd been driving all day and were so tired that no one answered at first. Dusty leaned forward, his hands gripping the steering wheel, trying to maneuver through the winding arteries of Berlin. The rush-hour traffic was nerve-wracking. Susana had been helpful directing and interpreting road signs, but now they were trying to navigate through town searching for a hotel. Bobby concentrated on a Michelin map he had spread across the dash. Fred now snored in the back seat.

Just as Sandy was going to ask again, Bobby said, "What? Sorry." He passed the map to the backseat. "Rotterdam has been on the smuggling route for centuries. Animals coming from all over the world, especially Africa, find their way there. It's the perfect location to ship them almost anywhere."

"How so?" Sandy pushed the map over to Susana.

"Well, for one thing, it's one of the busiest ports in Europe and centrally located for reaching the States. Trainers on half the circuses I've worked for have bought animals from smugglers on the black market."

"The route's like this," Ken said. "A trapper, usually Portuguese or Belgian, captures, say, a chimp. He sells it to a smuggler who gets it to Istanbul. From there, it's trucked to Rotterdam and concealed in some way—often in a container—

and then loaded onto a cargo ship bound for the States. It's then offloaded before reaching port, thus avoiding customs and Fish and Wildlife Department agents."

Bobby raised an eyebrow, surprised that Ken knew so much about smuggling. "That's right, and the fines and penalties are huge if you're caught with restricted animals like chimps." Smirking at Ken, he asked, "How do you know so much about smuggling?"

Ken smiled. "Contrary to what you suspect, I was on an international task force, led by the Dutch, investigating the enforcement of the CITES treaty."

"The what?" Sandy asked.

"Under the Endanger Species Act of 1973, the importation of threatened and endangered species is strictly monitored and controlled, and requires a permit," Ken replied. "The US is part of the treaty, the Convention on International Trade in Endangered Species of Wild Fauna and Flora, or CITES as we refer to it. Anyone landing with one of the creatures would have some explaining to do—explaining I'd rather not have to do."

"Even if we convinced Fish and Wildlife that the creatures were some kind of chimp, we'd still have them without a permit, and be in violation and face confiscation and jail time," Bobby explained.

"I'm sure Vandusen knows that as well, besides just wanting to keep them secret," Dusty said, looking over his shoulder long enough to hit a pothole.

"Keep your eyes on the road!" Bobby exclaimed.

Dusty smiled.

Fred yawned from the back seat and stretched after his nap.

"So this is all about some apelike creatures you and the government are fighting over?" Sandy asked.

Fred and Ken looked at each other. Everyone remained silent as Dusty wove through traffic and joined the *Grober Stern* roundabout. After their second rotation around the Victory Column everyone began to give directions.

"Shut up! I got this." Dusty veered through honking traffic and headed toward the entrance of *Tiergarten*.

"We discovered a possible chimpanzee hybrid the government would like to put to use," Ken said, picking his words carefully. "A use we don't agree with, and so we would like to find them and keep them safe."

Fred added, "This has put us on the wrong side of these agents, and they're people who'll stop at nothing—they'll even kill—to get their way. They care nothing that this is the scientific find of the century."

Sandy nodded and, deep in thought, said nothing more until Dusty made a sharp turn. "Who are these people?"

"Bad people," Bobby replied. "Contractors for the Department of Defense."

"Is Dr. Melon involved?" Sandy asked.

Ken nodded. "We think so."

"And this Vandusen?"

"One of the alphabets: CIA, NSA or the mob—who knows?" Fred said.

"I have a good friend and fellow officer named Johnston. He disappeared, and everything seems to lead to Dr. Melon and this Vandusen character. Childs, Melon, Johnston—and who knows who else …" Sandy's eyes welled up after mentioning

Johnston. "I want to find out what happened to my friend and make whoever is responsible pay," he finished, fighting to modulate his voice.

"I think if we find where Vandusen and his cronies have disappeared to, you'll get your answers, and we'll find the creatures," Ken said in a grave voice, then all fell silent except for the cadence of the wipers.

"So let's go to Rotterdam for chrissakes," Dusty said a moment later.

***

Susana had difficulty finding the hotel. They lost their way several times before finally turning down a dark alley that led to the dimly lit backdoor of a seedy, run-down little place that had seen better days.

Fortunately, Susana spoke German, as the establishment wasn't used to receiving tourists. In the end, they managed to get the last vacant rooms, with Bobby and Susana sharing one overlooking the alley. Ken wasn't sure if this was by chance or design on Susana's part.

After settling in, they had schnapps and coffee in the lounge. The strain of the last few days had put them on edge, and a waiter startled them when he opened the double doors and came in balancing a tray of pastries.

"We can book our flights out of Amsterdam after we pay a visit to the Port of Rotterdam," Ken said.

"We can reach the port by tomorrow if we leave early," Susana said. "But, first, I think you need to meet someone who might be able to help."

"Who?" Ken asked.

"Someone with experience in smuggling," Susana said.

The double doors opened again and a midget dressed in a suit entered the lounge. His rough and stubby features contrasted with Bobby and Susana's fine proportions. Before anyone spoke, the little man said, "Joel, at your service."

The group stared at the little man, then Ken found his voice and introduced everyone.

Joel's dark eyes took in his surroundings as he politely bowed at Ken's introductions. "I understand you're looking for some misplaced people and animals," he said when Ken had finished.

Ken nodded. "Please have some coffee."

Joel slid into a chair and accepted a cup and saucer, but waved off a plate Susana offered him. "Some men passed through a few days ago with live cargo on their way to Rotterdam. I think they're who you're seeking."

"Do you know their final destination?" Ken asked.

"I do. I had the honor of helping them with shipping papers." Joel smiled at Susana before continuing, "But it'll cost you."

"How much?" Ken asked.

The group grew uneasy. Bobby got up and looked out the window, then began pacing. Fred and Dusty stood from the couch they'd been sharing with Susana.

Joel waved his hand. "I don't want money."

"What do you want?" Ken asked.

"I want you to take my daughter with you," Joel replied.

"Your daughter! Who is she?"

Joel smiled and nodded toward Susana. No one spoke as they watched Susana take her father's hand.

***

The port of Rotterdam was chaotic to anyone who didn't know it. Tractor trailers honked as they roared down the tight lanes leading to the docks, and cranes squealed as they swung large, wooden crates onto the decks of towering cargo ships. Piercing beeps blared from backing forklifts that weaved through crowds of longshoremen.

"Just give me a few minutes," Joel said before being swallowed up into the activity of one of the busiest ports in the world.

The group gave up trying to speak over the noise, so they had nothing to do but wait. They stood on one of the few empty docks, but still men jostled by paying them little attention. A chalkboard nailed to a post read *Star of Rotterdam* - Seattle. Eventually Joel descended some steep wooden stairs leading down from the shipping office at the end of the dock.

"Show me the airline ticket," Joel said as he tried to catch his breath.

Ken found the ticket he'd bought for Susana and handed it over. "She'll be flying out with us, but she'll have to have a passport and visa."

"You let me worry about that," Joel said, taking the ticket. "They're on the *Star of Rotterdam*, and will be in Seattle in about a month. But I wouldn't expect them to be on board when the ship reaches there."

Ken nodded. "What about you?" He wasn't sure why he asked, but wondered what would happen if Vandusen found out that he'd betrayed them.

"I can't leave my business," Joel said, smiling at Susana, who'd started to cry.

Father and daughter embraced. It made a strange sight even to the passing longshoremen, who were used to seeing the wonders of the wide world. Several slowed their pace as they passed.

Lieutenant Sandy broke the spell. "Let's go home."

Chapter Forty-six

Vandusen peered out of the wheelhouse. Dense fog swirled around the windows, blinding them, and the bow cut a wake that disappeared in the dense grayness. The wipers worked double time but barely kept up with the streaks of heavy drizzle.

Vandusen had asked the captain to double the watch as they neared the coast. Now he could hear them calling out the depths as they neared the cove. After several months, they'd finally made landfall off the coast of Northern California. The trip from Rotterdam had been long and arduous. He'd gone to great lengths to have the captain avoid the shipping lanes wherever possible, even rounding the tip of South America through the Straits of Magellan, thinking it better than registering and crossing at the Panama Canal. This had doubled their time and effort. But money could buy almost anything. He was able to stay in touch with the General and was relieved to know they had a destination waiting in the Pacific Northwest.

"We need to offload these animals into the launch as soon as possible so the ship can continue to Seattle. Get them ready to load. Once we make it to the beach, we'll truck them to the airstrip," Vandusen said to Bauer.

"We don't have room on the plane to load them all at once, especially in this weather," Bauer said.

"Load as many on as you can and fly them out ASAP," Vandusen ordered.

"In this soup?" Bauer asked.

"Yes, I want them out of the area and hidden."

They planned to rendezvous with some of the General's agents in Shelter Cove on the Lost Coast, which would be a tricky piece of navigation even in the best of weather, but in this fog it would be a miracle if they made it. Vandusen thought the "Lost Coast" was a fitting name for the end of their voyage. They needed to use the cloak of fog and the dead of night to truck the creatures to a private airstrip and fly them to their new home. If their luck just held out a little longer, his mission would be finally accomplished.

The General had purchased an abandoned logging camp clustered deep in the woods near a town called Willow Creek. Vandusen had been amused when he later learned that the town had a Sasquatch museum. It would be a perfect place to conduct their experiments, and its remoteness would afford them the privacy they needed for the other aspects of their business such as interrogation.

The General had been able to keep the whole project on the down low by classifying it Top Secret. No one knew what its purpose was. He was amused when the General informed him that that little shit Dr. Melon was now in their employ. With his help, they could build relationships with the nearby universities. He laughed to himself when he thought that they'd look almost respectable.

The General had shared that while it was an unusual place to build their facility—most primate facilities were built in climates that resembled the jungles from which they came—it was remote, and that was important. It seemed that the General had learned much from Melon already. He still hoped to get a chance to capture some more of the creatures if that idiot Gabriel didn't kill them all before they dealt with him. He was pretty sure that sneaky Portuguese had been behind the problem they'd had in Germany. But he wouldn't find much there if he showed up to double-cross them. He'd made sure no one would.

The General's ingenuity and versatility impressed him. It seemed there was no limit to the money and resources the General could raise when he was put in charge of a project. The cover they were using was one of the General's best yet. Melon would be leaving his post at the National Science Foundation, N.S.F., and would be taking a position at the Department of Defense, D.O.D.

And there was Dr. Turner and his crew to deal with. They'd lost touch with them after their fortunes had changed with the counterattack of the Belgians, but now they'd be back on his turf, it would be time for a little revenge. He smiled at the prospect of having Dr. Turner and his whole crew as guests at their new place of operation.

He realized Bauer was still standing next to him, hesitating. "To hell with this weather," he growled. "Get your ass moving. I want those freaks loaded and in the air before daybreak and this damn fog lifts."

Bauer turned to make his way down to the lower deck and was swallowed in the fog.

Idiot, Vandusen thought.

***

"Well, at least we got half of those freaks of nature to the General," Vandusen said as he surveyed the damage. The wreckage of the Cessna was strewn across most of the valley. It looked as if the pilot had almost been able to set it down, even in the fog, had it not been for the trees on the edge of the meadow. One wing had been torn off in the treetops and the fuselage was broken into several pieces.

"We need to clean all this up right away before the Forest Service comes snooping around," Vandusen added. He frowned, worried about the absence of any of the creatures. The pilot and crew were accounted for but not the two creatures they'd loaded for the last trip to the new facility.

Bauer surveyed the dense conifers and steep rocky crags surrounding them. "I doubt they'll survive in this wilderness."

"I wouldn't count on it. Form a search party and start tracking them. They couldn't have gone far. Look at this mess!" Vandusen yelled. His voice echoed off the peaks surrounding them.

***

The creatures stopped at the ridge when they heard the echoes. They could just make out the tiny forms of the humans in the valley below. They were hungry and shivered in the cold but had to get far away from the valley where they'd awakened in fear. They turned, headed down the other side of the ridge, and disappeared into the trees. Night was coming.

Chapter Forty-seven

An unseasonable mist rolled into the meadow, leaving everything cold and damp. The tops of the towering redwoods disappeared into the brooding fog where the sun swallowed what was left of the day. A chill had replaced the sunny afternoon and the family of campers busied themselves, trying to gather enough dry wood to make a fire.

"Don't wander off!" Jason yelled to his children. The cloak of fog muffled his voice.

"Jason, watch your tone! You'll scare the children," his wife chided him. She felt unnerved by this abrupt change in the weather. In fact, the whole group felt uneasy, even though they knew this could happen any time of the year in the thick cedar and redwood forests of the Pacific Northwest. But somehow this felt different. It had been sudden. So they hastened to build a fire, hoping its glow and warmth might help take the gloom out of this place.

Just as Jason knelt to light a campfire, it started to rain. He shivered, feeling as though something evil had come to visit them and didn't want them to succeed with building the fire.

The families decided to pool their wood so they could huddle around just one campfire and make it bigger, so it would last. But as hard as they tried, they couldn't keep the wood dry enough for the fire to take.

Though the sun was hidden, the gathering darkness indicated the end of the day. The evening seemed to be growing out of the very shadows surrounding them.

Finally, Jason sacrificed some of the moonshine he kept in a flask hidden in his coat pocket, and the flames took. The withering glow grew, little by little, as they carefully added the driest of what they'd gathered until the first tendrils of flames grew into a roasting fire. The hovering mist swallowed up a crackling stream of sparks, but the families gathered around, reassured by the radiating warmth.

The moms pooled what they had left in their Coleman coolers to make a menu that would serve all of them while keeping them near and around the fire. As the fire grew, the small company of families relaxed a little, feeling safe again.

"God, this is getting spooky!" Jason said. He zipped up his faded Carhartt jacket after throwing another log on the fire, which sent sparks flying into the faces of all sitting downwind.

"Dad!" a teenage girl yelled as she and several other girls jumped up and frantically brushed sparks from their clothes. A faint breeze sent the fog swirling into mysterious forms around them.

"Sorry, dear. Didn't they teach you in the Girl Scouts not to park your butts downwind of a campfire? I think you'd want a fire, as creepy as it is tonight."

His wife shot him a disapproving glance.

"What?"

She warmed her hands and lowered her voice. "Enough of this spooky stuff. It's bad enough without you commenting on it."

He opened his mouth but paused, thinking better of it, especially when he got a second glare from another mom. "I don't like this," he whispered. "Hell, it's August. If it wasn't so late and dark, I'd say let's pack up and vamoose outa here."

"I think you should talk to the other dads and set up a watch or something," his wife said.

Relieved to have something to do, he nodded and made his way around the camp, whispering to the other men.

"Hotdogs, anyone?" Several of the moms closed in around the fire with trays of makings and everything seemed normal for the moment.

Later, the women and children climbed into their tents to sleep, but the men could not, or would not, sleep. The breeze died as night fell, and the mist thickened. They were running out of wood and worried they'd need to gather more before dawn—if there'd be one—and no one liked the prospect of leaving the security of the fire.

"I tell you I heard something," one of the dads said as he pointed out into the mist.

"Quiet! Keep your voice down," hissed another dad. "You'll wake up the girls." He anxiously looked over at the tents but only heard the soft breathing of the sleeping girls and their moms.

It had been an odd coincidence, but by chance or ill fate, of the four families who'd decided to go camping, all their children were teenage girls. They'd laughed at the time, thinking that at least they wouldn't have to set night monitors and deal with all the histrionics of teenage boy-girl drama, but now they weren't so sure.

A loud crack followed by a heavy thump of something hitting the ground, startled all four men.

"Shit!" a short little man said.

"Bill? Did you bring your pistol?" Jason asked.

He nodded.

"Well, go get it, damn it," Jason ordered.

Bill hesitated and stared in the direction of where he guessed his truck to be parked. It was impossible to see anything in this soup.

This is crazy, he thought. He knew his truck was only a few yards away, but the mist shrouded it from view. He took one last look around camp, shook his head, and disappeared into the mist.

Silence grew across the meadow as they waited for him to return. They couldn't see or hear him, as though the mist had swallowed him whole.

"It's been several minutes. Should we go check on him?" one of the dads whispered. They were reluctant to call out into the night, afraid to bring attention to the camp or wake the girls.

"It just seems like a long time," Jason replied. "Anyway, the hell with that. There's no sense getting picked off one by one."

"What the hell does that mean?"

"Nothing—just wait." No sooner had Jason spoken, they heard someone running toward camp. The men stood, grabbing anything that would serve as a weapon.

Bill stumbled into the light, waving his pistol in the direction from which he'd come. "I heard what seemed like a number of large animals and then saw several dark forms in the fog out toward the tree line."

"What were they?" Jason asked, picking up a piece of firewood. "I've heard that Big Foot is supposed to wander in these parts."

"Big Foot? I … I don't know."

"It's probably just a herd of elk."

"Only if elk walk upright like a man."

They all started to talk at once before Jason interrupted. "Let's be quiet and listen. We can't do anything until it grows lighter." He paused and asked Bill, "How much ammo do you have?"

"Just an extra clip, but I left it in the truck." Bill looked back toward where their trucks were parked.

"Terrific. Everyone stay calm. I'm sure it's nothing; just bumps in the night." He no sooner threw the last log on the dying embers than the sky started to grow lighter, and relief washed over him when he could finally make out the green of the meadow. The early morning was winning its battle with the night. A meadowlark startled them, reminding them that dawn had arrived. They could hear the girls stirring in the tents, whispering and giggling.

"Is that all they do? Giggle?" one of the dads asked.

"Let's get moving and load the trucks," Jason said.

The men began packing up. The girls unzipped the tents, chatting away, unaware of the events of the evening.

Suddenly, a loud cry rose up from the woods, followed by the crack of what sounded like large trees being broken in half.

Jason turned toward the girls and yelled, "Stay in your tents!"

To their horror, two massive, black creatures raced toward them through the tall grass of the meadow, running upright. The ground shook as they neared.

Without saying a word, Bill knelt and began firing. Shots rang out, echoing off the surrounding mountains and drowning out the screams from the tents. One of the creatures fell some distance away, but the other kept charging before falling at Bill's feet. Shaking, he looked at Jason. "I'm empty." He took off, running for his truck.

Jason crept toward the bodies but froze when one of the creatures opened its eyes. It struggled to its feet and looked around, as though getting its bearings. Its coarse black hair bristled, its eyes grew red, and it let out a deafening scream that filled the meadow. For several heartbeats there was silence, and then the forest echoed with the answer of deep, bellowing calls.

The girls' screams filled this once-quiet part of the woods.

***

A Note from the Author

It would be immensely helpful to me if you could write a review for *Becoming Human* and publish it at your point of purchase. I need your reviews to help find the readers who will enjoy my work.

Also, please sign up to my newsletter to hear when *More Than Human,* the sequel to *Becoming Human*, is published and receive some true stories of my life with chimps **FREE**. Just type the following web address into your browser:

http://bajamotoquest.com

Then scroll to the bottom of my blog and click on where it says:

PLEASE SIGN UP FOR MY NEWSLETTER.

And please stay in touch:

Follow "@KenDecroo" on Twitter
Like "Ken Decroo" on Facebook

Acknowledgements

The journey of writing a novel is long and winding. There are so many humans and non-humans to thank. The characters of this book, this series, are based on my experiences in the world of wild animal training and research. I am grateful to have worked with many unique people and lived in the company of chimpanzees and other wild animals. They have taught me a lot about humility and love. I thank them all.

This book has evolved and grown as the result of the mentoring and guidance of my world class editor, Tahlia Newland of AIA Publishing. The cover was done once again by Velvet Wings Media. I would like to thank AIA Publishing for taking a chance on another of my books.

And now, I would like to thank the most important people in my effort; my beta readers. These are colleagues who read the manuscript in its entirety and gave me valuable feedback on what was working or not. Some read several versions of my story as it evolved. I am grateful for your hard work and honesty: Dorothy and Steve Clark, Jamie Stortz Morris, Joanne Larsen, and Tamara Lynn Decroo.

And finally, I would like to acknowledge my parents, Ken and Lois Decroo. I am sad to say, mom passed away recently, but I hope she enjoys this story between performing her duties as an angel. As for my dad, he is still going strong and is an inspiration to what I write. He is ninety-four and tough as Lester.

9 780648 417125